WAITI
THE

WAITING AT THE GATE

HEATHER INGMAN

FOURTH ESTATE · London

First published in Great Britain in 1996 by
Fourth Estate Limited
6 Salem Road
London, W2 4BU
Copyright © 1996 by Heather Ingman

A catalogue record for this book is available from the British Library.

ISBN 1–85702–480–X

This novel is a work of fiction. Any references to historical events or
to real locales are intended only to give the fiction a sense of reality
and authenticity. Other names, characters, places and incidents are the
product of the author's imagination and any resemblance to real-life
counterparts is entirely coincidental.

Typeset by Palimpsest Book Production Limited,
Polmont, Stirlingshire
Printed in Great Britain by Clays Ltd, St Ives plc

For Lindy
in memory of Malcolm

WAITING AT THE GATE

Chapter One

....

Harriet Lee arrived at the school gate.

'Well, here we are again,' she commented.

Alix Greenwood turned, saw who it was and grimaced. 'I've been trying to work out how much of my life will be spent standing outside this damned gate. One more year of nursery. Three of infants. How many in juniors? I forget.'

'Four years,' Peggy Murray chimed in. 'But in the last year in juniors some of them stop being collected.'

'Great!' snorted Alix. 'Only another seven years to go! Seven years of twice a day for fifty-two weeks —'

'Minus holidays,' Fiona Wilson-Smith reminded her.

'Minus, say, twenty weeks is . . . Oh, I give up!'

'A lot, anyway,' agreed Peggy.

'Too much!' Alix frowned and flicked her blonde plait over her shoulder.

'You could always do as I do, Alix, and employ a childminder,' suggested Fiona.

Fiona Wilson-Smith ran her own PR company and was to be seen at the school gate only once or twice a week. Small and slim, dressed in high heels, short neat business skirts and freshly ironed shirts (she employed a housekeeper as well), Fiona was the object of much barely articulated envy amongst the other mothers at the school gate.

'It's all right for you to talk. You've probably pinched the only really reliable childminder in the whole of Apple Burton,' muttered Alix.

'I hope so.' Fiona grinned. 'I say,' she said, suddenly serious. 'Did any of you receive anything odd via e-mail yesterday?'

'What's e-mail?' asked Peggy.

'Don't have a computer,' replied Harriet.

'How do you mean odd?' enquired Alix.

Fiona wrinkled her pert little nose. 'Can't explain. Nothing you could put your finger on. Hinting at things, you know. It gave an e-mail address in Finland. Finland! Who knows anyone in Finland, for God's sake? Oh well, it's probably nothing. There're a lot of loonies out there on the Internet.' She looked round at their blank faces. 'I say, girls, you don't seem very *au fait* with the computer world. Hadn't you better buck up your ideas? There won't be any jobs for computer illiterates in the year 2000, you know.'

Leaving them with that cheery thought, Fiona moved off to greet someone else. Unlike the other mothers, Fiona didn't stick to one group of parents but socialised amongst all the groups. 'Networking', Alix called it. It was generally assumed that Fiona was making a bid to get elected to the board of school governors.

'Did you understand any of that?' whispered Peggy.

'Not much,' admitted Harriet. 'There's not much call for computers in my line of work. What about you, Alix?'

'Oh, I know nothing about computers.'

'I wonder if I should go back to work? It might be one way of losing weight.' Peggy sighed and looked down at herself. She was a small, plump woman in her mid thirties with a freckled face and masses of fluffy, rather faded red hair. Despite her plumpness, there was something rather fragile about Peggy's face, Harriet had always felt. 'You'd hardly believe it – I've put on yet another half stone! It's Ben's tea, he just won't eat it. I end up eating it myself and then having another meal in the evening with Frank.'

'What does it matter?' said Harriet. 'As long as you're happy. Many men prefer plump – er, dislike skinny women.'

'Huh! I don't believe that! It's a miracle Frank puts up with me, looking like this. Mum was on at me again about my weight this morning. She's read about this amazing new diet in *Woman's Weekly*. You eat nothing but grape nuts for a fortnight. I'm thinking of trying it.'

'I hate diets,' remarked Harriet. 'They make me think about food all the time. I'm sure I get fatter when I'm on a diet than when I'm not on one.'

Alix grunted. 'Yes, that's the whole idea. That's how these people make their money. You go on a diet, put on weight, decide the book's useless, chuck it away and buy a new one. The market's insatiable.'

'A bit like my stomach,' joked Peggy. 'It's all right for you, Alix,' she went on, 'you don't need to diet.'

Tall and willowy, Alix cut a striking figure amongst the group of mums, grannies, aunts, neighbours and dads gathered outside St Cecilia's school gate. She had long blonde hair tied back in a plait and was always immaculately turned out. Today it was a pair of Katharine Hamnett jeans and a white shirt that looked as if it had come straight out of a Ralph Lauren catalogue (it probably had). It always gave Harriet hope to look at Alix – if a woman could look that good at forty-one!

Harriet herself didn't stand out from the rest of the waiting mothers in any way. She had shoulder-length brown hair in need of a cut, a pair of large brown eyes (her best feature) and a bad complexion. She had, in her opinion, slightly too much weight around her stomach and hips and too little around her breasts. Hers was an average English face and an average English figure. The only thing that might have surprised an observer was her exceptionally filthy hands. Harriet was a painter.

'You're not really thinking of going back to work, are you, Peggy?' asked a woman in her sixties who'd been hanging around on the edge of their group. She was called Mrs Parsons and she was the grandmother of twins.

'I suppose not. Frank likes to have me at home. Besides, Ben's still only three.' Peggy sighed again.

'That's right. The kiddies do love to be with their mummies, don't they?' said Mrs Parsons.

'Do they? Do they really?' snapped Harriet. She felt this was about as far as she could go in the circumstances, since they were standing outside her son's school. Her preferred response to Mrs Parsons' inane statement would have been to punch her on the nose. She avoided catching Alix's eye. She knew Alix well enough to know exactly what kind of expression would be on her friend's face.

Moving back up to Apple Burton from London six months ago, Harriet had contacted those few of her old school friends still living in the town. Alix and Peggy had been among them. Harriet and

Peggy had been in the same form at Apple Burton High. Harriet remembered Peggy, her frizzy red hair tied up in two navy blue bows, weeping buckets that first day in nursery school. Harriet had sat and stared and then burst into tears herself. They'd been friends, not close but part of a group, till Peggy left at sixteen to go on to secretarial college. There was a bit too much of 'Frank thinks' or 'Frank says' about Peggy nowadays. Alix was the mother with whom Harriet felt she had most in common, though Alix's sharpness was on occasion unnerving. Alix had a low tolerance threshold for the slow, the slovenly and the pathetic, which sometimes made her hard to keep up with.

At school Alix had been one of the cool set. Several forms higher than Peggy and Harriet, she'd been one of the glamorous older girls whose shirts never looked crumpled and whose skirts didn't hang off their waists. In those days, Alix had been school prefect and was talked of as having a brilliant future. Harriet sometimes wondered what had become of it. What exactly had Alix done between leaving school and marrying Tim Greenwood five years ago? Apple Burton wasn't the sort of place Harriet would have thought someone like Alix, or the girl Alix had been, would have wanted to stay in for long.

For Apple Burton was a small, rather sleepy East Yorkshire market town. Its heyday had been in the fourteenth century when it had been a centre for the cloth trade and for pilgrimages. Remnants of that era lingered on in the street names (Dyer Lane, Fuller Road), in the crumbling town gate, the Minster, the Friary and the oversized parish church. Unusually for an English market town in the late twentieth century, Apple Burton had managed to hang on to its market which was held once a week, on a Saturday. But in the high street, branches of national chains were gradually replacing local shops and six or seven buildings in the centre of town stood empty. It was a town with a lively and interesting past, but where nothing much had happened for centuries and nothing much was expected to happen in the future.

It was a long time ago, thought Harriet. I expect we've all changed. It was strange, this relationship between parents at the school gate. They saw and chattered to one another twice a day every day during term time and that gave them the illusion of knowing each other very well whereas in fact, she reflected, the only thing they had in common was that they all had children of the same age.

'Hi, Muriel,' she said as a short, dark-haired woman joined them. She was pushing a baby in a buggy and tugging a toddler by the hand.

'Hello.' Muriel Winter paused beside them and wiped her face with a grubby handkerchief.

'Hot, isn't it?' said Peggy sympathetically.

The other mothers were all in T-shirts and jeans or short skirts but Muriel was wearing a long-sleeved pullover and thick black stockings. She nudged back a sticky strand of hair from her forehead.

'It is rather,' she agreed in her small, timid voice. 'I didn't realise it was going to turn out to be so hot.'

'Didn't you?' said Alix lightly. 'But it's been like this for three days now. I'd have thought it was obvious we're in the middle of a heat wave.'

Harriet started at Alix's sharp tone. What had got into her? Why on earth was she putting the knife into Muriel? As the mother of four children under seven, Muriel Winter generated a certain amount of sympathy at the school gate. She was a shy, gentle sort of person, overburdened by her children. She flushed now at Alix's words. Harriet tried to think of something to say to cover the embarrassed silence but failed, as usual. Was it because she was a painter, she wondered, that she was so inarticulate? No, it was more than that. Harriet distrusted words. They were deceivers. Geoffrey, her ex-husband, was good with words. Good at making speeches in Parliament, good at persuading people into things – he'd been an art dealer before reinventing himself as a Tory MP. Nicky had inherited his father's gift. Already, at three, he was in the habit of finishing his mother's sentences for her. Harriet could never say what she meant half so well in words as when she was standing in front of a canvas with a clear vision in her head.

She gave up thinking about Muriel and became absorbed in watching the play of light through the trees in the field surrounding the school.

'Here they come!' Peggy's voice broke into her thoughts.

Alix nudged her. 'Come on, head in the clouds, time to do your mummy stuff.'

Harriet grinned and began waving as a line of three-year-olds trotted round the corner and across the playground, holding hands and singing 'The Grand Old Duke of York', led by Mrs Parker beating time with her hand.

'Aren't they sweet?' murmured Mrs Parsons.

'At the moment,' said Peggy. 'But wait till the walk home. Mummy, I'm tired. Mummy, my leg hurts.'

'Mummy, I've got tummy ache. I want to do a wee-wee,' added Alix.

'Or poo,' put in Harriet.

'Christ, yes! Hellish in the middle of the street.' Alix rolled her eyes. 'That kind of thing just makes me want to tear my hair out.'

Mrs Parsons sniffed. 'I don't know why some people have children.'

Harriet stifled a giggle. She opened her arms and bent down to give Nicky a kiss. 'Hello, darling. Have you had a lovely morning?'

He wriggled out of her arms and thrust a picture in front of her nose. It was a brown cow jumping over a silver moon.

'Look,' he said, 'it moves.' He pulled a string. The cow jumped sideways over the moon. 'Hey diddle diddle, the cow and the fiddle – isn't that clever?' He stared up at her through his grimy glasses.

'It's lovely.' Harriet gave him another kiss. Nicky made a face and pulled away. Sometimes he reminded her very much of his father.

'She's so gifted, Mrs Parker. Puts me to shame. I can hardly even draw a decent cat.' Peggy groaned. 'Well, see you both tomorrow.'

She moved off with Ben. Peggy lived on a modern housing estate on the edge of town whereas Harriet and Alix lived in older houses, nearer the centre. They usually walked part of the way home together.

'Wait, Harriet.' Alix caught her by the elbow.

'What is it?'

'Let her go first.' Alix nodded in the direction of Mrs Parsons who'd set off at a brisk pace, a serious-faced twin trotting sedately on either side of her. 'I don't think I could bear to walk home with that woman.'

Harriet smiled. 'It's all right. She's turned the corner.'

'Thank God. One of these days I swear I'll take a swipe at her.'

'Great! Do it when I'm there to watch.'

They grinned at each other and set off to walk home, with Nicky and Alix's daughter, Imogen, skipping along beside them. Nicky was singing his favourite song.

'Daisy, Daisy, give me your lancer do. I'm half crazy, all for the lunch of you.'

An odd child, Harriet thought, looking at him affectionately. I wonder where he gets his eccentricities from? Aloud, she said, 'I wish Peggy wouldn't always do herself down. I don't mean about drawing cats, but in general.'

'I know.'

'Take her weight, for instance. She always was plump, as far as I can remember. It suits her. And we're all gradually catching up on her anyway. At least I am.' Harriet sighed and drew in her stomach muscles.

'Don't I know it!'

'You? You don't need to worry. You're skinny, lucky devil!'

'Not by nature. It takes a lot of hard work, I can tell you. Sometimes, when I'm down at the gym working out, the sweat dripping off me, stomach hollow with hunger, I wonder whether it's really all worthwhile. Tim never notices what anyone looks like so I'm not doing it for him. It's just a habit. As women we're brought up to police our bodies, to keep a look-out for the first sign of fat. Some of us spend so much time doing that we haven't time for anything else. Which of course is the point of it all.'

Harriet wondered for a second at the bitterness in Alix's tone. Then she remembered that Alix's younger sister Frances was, or had been, anorexic. She still looked skeletal. Many were the times when Frances had appeared at the school gate to pick up her two from juniors and Alix had asked her what she'd eaten that day. Harriet flushed. She'd been tactless going on about weight. She opened her mouth to say something when Alix went on, 'Have you ever met Peggy's mother?'

'Not since I moved back here. Years ago I must have met her, when we went round to each other's houses to play. But I can't remember her.'

Alix shook her head. 'There's no pleasing that woman. It's no wonder Peggy's got such an inferiority complex.' Alix looked as though she was about to elaborate on something, but didn't. Instead, she asked, 'What have you done with your morning?'

Harriet adopted a solemn air. 'I stood in front of a blank canvas. Then I cleaned all my brushes very, very thoroughly. Then I drank a cup of coffee. Then I stood in front of the canvas again and smoked five cigarettes, one after the other.'

'Thought you reeked a bit.'

'Nothing gets past you, does it? Come here, imp!' Harriet caught hold of Nicky's hand. Alix grabbed Imogen and they all crossed the road. 'The canvas is still blank.' Harriet let go of Nicky's hand. 'It's been one of those mornings when I can't help feeling I'd be more use to society if I went out and trained as a social worker.'

'You wouldn't. Believe me.'

'No, probably not. I'm hardly cut out for that. What did you do this morning?'

'Shopped.'

Alix was a frequent and prolific shopper. Harriet, who hated shopping for anything except paints, was always amazed at the amount of time her friend put in at the shops.

'Buy anything?'

'Couple of shirts. Oh, and a party dress for Imogen,' she added rather shamefacedly.

'Another one? Alix!'

'I couldn't resist it. It's pink with frills and things.'

Imogen, all long legs and blonde curls, was one of the most spoilt children in Apple Burton. Having had her only child relatively late in life, Alix lavished affection on her.

'Don't say anything. Just don't say anything,' she added. 'It's one of my greatest pleasures in life, buying clothes for Imogen.'

'I know,' answered Harriet warmly. 'You shop. I stand in front of blank canvases. Do you think we're making the best use of our lives?'

'As Miss Barnesley used to say.'

'The witch with the warty hands whose stony stare could silence a hall of three hundred girls.'

They smiled at each other.

'It's this place.' Alix stifled a yawn. 'Nothing ever happens. It must seem terribly dull to you, after London.'

'Well –' began Harriet.

'Mummy! Mummy! Lucinda got stung by a wasp!' Nicky interrupted her excitedly.

Harriet looked down at her son. She brushed back his fine brown hair, inherited from her. 'Did she? That must have hurt.'

'It did.' He nodded, full of his important news.

'She cried,' added Imogen.

'I bet she did,' said her mother. 'Most people would.'

'What happened then?' asked Harriet.

'Mrs Parker rubbed something on her arm, then she cuddled Lucinda. We all sat round and sang a song,' Nicky informed her.

Harriet and Alix glanced at one another. Their faith in Mrs Parker was constantly vindicated by little episodes like this.

'What did you sing?' asked Harriet.

Nicky shrugged. 'Can't remember.' With all the flightiness of a three-year-old, he'd suddenly lost interest in the topic. He whispered something to Imogen and they ran on ahead to inspect some flowers. Alix resumed their discussion.

'What gets me about Apple Burton is the sheer smugness of its inhabitants. We're all right Jack up here, prosperous farming community, low unemployment, little vandalism, no serious traffic problems, the rest of the country can go to hell. Doesn't it seem dull after London?'

'Well, yes it does. Though the things that kept happening there – muggings, tyres let down, windows smashed – weren't necessarily the things one wanted to happen. But you see, Alix, that's why I came back to Apple Burton. It's dull but it's safe. After Daniel, that's all I ever wanted to be – safe.' A shadow passed over Harriet's face. It often did when she spoke of her elder son.

'I can understand you feeling like that,' said Alix, after a moment.

'However, things may be about to happen.' Harriet changed the subject. She never could bear talking about Daniel for long. He belonged to her most private thoughts. 'I've sent off the form.'

'The form? Oh, the form!' Alix halted and gazed at her. A gleam of excitement appeared in her eyes. 'Harriet! That's great! I never thought you'd do it.'

Harriet looked smug. Two months ago, her divorce from Geoffrey had been finalised. Ever since then Alix had nagged on at Harriet about getting out and meeting new people. By which Alix meant men. 'Your job's hopeless,' she'd said. 'You'll never meet anyone painting alone in your studio all day.' 'I see buyers,' Harriet had protested in her defence. In fact most of her paintings were sold through a local art gallery where she had a standing arrangement with the owner, Douglas Hornby. True, that's how she'd met Geoffrey all those years ago, when she'd turned up at his London gallery one day hoping to persuade him to buy some of her paintings. He hadn't; instead, with his usual way with words, he'd persuaded her to have lunch with him. But there was no chance of a romance with Douglas Hornby, who'd been living very happily with a man for the past fifteen years.

Douglas stood between her and the people who bought her pictures. This suited Harriet very well. After all, she reasoned, women giving up their babies for adoption never see the future parents, do they? But Alix was right, it did limit her social life. The only men she met regularly were fathers at the school gate and in the nature of things they were likely to be married or in stable relationships. The ones who weren't looked downright dubious. That ginger-haired man in the shabby jeans with his scruffy Alsatian on a piece of string. Or that bad-tempered-looking man who never spoke to anyone and was rumoured to be a writer. She could imagine what sort of books he'd write – nasty, sour things with a hint of misogyny, if not misanthropy. Nevertheless, with all these cards stacked against her, Harriet had been horrified when Alix had suggested she join a dating agency.

'They're for social inadequates, no-hopers, mummy's boys,' she'd said.

'Not at all. They've become a perfectly respectable way for busy professional people who haven't the time to spend in pubs and night-clubs to meet each other.'

'You've got to be joking! I'd rather join an evening class on car maintenance!'

'Good idea. Why don't you?'

'I don't have a car. Besides, what with my painting and Nicky, I'm a basket case by nine in the evening. I haven't the stamina for a social life.'

'That's where a dating agency comes in. Saves you the hassle. Matches you up with suitable partners without you having to lift a finger.'

'Why are you so keen on them? Is that how you met Tim?'

'No. We met at an evening class, actually.'

'What in?'

'Do you know, I can't remember.' Alix laughed. 'But when I was working in the Citizens' Advice Bureau –'

'I didn't know you'd worked in a Citizens' Advice Bureau.'

'You'd be surprised what I've done in my time. Anyway, when I was working there, I sometimes used to recommend dating agencies to my clients. Divorced people or people just out of prison, for instance. It was a way of getting them to break with old associates.'

'There you are, I'd probably meet up with an ex-con.'

'What's wrong with that? So long as he *is* ex? Mind you, you've got to be choosy about which agency. I'll hunt out some information for you.'

So Alix had handed her a wad of information on dating agencies and in an idle moment Harriet had leafed through it and casually filled in a form. Work: children and painting. Hobbies: children and painting. Seeks male friends any age from thirty upwards. Colour, race, religion immaterial. It wasn't an exciting profile. No little extras such as 'Fun-loving sex kitten seeks daring romps with male wild cat' or 'Antarctic ice-queen wants hot man to melt her heart'. She'd probably sound too boring to attract any partners. For ten pounds extra you could have your photo published in the agency's magazine. Harriet declined this opportunity. She thought it best to be as vague as possible about her physical appearance. Most of the ads at the back of magazines these days seemed to specify long-legged blonde-haired women under the age of thirty. Except the ones that pleaded for an understanding female – and anyone in their right minds would run a mile from those.

'God, it's so exciting!' Alix clutched her arm. 'I wonder who they'll match you up with? You know, I almost envy you.'

'I can't think why. Tim's all right. Isn't he?'

'Oh yes. He's all right.'

A shy, gentle man, Tim worked in the law department at Humberside University. Harriet had run into him once or twice at the school gate. Alix rarely mentioned him. The conversation between the mothers at the gate was always firmly child-centred.

'Which agency did you choose?' went on Alix. 'Shall I come in for coffee and we can discuss it?'

They'd arrived outside Harriet's house, a three-storey red brick Victorian terrace, screened from the main road by a row of chestnut trees.

Harriet hesitated.

'I'd planned for Nicky to have a nap. I'm taking him to his grandfather's in a little while.'

'Oh yes?' Alix looked at her knowingly. 'We'd better postpone our chat then. You'll want to change.'

Chapter Two

Yes, I must change, but what into, Harriet wondered, standing in front of the full-length mirror in her bedroom while Nicky took his nap on the sofa downstairs. The walls and ceiling of Harriet's bedroom were painted a deep glossy red. The wooden floor was a tranquil sea-green. She'd mixed the colours herself. Every conceivable surface – the wardrobe doors, the chest of drawers, the small table by the window – was covered with painted flowers or abstract swirling patterns. For Harriet, art wasn't just something you did on canvas. It was a way of life.

She laid out on her four-poster bed two skirts, a short one and a long one. She stood considering them, aware of the absurdity of the fact that she dressed more carefully to visit her father than she ever did to meet prospective buyers. 'Honestly, Harriet,' Alix had said once, 'you make as much fuss over a visit to your father as you would for royalty.' 'Nonsense,' she'd replied. 'I'm a republican. I wouldn't lift a finger for royalty.'

Harriet tried on the short pleated skirt. It made her look young and sporty, certainly. But did it make her look too young? Would remarks be made about women of a certain age having to be careful how they dressed? If she stood sideways was the slight bulge visible where Daniel and Nicky had been and which had never returned to its proper shape? Yes, it was. She discarded the short skirt and tried the long flowered one. Better. She put on a long white T-shirt over it. Good. Go for the flowing, innocent, tripping through the cornfields look.

Tying a cotton scarf around her neck, Harriet mentally reviewed her life. Two paintings sold in the last month. Make a big thing of that. Some slates fallen off the roof during a recent storm. Make a small thing of that. She'd get it seen to some time – in the fullness of time, as civil servants said. The house belonged to her father. It was where Harriet had grown up. Her father had given it to her when he'd moved into his retirement home, a sheltered flat near the Minster. Or rather, he allowed her to live in it. Which was generous of him, she had to admit.

After years of battling with local authorities to get decent provision for Daniel, Harriet had been glad to move out of London. There was less pressure on resources up here. The school Daniel was at now was better than anything she'd found in the south. Besides, the house in Fulham had belonged to Geoffrey. Although he'd been decent about moving out into a rented flat, in the long run pride wouldn't have allowed her to go on living in his house for ever without paying him rent and rent, in her precarious financial position, was just what she couldn't afford, especially at Fulham prices. Life was cheaper up in Apple Burton and her father had never asked for rent. If only, though, he wouldn't always assume that his house was running to rack and ruin since she'd taken it over.

It was a large house with many stairs. A mysterious place, full of light and shadow. Turning a corner, you suddenly came upon a dazzling shaft of light or an unexpected pool of darkness. Like life. She was gradually repainting it, room by room, getting rid of the insipid pastels, the magnolias and off-whites of her childhood. The kitchen, for instance, was now a rather startling navy blue with white tiles on the floor and a bright white ceiling. It wouldn't be to everyone's taste. But it pleased Harriet.

She went on with her review. Nicky settling down well at nursery school. Had come out of his shell and was beginning to play with the other children. No, don't mention shell. That made it sound as though something was wrong with him. Which would be put down to the way he'd been brought up. Which would be put down to her.

Daniel was doing his best at boarding school. Enjoying the routine, which was what she could never give him; at least not in the quantity he required. Geoffrey . . . God knows what Geoffrey was up to. She hadn't heard from him for months except via her solicitors. Harriet glared into the mirror. Was her life in order? No little chinks through which failure could be glimpsed? The main thing was to avoid detail. Her father was good at tripping people up on detail. It was what had got him so far in his job. All the way from the shop floor to company director. Not chairman, though. He'd trodden on too many toes for that.

She went downstairs and gently stroked Nicky's cheek. 'Time to wake up, darling. Time to visit Grandpa.'

He was awake in an instant. 'Goody. Now,' he sat up and looked around him, 'the first thing to do is find my shoes.' Like Alice in Wonderland, Nicky was full of little pieces of good advice for himself. It was a constant amazement to Harriet that she'd managed to produce such a practical child. Probably he took after Geoffrey.

Nicky glanced out of the window. 'It's a nice sunny day, isn't it, Mummy? I think I'll wear my pencils.'

He slid off the sofa and went to fetch his plimsolls. He sat on the floor, puffing and sighing. After a moment's struggle, he looked up at her. 'It's a bit tricky.'

She smiled and knelt down to help him. He was so independent. Determined to do everything for himself. So was Daniel, for that matter. Only his independence was quite a different thing from Nicky's. She hoped. Harriet was constantly on the look-out for signs of Daniel in Nicky, though the doctor had told her, when she'd discovered she was pregnant with Nicky, that it was unlikely the same family would have two children like Daniel. 'God rarely makes the same mistake twice,' he'd said. She'd thought it odd to bring God into it.

She finished pushing Nicky's feet into his plimsolls and said, 'I wonder what Daniel's doing now?'

'Will he have got the picture I drawed?'

'Probably. Yes, I should think so.' She stood up. 'You can take some toys to Grandpa's if you like.'

'No thanks, I wouldn't.'

Her father's flat was small and crammed with too much furniture. He had a bedroom, a kitchen, a bathroom and a sitting room with a view of the Minster. All the rooms were painted magnolia.

'Well, what have you been doing with yourself?' he enquired, settling himself into the armchair. He was a small, slim man with only traces now of a businessman's paunch. His hair which had once been black had turned, in recent months, completely white. To complement it, he'd taken to wearing vivid pink or yellow jumpers. He'd always been careful of his appearance. He played golf three times a week to keep himself in shape, and had recently been elected captain of the seniors for the third year running.

Harriet took the hard-backed chair. Nicky trotted off to the cupboard in the kitchen where toys were kept for him.

'What have I been doing? The usual,' she replied. 'Painting. Looking after Nicky.'

As usual, the usual didn't sound up to much. Nothing to compare with her father's busy productive days as a company director. 'Why are you wasting your time on that?' he'd ask, coming in from work and finding his daughter painting at the kitchen table. 'Leave her be, Anthony,' her mother would protest. Always now, alone with her father, Harriet missed her mother's gentle presence.

'And Nicky? Are they teaching him to read yet at that school of his?'

Her father disapproved of state schools. He'd been educated in one himself. So had Harriet, so had his two sons. He'd hoped for better for his grandson. He'd twice offered her money for private schooling. So far, Harriet had resisted taking it. St Cecilia's was a warm, friendly school, just the kind of school she'd hoped to find when she'd moved up from London, and when Nicky was a bit older, he'd have friends nearby to play with.

'They don't do reading yet. They think it's too early. But they've started him on letter recognition.'

'Hmmph! He's got a woman teacher, I suppose?'

'Two women teachers – Mrs Parker and Mrs Moss. They're very good.'

'I had a woman teacher once. Never any use. She beat me,' he added, rather surprisingly.

'What for?' she asked.

'She thought I'd done something I hadn't.'

'Oh? How did you feel about that?'

'I despised her.'

There was a silence.

'Daniel's doing well,' she ventured. 'I got a letter from his headmistress last week.'

'Mm.'

Her father moved restlessly in his chair – whether because his gout was playing him up or because he disliked any mention of Daniel, his other grandson, who'd never be able to read properly, was an open question. Harriet held her breath.

'Any news from their father?' he shot at her.

His old trick – because it hurt too much to think of Daniel, he shifted the hurt on to someone else. His sharp black eyes rested on his daughter's face. Harriet willed her expression not to change.

'No news,' she said slowly. 'Geoffrey and I lead separate lives now.' How often would she have to explain that to him? 'For all I know, he may be preparing to get married again.'

'Aye. I should think so. Bright lad like that. Saw his name in the paper again yesterday. Some speech in the House. Interesting life he has. At the centre of things.'

The old man looked round his quiet sitting room with an air of regret. Once he'd been at the centre of things and, if his daughter had played her cards right and remained married to Geoffrey, he might still have been at the centre. There were times when Harriet thought her father was fonder of his ex-son-in-law than he was of her. The two had got on like a house on fire from their first meeting. Launched straight into a political discussion while she'd been left silent on the sofa.

Not enough get up and go, that had always been her trouble as far as her father was concerned (it was how he would have expressed it, too). He'd wanted her to be a barrister or a surgeon, or even a buyer for some large company, say, Marks & Spencer. Anything rather than painting at home all day, never meeting anyone, never bringing him interesting gossip. Well, she met lots of mothers at the school gate, but he wasn't interested in them. His two sons, Harriet's elder brothers, they'd done all right. One was a merchant banker in Australia, the other worked in Detroit. But they were too far away for regular contact. It was a sad irony in his old age that the child with whom he had the least in common was the one who lived closest to him.

If Geoffrey had any heart about him, Harriet thought, he'd give the old man a ring now and then. But it was out of sight, out of mind with Geoffrey (that went for his sons as well). And it hadn't been for his heart that she'd married him, but for his boyish good looks and because she'd been three months pregnant with Daniel and Geoffrey had represented the sort of financial stability she was afraid she'd never be able to give a child. When she met Geoffrey, Harriet's career as a painter had been going through one of its increasingly frequent low spots. She'd been reduced to living on the dole again and was beginning to wonder whether she'd ever in her life earn more than starvation wages. It was because her motives for marrying Geoffrey had been so mixed that, when they broke up, she'd refused to accept any money for herself; for the children, yes, but not for herself.

In marrying Geoffrey, Harriet had thought she was marrying an art dealer but, four months after their marriage, his political ambitions won out over art and he got himself selected as prospective Tory candidate for an affluent London constituency. There was a by-election, and Harriet had swallowed her convictions, bought a proper maternity frock and done her bit as a Tory wife. Geoffrey was elected by a comfortable margin. He sold his galleries, and soon after Daniel's birth he began working longer and longer hours in the House. She'd never been interested in politics, and as time went by they found less and less to say to each other. She'd been too exhausted to care, too wrapped up in Daniel's problems and with snatching odd hours, often in the middle of the night, to do her painting which seemed suddenly, perhaps as a result of Daniel, to have taken on a new direction and a new urgency. There'd been, well out of the public eye, breakups, reconciliations, breakups, more reconciliations (usually around election time). Nicky was the unforeseen result of one of these. Back in her home town, Harriet wondered how on earth she and Geoffrey had managed to remain married to each other for so long.

She glanced at her father who was examining a train his grandson had brought him from the toy cupboard. Perhaps he'd had some influence over her after all. He'd so thoroughly approved of Geoffrey who, even before his selection, was something of a name in Tory party circles. Geoffrey represented all she'd been brought up to aspire to. At their wedding her father had called for 'A toast to the bridegroom', until someone reminded him there was also a bride. And then it had only been a year since her mother's death. Still disorientated, and further confused by her pregnancy, Harriet had plunged into marriage as a way of shoring herself up against the chaos which had seemed about to break over her. She'd missed her mother's gentleness, her sensible words of advice. When Daniel was born, Harriet's first thought had been, 'I wish Mum could have seen him.' Later she was glad her mother had never seen Daniel.

Her father glanced over at her. 'Hadn't you better be off if you're going to the gallery?'

He wanted to be left alone with his grandson. Nicky was her father's last hope. He was centring all his remaining ambitions on him. He was forever sticking public school prospectuses under her nose. 'You're depriving Nicky of all this,' he'd say.

She rose to her feet.

'Will you be all right with Grandpa for a while?'

Nicky nodded.

'I won't be long.'

'Be as long as you like,' replied her father. 'We'll be all right, won't we, Nicky?'

Harriet, leaving them together, wondered uneasily whether Nicky was too young to be indoctrinated into her father's vision of life.

She went through the accounts with Douglas at the gallery and then, since it was too early to go back to her father's, she slipped into a nearby café. She sat sipping her cappuccino, thinking about her father being beaten as a boy for something he hadn't done. Was this where his lifelong resentment towards women had begun, from this one small incident in his childhood? She and her mother had lived under its shadow all their lives. In the end, her mother hadn't been able to put up with it any longer. The relationship between her parents had degenerated into endless bickering about the most trivial of things. They'd lived apart for the last three years of her mother's life, although quite why Harriet, down in London, had never been able to figure out. She'd always suspected some unfaithfulness on his part. But perhaps it had been nothing so specific, simply the accumulation of a lifetime's irritation with each other?

She took out a cigarette and lit it. The waitress, a sharp-faced woman in her fifties, came up to her.

'Ner smirkin'.' She pointed to a sign on the wall. 'This is a ner smirkin' café. If you want to smirk, ger off erm.'

Harriet, whose ears after six months back in the north were now reattuned to the local accent, obediently stubbed out her cigarette. 'Sorry,' she said, as meekly as if she'd been caught robbing a bank (for many people nowadays, smoking *was* a more serious offence than robbing a bank). She smiled to herself as she remembered Miss Barnesley one day in class telling her to 'Wipe that smirk off your face, Harriet.' She'd had to go home and look up smirk in the dictionary. The waitress eyed her suspiciously and moved away.

Harriet glanced around. At the table next to hers, a middle-aged woman sat tapping her ringed fingers as she waited impatiently to order. Tap, tap her fingers went on the Formica. Just as her mother's fingers had tapped all through Harriet's childhood. It was the anniversary of her death tomorrow. Nine years ago tomorrow she'd left them all. Her father wouldn't mention the anniversary. Her mother's name hadn't passed his lips since the day she'd moved out. Masculine pride. Harriet sighed and finished her coffee. Why aren't you here, Mum, to help me with Daniel? With Nicky? With Dad? With all of the life I've got to get through without you? She left the café in a blur of tears and had to sit down on a bench to steady herself before she could face her father again.

On the way home from his grandfather's, Nicky had a tantrum and in calming him down Harriet forgot to think about her mother. But the thoughts returned after she'd bathed Nicky and put him to bed. She made herself a cup of coffee and went up to her studio on the second floor. It was a large, bright room overlooking the street. The ceiling was white, the walls a quiet grey, restful for her eyes in between painting. There were no curtains at the windows, to maximise the light.

She stood in front of the blank canvas, thoughts crowding her mind. No, it was no use. She wouldn't be able to paint tonight. She sat down on the old sofa worn bare since Daniel and Nicky had clambered over it, dribbled on it and been sick on it as babies. She lit a cigarette. What she chiefly thought about death was this: you went calmly along, painting and looking after the children, thinking life was going to go on for ever, and then death revealed that all the time you'd been walking on a tightrope suspended over a yawning chasm. Her mother's death had made her feel like that. It had made everything wobble for a bit. Brought her own death that little bit nearer.

The sound of the phone ringing in her bedroom below broke in on her thoughts. She ran down to answer it.

'Hi. Alix here. I rang up for a chat. Tim's busy surfing.'

Harriet glanced out of the window. 'Surfing? In the dark?'

'Not that kind of surfing. Surfing the Net. Tim's been wired up for the World Wide Web. He thinks he's got friends all over the world. He spends ages chatting to a bloke in Australia about

EC law. I say to him, Tim, get real, these aren't proper friends. They aren't going to be there to hold your hand if you get fired from your job or if Arsenal lose at Wembley. He used to spend weekends under the bonnet of his car. Now he spends them staring at a screen. I'm an Internet widow. Beep beep, buzz buzz from the spare room till three in the morning.' She groaned. 'Pathetic, isn't it? Why would anyone want to communicate in such a dysfunctional, anti-social way?'

'I don't know. As Fiona demonstrated this morning, I don't understand computers.'

'Neither do I. Nor do I want to. Anyway, I know you never go anywhere in the evening, so I thought I'd give you a ring. You could tell me a bit more about this dating agency.'

'Can we do it some other time, Alix?'

With the quickness Harriet liked her for, Alix said, 'Gosh, you sound down. What's the matter?'

'I was thinking of my mother. She died nine years ago tomorrow. It's funny how it still seems like yesterday.'

'I know, it never goes, does it? My father died twenty-three years ago and I can still remember exactly what it felt like.'

'I didn't realise he was dead, Alix. You must have been just out of school.'

'Just finishing. He was forty-two. He had cancer.'

'My mother had a stroke. She was fifty-three.'

'Some people get a crap deal out of life, don't they?' Then, as Harriet couldn't answer for tears, Alix added, 'I'm sorry, Harriet. I've caught you at a bad time. I'll see you at St Cecilia's tomorrow.' She rang off.

Harriet put the phone down, went back upstairs to her studio and lit another cigarette. She wondered whether Alix's mother was still alive. There'd been something funny about her. She'd been ill or something. Strange, then, that it had been her father, that tall, rather good-looking man, who had died. But perhaps Alix's mother was dead too. Harriet didn't know. Parents were another topic rarely discussed at the school gate.

Harriet sat for a long while in the dark, thinking. Death always made her think of Daniel for some reason. Perhaps because the doctor had said it was unlikely he would have a normal life span. For some women that would be a consolation, the thought of their son being released into a better life. Not believing in an after-life, Harriet was denied that comfort. In her view, any kind of life was better than none. Marginally.

That night she had a dream. She was three feet eight inches tall. Dressed in jeans, yellow anorak and trainers, she was walking along a busy street. Fear walked in front of her. The pavement was uneven. From time to time she stumbled. It was raining. She wanted to do up her anorak, but she couldn't remember how. All around her, above her head, was a buzz of voices. She couldn't make out what was being said. The words made no sense; they were disjointed grunts coming out of the backs of people's heads. She wasn't tall enough to see their faces. They were giant shapes moving backwards and forwards in a confusing way. They jostled her as they passed. To escape them, she stepped out into the road. There was a screech of brakes, a thud, and then all went silent.

Harriet opened her eyes and screamed. Then she lay very still in the darkness, adjusting to her proper height. There was no sound from upstairs. Nicky hadn't woken. She switched on the light and reached for the phone. The night nurse wasn't pleased. No, there'd been no accident. The children were quiet in their beds.

Harriet replaced the receiver. It's all right, Daniel, she thought. Only a bad dream. Go back to sleep now. She didn't doubt it had been Daniel's dream that had woken her up. She'd put space between them, she'd had to, for the sake of her own sanity and Nicky's; but he was always with her, day and night, thoughts of him, no matter what she was doing. He was her life-sentence. He was also her joy. Her astonishingly beautiful first-born.

Chapter Three

....

The next day brought post for Harriet. 'We are thrilled you've taken the plunge and decided to join Sweethearts. Choosing your partner for life is the most important decision you will ever have to make. We are here, with our sophisticated computer analysis and experts in psychology, to make that decision a little bit easier. The preliminary form you filled in has matched you with Andrew, thirty-nine, and living in Hull.'

Harriet pulled a face. Andrew wasn't a name that appealed to her particularly and she bet thirty-nine meant forty.

'When you go on to the next stage' (send us the money) 'we will post you a full list of names matched personally for you by our computer. Why delay? Send off the fee today and find the partner of your dreams.'

She put down the letter. It was a long time since she'd had dreams about the perfect partner. A few new friends of the opposite sex was what she'd gladly settle for. She glanced at Nicky sitting on the kitchen floor in pyjamas, wellington boots and a sun hat, his mouth smeared with chocolate from the leftover Easter egg he'd insisted on having for breakfast. With two young children what else could she hope for?

Half an hour later, having changed Nicky into shorts and brushed his teeth, Harriet stood outside St Cecilia's school gate.

'Hi, Alix. Hello, Peggy.'

'I say Peggy, are you OK?' Fiona Wilson-Smith paused at their group as she made her way along the line of parents. Like royalty, Harriet always thought. You felt privileged to have a word. 'You're looking a bit peaky. Is it the diet?'

'I'm all right,' mumbled Peggy.

Harriet glanced at her. Peggy's face was pale, her expression indecipherable behind a pair of dark sunglasses. Red-haired Ben stood by her side, waiting to go in. Her elder son, Simon, was playing in the infants' playground.

Harriet waited till Fiona was out of earshot, then said, 'Are you really all right, Peg? You don't look it.'

'Tell you later,' she replied in an undertone, making Harriet feel quite anxious. What on earth was wrong? She glanced down at Ben. The children weren't ill or Peggy wouldn't be here. She hoped there was nothing the matter with Frank. He and Peggy had been married for over ten years.

'Gosh, Muriel! Whatever have you done to the side of your face? That's a really nasty bruise.'

Brenda Barlow's strident tones rang in Harriet's ear, distracting her attention from Peggy. Brenda, a small, thin woman with eyes like coal nuggets, was the local busybody. Mention anything to Brenda and it would be all round Apple Burton in less than half a morning. Harriet was always extremely cagey in her presence.

'N . . . nothing. I . . . fell.' Muriel bent down to retrieve a shoe the baby had thrown out of its buggy, then moved further down in the direction of the school gate, clutching her three-year-old by the hand.

'She's so pathetic,' muttered Alix, when Brenda's back was turned. 'Why doesn't she just leave him?'

'I know. It's dreadful.' Peggy sighed.

Harriet looked at them both. 'Why? What do you mean?' She thought for a moment, then said in horror, 'You don't mean Ted gave her that bruise?' Ted was Muriel's husband, a short, stocky man, going bald.

'Darling, you'd never know anything about anything, would you, if we didn't keep you informed? Why do you think she wears all those clothes, even in the middle of a heat wave? It's to cover up the bruises.'

'It's been going on for years,' added Peggy. 'I've had a talk with her, even given her the address of a refuge in Hull. She says she can't leave him because of the children.'

'Pathetic!' snorted Alix. 'He'll start on them next.'

'How awful!' exclaimed Harriet. 'Can't we do something?'

Alix gazed at her ironically. 'What do you suggest we do? Camp out on her doorstep and rush in the moment we hear screaming? No. These women learn to scream with their mouths shut. Oh, hello, Frances,' she added, as her sister came up to join them, which she sometimes did after dropping her two off at junior school.

Frances, unlike her sister, was small and dark, and excessively thin.

'What have you eaten today?' Alix asked. 'Did you have breakfast?'

Frances frowned. 'Of course I had breakfast.'

'What did you have?' persisted Alix.

'Half an apple.'

'Frances! Really!' said her sister, exasperated. 'Go home and get some carbohydrates down you, for God's sake!'

'Alix! Stop fussing! I eat like a pig, you know I do.'

'You don't, that's the trouble. I wish you did.'

'You need talk, all that exercising you do.'

'I exercise so that I can eat. You don't exercise and you don't eat. That's not a healthy option.'

'I'm not going to talk to you, Alix, if you're in that sort of mood.' Frances walked off.

Alix stood looking after her, biting her lip and frowning.

Harriet, observing this bout of sisterly squabbling, wondered whether things had always been like this between them, whether Alix had always had to look out for her younger sister.

'Here she comes,' said Peggy as Mrs Parker emerged from the nursery door, ringing her hand-bell.

There was a general movement along the line as parents stooped to kiss their children, smooth down their hair and straighten their collars.

'Have a lovely morning, Nicky.'

He wriggled out of his mother's embrace and ran off into the playground. Harriet stood remembering, half with regret, those mornings early on when he'd refused to let go of her hand and she'd had to walk with him right into the classroom.

'Can I come some of the way with you two?' muttered Peggy.

Harriet looked at her. 'Of course, Peg. What's wrong?'

Peggy walked alongside her for a moment in silence. 'Did you have a letter this morning?'

'Yes I did, as a matter of fact, but –'

'Oh, poor you! Horrible, aren't they? I feel really shattered by mine.'

'Well they are a bit sleazy, perhaps. How did you know I'd had one?'

Over her shoulder, Harriet glared at Alix walking a couple of paces behind them. How could Alix have been so tactless as to reveal her secret about the dating agency to Peggy? It would be all round the school gate that she was looking for a man. That guy with the ginger hair and the Alsatian on a piece of string might even offer his services.

'Anyway, I don't understand,' she continued, 'I thought you were happy with Frank? Why would you want to go and join something like that?'

Harriet glared at Alix again. If this had been her way of cheering Peggy up, it was a pretty poor one. With a husband and two children, how on earth would Peggy find time for an affair? To say nothing of the morality of it.

'Join? It isn't a club,' replied Peggy. 'Though perhaps it'll turn out to be. Denise Potter has had one too. She told me last week.' Denise was another of the mothers at the school gate.

'Denise?' said Harriet, bewildered. 'But she's only just got married again.'

'I know. That's what the letter was about. Made her feel quite sick. So did mine.'

'Well I know the marketing jargon they use would make anyone want to throw up, but –'

'Look, I think you two must have got your wires crossed somewhere,' interrupted Alix from behind. 'What exactly are we talking about here?'

'Anonymous letters.' Peggy turned round. 'I've had one. Denise has had one. And now Harriet says she's had one too.'

'No, no,' put in Harriet hastily. 'I thought you were talking about something else. My letter was about – something quite different.' She glanced sheepishly at Alix who said, 'You don't mean to say there's a poison pen at work in the community?'

'Apparently. My letter was quite awful. It accused Frank of, well, of having an affair with his secretary. Bonking, is how the writer put it. There was a drawing. It can't be true, it just can't!' added Peggy. 'Shirley's near retirement. She's sixty if she's a day.'

'I'm sure it's not true,' said Harriet quickly. Though she only knew him from bumping into him occasionally at the school gate, Frank Murray had always seemed to her exactly the right sort of husband for Peggy. Solid and reliable, he worked for a large company in the centre of Hull.

'Did Frank see it? What did he say?' Alix came up beside them as the pavement widened.

'He said it was a load of rubbish and I should ignore it. He wants me to burn it.'

'Have you?'

'Not yet.'

'Perhaps you should take it to the police?' suggested Harriet.

'Oh, they wouldn't be interested. It's printed on a scrappy bit of paper. Frank said it's the type of paper they use at the office for computer print-outs.'

'Sneaky,' remarked Alix.

'Yes. Sneaky and rather horrible. Frank says I should forget all about it and I suppose I should. But it's made me feel all quivery inside. To think that anyone could hate me enough to send me a letter like that.' Peggy's plump freckled face crumpled. Behind the dark glasses, tears rolled down her cheeks.

'It might not have been anything personal,' said Harriet slowly. 'Did it mention Frank by name?'

Peggy sniffed, took off her glasses and wiped her eyes on her sleeve. 'No, I don't think it did. "Your husband" is what it said. It didn't mention my first name either. It was simply addressed to Mrs Murray.'

'There you are then. The letter writer probably picked your name at random out of the phone book. After all, you aren't the only one. Didn't you say Denise had had one?'

'Yes, she got hers last week. She was so upset she didn't show it to anyone, not even to Peter. You know they've only been married a month. She only told me about it because I found her crying her eyes out behind the frozen vegetables at Sainsbury's.'

'What did hers say?'

27

'It said that her husband – I don't think it mentioned him by name either, now I come to think of it – had gone to prostitutes before they were married. There was a description of the things he liked done to him. Rather beastly. And, like mine, it had a drawing. Hers was of a woman in boots and a corset with a whip in her hand.'

'The writer's obviously unhinged,' said Harriet. 'Some kind of pervert. I should ignore it.'

'I wonder if anyone else has had one?' mused Alix. 'I imagine it's the sort of thing people would normally want to keep quiet about. Yes, I wouldn't be surprised if one or two other people in Apple Burton had received one. After all, why should he pick on you two? Was the postmark local?'

'I think so. It was a bit smudged.' Peggy walked on for a moment in silence. 'Perhaps you're right. Perhaps it was nothing personal. Maybe I was unlucky. Look, you two, you won't mention this to anyone, will you?'

'Of course not,' replied Harriet.

'I'm going to forget all about it now. I just felt I had to tell someone. I was going mad on my own thinking about it. And I couldn't tell my mother. She'd have said something like there's no smoke without fire and spent half the day interrogating me about Frank.'

'It's all best ignored,' said Harriet firmly. 'It was probably something that's happened once and you two were unlucky. Now that he or she has let off steam that'll be the end of it.'

'I hope so.' Peggy sighed. She stood still on the pavement. 'I think I'll go back home now. I can't face going into town this morning.'

'That's right,' agreed Alix. 'Go home, make yourself a cup of coffee and listen to *Woman*'s hour or something.'

'Take care,' said Harriet. 'Poor Peggy,' she murmured, as the two of them walked on. 'I wouldn't like to get a letter like that.'

Alix nodded. 'Pretty unnerving, all right. But you know, Harriet, though I didn't like to say so in front of Peggy, these things don't usually stop there. Once a writer has got the steam up to write this kind of thing, he often goes on and on, especially if they're as random as these appear to be.'

'How do you know about it? I've never in my life come across this kind of thing.'

'I worked in the Citizens' Advice Bureau, remember? It's surprising how often people do receive nasty anonymous letters through the post. I saw quite a few of them.'

'I hope you're wrong. I hope this is the end of them.'

'So do I.' They stopped outside Harriet's house. 'Well, cheerio. Don't let it interfere with your morning's painting. I say.' Alix turned. 'Wouldn't it be awful if the letter turned out to be true?'

'What do you mean?'

'I mean if Frank really *is* having an affair with his secretary.'

Harriet stared at her. 'Oh no, that's impossible. It'd kill Peggy. She depends on him so much. And Frank, well, he seems so – so reliable.'

'He does,' agreed Alix. 'See you at lunch-time.'

'Bye.'

Harriet went inside her house. It had been quite an eventful morning, what with her letter from the dating agency and Peggy's anonymous letter and finding out that Muriel's husband beat her up. Peaceful Apple Burton, she thought, where nothing ever happens. She hoped nothing was going to happen to disturb that peace. Harriet had always maintained that a dull life was the only way to get any painting done.

She cleared away the breakfast things and went up to her studio. Standing in front of her easel, she suddenly found it quite easy to dismiss Peggy's letter from her mind. The daily struggle to record light, colour and form – for Harriet that was what spelled happiness. She lit a cigarette and selected a brush. The ninth anniversary of her mother's death. She painted all morning in a sudden burst of energy. Rage over her mother's stroke seemed to spur her on, as if by creating something on canvas she could somehow counteract the disease that had so suddenly destroyed her mother's body. Nonsense, of course. It was science, not art, that would one day find the cure.

At twelve-thirty, Harriet laid down her brush, stood back and gazed at the three angry red stripes horizontal on the canvas. It reminded her of Rothko, except that this painting wasn't restful. It had been painted in rage. Well, there were a lot of angry people about these days. Perhaps someone would like it enough to buy it. She cleaned her brush and went downstairs to grab a sandwich before it was time to pick up Nicky.

She approached the school gate with something like dread, but the mothers were all talking cheerfully to one another and Peggy even gave her a wave and a smile. It's nothing, Harriet thought; that letter was a one-off, a flash in the pan. She looked for Denise and saw her waiting calmly by the gate, tall and pretty in a flowered summer dress, her long hair fastened up in a ponytail. Harriet gazed along the line of chatting parents. How could she have thought that anything bad would happen here, in this most innocent of settings, where parents waited for their children to come out of nursery?

Chapter Four

....

Two days later, Harriet received another letter. It contained four names and phone numbers, with the promise of more to follow. She looked at them. Andrew (again), James, Derek and Mick. All pretty innocuous, as men's names went. What the hell, she thought. She was tired of doing nothing but paint and look after Nicky. It would be nice to go out for a change, even if it was only down to the pub.

While Nicky was eating his Coco Pops, she dialled Andrew's number.

A breathless voice said, 'Hi! This is Andy. I'm not in at the moment, but if you leave your name and number, I'll get back to you ASAP. Cheers!'

She hesitated. Didn't Andrew sound just a little too cheerful? Was he on something? Did he work in PR? Was he a manic depressive in the manic phase? She left her name and number anyway.

There was a peculiar hush at the school gate when Harriet arrived with Nicky. Some of the parents were huddled together in groups, speaking in whispers. Others were standing apart looking worried.

'What's happened? What's the matter?' she asked Alix. She felt obliged to whisper since everyone else was.

'There've been more letters.'

'And not only letters,' put in Brenda Barlow eagerly. 'It's been coming up on people's computers.'

'What has?' asked Harriet.

'She means e-mail,' explained Fiona. 'You know I mentioned something funny came up on my computer a couple of days ago? Well, something really strange came up yesterday on my computer at home. God knows how he or she does it. It's quite difficult to send e-mail anonymously.'

'What did it say?' asked Brenda.

Fiona glanced at her coldly. 'I can't remember. I erased it immediately.'

Disappointment flashed across Brenda's face.

'I knew he wouldn't stop,' said Alix.

'Mary's had one,' added Brenda with relish, 'and Jane and someone else over there,' she waved a hand, 'had one come up on his computer at work.'

'This is awful,' said Harriet. 'It's got to be stopped.'

'I agree.' Peggy joined them. 'But what can we do?'

'We could go to the police,' said Fiona slowly.

'Yes, I'll come with you. Perhaps the others will come too.' Peggy darted over to where Mary and Jane were standing by the gate. A few moments later, she was back. 'They can't come. They've got to go to work.'

'*I've* got to go to work.' Fiona pursed her lips. 'But I think this is more important. We're none of us safe in our own homes at the moment. Try to get their letters off them at least, Peggy.'

'Why?'

'To show to the police.' Fiona was at her most patient.

'Oh yes, yes of course.' Peggy dashed back to Mary and Jane. They each reached into their handbags and pulled out a brown envelope.

'God! Fancy carrying them around,' muttered Fiona. 'I couldn't wait to erase mine.'

'You won't have anything to show the police,' Alix commented.

'No, but I can tell them what was in it.' Fiona glanced along the line to where Brenda was standing and lowered her voice. 'It said Julian visited gay bars. Have you ever heard anything more ridiculous?'

'Julian!'

No, thought Harriet, it didn't seem likely. Tall, dark and curly haired, Julian was one of the best-looking fathers at the school gate. He and Fiona had a four-year-old daughter, Angelica. Added to that, Julian was highly respected in the local community. He was a town councillor and sat on numerous committees.

'I've got the letters,' said Peggy, 'and we can pick up mine on the way to the police station. I'm glad now I didn't burn it if it's going to be evidence. I wonder what Denise did with hers?' They looked along the line but there was no sign of Denise. 'Oh well, we'll have to go on our own, Fiona. Why don't you two come along with us? We could do with some moral support.'

'Yes, all right,' agreed Harriet.

'Can't. Sorry. I've got a doctor's appointment,' replied Alix.

So Fiona, Peggy and Harriet went, in Fiona's open-topped BMW, to Apple Burton police station, stopping on the way to pick up Peggy's letter.

'Yes?' said the bored-looking police constable behind the counter. He folded up his copy of the *Sun* with an air of regret.

'We're here to report a crime.' Peggy leaned up confidentially against the counter. 'We've received letters.'

'What kind of letters?' The police constable stifled a yawn.

'Poison pen.'

The police constable raised an eyebrow. 'Been reading Agatha Christie, have we?'

'Now listen, this is serious,' put in Fiona indignantly. 'We've had the most filthy letters.'

Harriet didn't know whether it was Fiona's short skirt, her upper-class accent or the mention of filth that caused a spark of interest to appear in the policeman's eyes.

'Hand them over, then.'

'I beg your pardon?' said Fiona.

'If we're going to investigate this we need to see the letters, madam.'

'Here they are.' Peggy thrust them across the counter. 'I hope you'll be discreet, constable. These letters contain wild allegations which could be very damaging if they got out.'

The police officer gave Fiona a look. 'Which one is yours?'

'Mine came by e-mail,' she said, loftily.

'Eh?'

'It came up on my computer screen.'

'Oh? And what have you done with it?'

'I've erased it.'

'Pity.'

'Do you think they're connected? The letters and the anonymous e-mails?' asked Harriet. 'Do you think they were written by the same person?'

'Not necessarily. Though the idea of one, let alone two anonymous letter writers operating in Apple Burton seems unlikely.' He looked at them suspiciously. 'This isn't some kind of hoax you ladies have dreamed up at a coffee morning, is it?'

'I wouldn't be seen dead at a coffee morning,' replied Fiona. 'And it certainly isn't a hoax.'

'Good. There are penalties for wasting police time, you know.' He glanced down at the letters. 'No use testing for fingerprints, I suppose. They'll have been pawed over by the lot of you.'

'On the contrary, officer. We don't even know what's in two of them, Mrs Davison's and Mrs Harris's,' said Fiona drily.

'What will happen?' asked Peggy, after they had given him their names and addresses.

'There's nothing much we can do at the moment, Mrs Murray, apart from opening a file. It's not a prosecutable offence to send letters like these.'

'Well if it's not, it certainly ought to be,' put in Fiona.

The constable fixed her with a look. 'There are a lot of things that ought to be prosecutable that aren't, madam.'

'There haven't been any other anonymous letters reported in the area then?' asked Harriet.

'Not that I know of. It's not the sort of thing people go

around broadcasting. They usually prefer not to report it to the police.'

'I can see why,' muttered Peggy, as the three of them trailed forlornly out of the police station. 'Not very encouraging, was he?'

'No,' agreed Harriet.

They began walking back towards Fiona's car.

'We'll simply have to do the thing ourselves,' said Fiona, in determined fashion.

'What do you mean?'

'Be vigilant. Encourage people to come forward with their letters. Keep our eyes and ears open.'

'You're right,' said Peggy. 'If the police won't help us, we'll have to do it ourselves.'

'That's the spirit! Well, must dash. Got a business to run. Coffee mornings indeed!' Fiona gave a wave and got into her BMW.

They watched as she drove away.

Peggy sighed. 'It must be nice to be decisive.'

'Yes,' said Harriet. 'I wonder what it feels like.' She gave Peggy's arm a squeeze. 'Don't worry. Whoever wrote those letters is a loony. And now at least you know you're not the only person to have received one.'

'Yes, they're obviously the product of a sick mind and quite unfounded,' Peggy said cheerfully. She'd returned to her usual self. 'I think I'll go back on that diet. All this stress has played havoc with it. I feel better now.'

'Good.' Harriet glanced at her watch. 'There's not much point me starting painting at this late hour. Are you on for a coffee in the Apple Burton Arms?'

'Yes, why not? They do great Danish pastries.'

'I thought you were going on a diet?'

'Bugger the diet. I'll start it tomorrow.'

They lingered in the Arms until it was time to collect Nicky and Ben from nursery. At the gate of St Cecilia's, they met up with Alix.

'How did it go down at the police station?'

'They weren't interested,' replied Peggy.

'I thought they might not be.'

'Fiona says we must all be vigilant.' Peggy glanced along the innocent-looking line of mothers, fathers, grannies and childminders waiting for the children to come out. 'Though it seems hard to believe the writer of those letters is someone connected with St Cecilia's.'

'It does,' agreed Harriet. 'For all we know people all around town might be receiving letters and e-mails and simply not coming forward with them.'

'I bet the writer's a man,' said Peggy. 'All this obsession with sex.'

'Mm,' said Harriet. 'If it was man and say, for argument's sake, he was connected with St Cecilia's, who do you think it could be?'

'Some lonely frustrated man who gets his kicks out of sending filthy fantasies to females?' suggested Alix.

'How many men come regularly to the school gate?' asked Peggy.

'There's that man with the Alsatian,' put in Harriet. 'I don't know his name.'

'Tony Richards,' said Peggy. 'He's unemployed.'

'How do you know?'

'Frank sacked him three months ago.'

'So he's had plenty of time to hatch this up,' said Alix.

'Yes, Peggy!' Harriet pounced eagerly on Alix's suggestion. 'Perhaps it's all an elaborate revenge plot to get back at Frank through you?'

'But then why write all the other letters?' Peggy objected.

'Perhaps we should start getting friendly with him anyway.'

'Why?'

'To see what kind of man he is,' Harriet explained. 'To see if he's the kind of man who might write those letters.'

'It's no good me talking to him,' said Peggy. 'He knows exactly who I am. Ever since Frank sacked him there's been a frozen silence between us. If I tried getting friendly with him now, he'd simply be suspicious.'

'OK, Alix and I could do it then. Here they come.'

Led by Mrs Parker, the children marched across the playground, holding hands and singing 'Baa, baa, black sheep'. Peggy collected

Ben and set off home. The other two women turned in the opposite direction.

'If it is a man,' persisted Harriet, 'who else could it be besides Tony Richards?'

'The vicar has a daughter in the nursery. He sometimes drops her off.'

'Reverend Threlfall? I can't see it.'

'Neither can I, really,' Alix admitted, 'except that, being a vicar, he'd be privy to secrets about everyone's personal life. Everyone who goes to St Cecilia's church, that is.'

'If you're arguing along those lines, it could equally be Dr Wentworth. In fact more so. I bet more people attend his surgery than go to St Cecilia's church.'

'True. And what about that sour-looking man who never speaks to anyone?'

Harriet groaned. 'Oh, Christ, we'll never get friendly with him! Apart from Tony Richards, they don't seem very satisfactory suspects, do they?'

'No, but we have to start somewhere, I suppose.' Alix halted outside Harriet's house. 'After the weekend, let's see if we can get a line on Tony Richards, shall we? See you on Monday.'

Back home, faced with the thought of yet another weekend on her own without any adult company, Harriet was slightly disappointed to find no message on her answering machine from Andrew (or Andy). While Nicky took a nap on the sofa, she had another look at her list. She dialled James's number. He appeared to be out. She phoned Derek. An elderly sounding woman answered.

'I'm Derek's mother. How do you do? Just a moment please, I'll get him.' Like many women in the area, Derek's mother spoke in a broad Hull accent while attempting, vainly, to disguise it as South of England. This gave a most peculiar twist to her vowels. 'Who may I say is calling?'

'Harriet Smith.' She wasn't going to give her real surname. She didn't want Derek (or his mother) looking her up in the phone book.

'Just a moment, please. Derek! Derek!' Harriet heard her screeching down some corridor. 'Fern curl fer yer!'

'Hi. That was my mum. You're lucky to catch me, I was on my way out to the office. This is my lunch hour. I always come back home for lunch. Makes a nice break in the middle of the day.'

'You still live at home, do you?' Harriet consulted her list. Forty-one.

'Yes, it's just me and my mum. Dad died eight years ago. I couldn't leave her on her own. But it's not what you think. We lead separate lives. In fact it was Mum who suggested I join Sweethearts. I thought, what the hell? Give it a try. Anything for a laugh, eh?'

Thanks very much, thought Harriet. 'You work locally then, do you?' she asked.

'Yes, I'm with NatWest. Nice steady job, my mum said. What do you do – Harriet, is it?'

'Yes, Harriet Smith. I paint.'

'That's nice. My mum said you had a nice voice on the phone. She said you didn't sound common.'

'Oh well, that's good. If your mother says that, I must be all right.'

He failed to catch the sarcasm. 'Yes, she's generally right about people. She's put me right about quite a number of my girlfriends over the years.'

I bet, thought Harriet.

'So you're a painter, are you? What do you paint?'

'Pictures.'

'What's your favourite colour?'

'Cobalt,' she snarled down the phone.

'Eh?'

She made an exasperated noise and rang off. That computer of theirs must have been having a bad day when it matched us up together, she thought. She crossed Derek's name off her list. She'd kill Alix when she saw her.

Chapter Five

....

'You have to persevere. You can't expect the computer to get it right every time. Have you heard about Denise?' said Alix on Monday morning.

'No. Why? What's she done?'

'She's left Peter.'

'Bloody hell! Why?'

'Those things in that letter. They turned out to be true. Peter broke down and confessed last Thursday.'

'So that's why she wasn't at the school gate on Friday.'

Peggy came up to them looking white-faced and strained. 'Have you heard about Denise?'

'Alix has just told me.'

'I don't know what to think.'

'Peggy, just because one letter's turned out to be true, it doesn't mean the others are. It was probably a lucky guess on the writer's part,' Harriet comforted her.

'That's what I keep telling myself. I wish we could find out who's writing these letters, though.'

'Has anyone had any more?' asked Harriet.

'No,' replied Alix. 'Or if they have, they're not telling.' She looked along the line of waiting parents. 'I bet somebody's had one. What would you do if you got one?'

'Tear it up,' admitted Harriet. 'And not tell anyone.'

'There you are. So would I probably.'

'Yet if there is somebody targeting the parents at St Cecilia's, they ought to be stopped. It could get dangerous. One marriage is already under threat and . . .' She glanced at Peggy and stopped.

'Who do you think it could be?' wailed Peggy.

'Who knows?' Alix grunted. 'Somebody whose child was turned down for a place?'

'Exactly,' said Harriet. 'Ludicrous, isn't it? I really wouldn't take any notice, Peggy. Denise may have had other reasons for leaving.

I mean she may have found out something else about Peter. After all, they hadn't been married very long, had they? It's different with you and Frank. You've known each other for years.'

'Men do go off, though. You read about it in the papers all the time.' Peggy sighed. 'I wish I wasn't so fat! Very soon I won't be able to get into jeans at all.'

As they were speaking, Harriet noticed out of the corner of her eye that Tony Richards was edging closer and closer to their group. She nudged Alix. Was he eavesdropping on their conversation? Was he trying to find out how much they knew? Was he the letter writer? Alix gave him a hard stare and he moved away again, dragging his Alsatian with him.

'Interesting,' murmured Alix.

'Very,' replied Harriet, then the children came out and put a stop to their discussion.

Harriet took Nicky into town to buy him some new shoes. It took a long time as he insisted they had to be red. While she was in the shop, Harriet bought herself a pair of sandals.

'The'rr nice, therse,' said the sales assistant, wrapping them up.

'Comfortable,' agreed Harriet.

'Yer. Comfort's what yer lookin' fer nerr, isn't it?' said the assistant.

Harriet didn't like that 'nerr'. Did it mean 'now' as in nowadays? Or 'now' as in now the weather's turned hot? She feared it didn't. She feared it meant now you've reached that age when fashion's no longer relevant to you. She left the shop feeling thoroughly depressed.

Halfway home, Nicky sat down on the pavement and refused to walk any further.

'My legs won't go any more, Mummy.'

'Come on, Nicky.' It was embarrassing having one's child sit down in the middle of the pavement. People were having to walk round him. Not people Harriet knew. But still. 'Come on. When you get home you can have a lolly,' she added, resorting to bribery.

He gazed solemnly up at her. 'I'm at the end of my tether.'

'Oh, Nicky! Don't exaggerate!' she exclaimed, lifting him up in her arms.

She had to carry him the rest of the way home. She arrived back, exhausted and cross, to find the phone ringing. She sprinted down the hall to the kitchen to answer it.

'Hi. This is Andy returning your call.'

'What? I'm sorry, I can't hear you very well. The line's bad.'

'I'm on my mobile. Just coming out of a tunnel . . . Now! Is that better?'

'Yes. Who did you say you were?'

'Andy. From Sweethearts. Remember?'

'Oh. Yes.'

'Tell me all about yourself. Name, age, vital statistics. Only joking.'

'I'm Harriet. I'm thirty-six.'

'Nothing wrong with that. In my opinion, women are like cheese. They ripen with age.'

'How old are you?' She knew how old he was. It had said in the agency's letter. She wanted to make a point.

'Forty,' he replied, shaving two years off his age in the letter. 'I'm a sales rep for a computer company. Spend the week dashing around the country. Love the job but it plays havoc with relationships. What do you do?'

'I paint.'

'Lady of leisure, are you? I had a girlfriend once who went to painting classes. Never amounted to much. A few daubs that you certainly wouldn't want round the house.'

'I'm a professional artist. I do it every day.'

'Do you? Lucky woman. If I was doing it every day I wouldn't need to join a dating agency.'

'Look, it was nice of you to phone back, but I don't think this is going to work out, do you?'

'Bit hasty, aren't you? I haven't told you anything about myself yet.'

'I think you have.'

'But . . . oh, shit . . . another tunnel.'

There was a whirring noise. His voice disappeared into a black hole.

Harriet put down the phone. She hoped she'd been firm enough.

After all, he had her number now. She'd specified to the agency that they weren't to hand out her name or number to anyone, she'd do all the phoning. And now, stupidly, she'd given her number to Andrew. If this goes on, she thought, I'll have to go ex-directory.

At tea, as Nicky sat eating his boiled egg and soldiers, she reviewed her list. Andrew (crossed off). Derek (crossed off). Was she being too choosy for a woman in her position? James. Mike. On impulse, she rang James's number again. This time he was in, but he sounded frantic.

'Hello. Yes, that's me. Oh hell! Can you hang on a minute? I'm in the middle of feeding the kids.'

Harriet hung on, hearing children's shrieks in the background. This sounded more promising. More like real life, anyway. There were several more yells, then a thump, then James came on again.

'Listen, could I phone you back in half an hour?'

'Sure.'

'I'll get their tea finished, then I'll sit them down in front of a video and we can talk properly. Sorry to be in such a flap.'

'It's all right. Silly time to call.' She gave him her number and rang off.

Nicky looked up.

'Was that my daddy on the phone?'

'No, darling, it wasn't.'

'Ooh!' His face fell. He stared down at his plate.

She put an arm around him. 'Some day, Daddy will phone, Nicky. Some day he will. Just now he's busy with his camels.'

Nicky, who'd met up with his father once in the past year, had invented a story about Geoffrey being an Arabian prince who lived in a splendid palace and went out riding camels all day. Harriet was never quite sure what to do about this fantasy. It seemed to satisfy Nicky and gave him a certain kudos amongst his friends at nursery. She'd decided not to shatter it for the time being. Better an Arabian prince than a Tory politician who was too busy to see his son.

'I'd like to have a camel. Mum, I've finished my boiling egg. I need to watch a video.'

'Need to?'

'Yes, I need to.' He turned a serious face towards her. 'Oh please, Mummy, please. I like you very much. So much.'

She pressed her nose against his. 'I like you, you old flatterer.' She was about to add, 'just like your father', but thought better of it.

They went through into the playroom at the front of the house. When Harriet was a child, this had been a formal dining room and hardly used. She'd painted it bright yellow and sketched an animal frieze round the walls. Her father had practically had a fit when he saw it for the first time. Later he'd grudgingly admitted that at least she'd found some use for the room. She switched on the television. 'What video do you want, Nicky?' she asked, thinking that already she'd found something in common with James. She had just put in a Peter Rabbit video when the phone rang again.

'All right, Nicky? I'll go and see who that is.'

'Hi. James again. Sorry about that. Things have calmed down a bit now.'

'It's all right. I understand. I have children too.'

'I knew you must have. I told the agency I particularly wanted to meet women with children.'

'Did you? Why?' A sudden chill ran down her back. He wasn't some kind of pervert, was he?

'I'm not interested in women who go clubbing. I've got beyond all that.'

That sounded reasonable enough. So had she, for that matter. 'Why did you join Sweethearts, then?'

'My wife left me. About a year ago. It knocked a hole in my confidence.'

Join the club, thought Harriet. For once the computer seemed to have used its brain.

'And with the job and the kids I don't have time to go out looking for new people to meet. Why did you join?'

'Same reasons, basically. My husband and I split up. We got divorced two months ago. I have two children. Boys. My work is – well, I'm freelance. I work at home all day so I never see anyone.'

'You're in a similar position to me then.' There was a new note of interest in his voice.

'Y-yes,' she said uncertainly. It had suddenly occurred to her that what James might really be looking for wasn't so much a date as a mother for his children. 'Er . . .'

'Yes?'

'Er . . . when your wife left you, she didn't take the children then?'

'Yes and no. Weekends the girls are with me. During the week Trish has them. Tonight's a bit of an exception. Trish had to go away on a conference.'

'I see.' Harriet couldn't think of anything else to say. No doubt she should be asking James all sorts of searching personal questions.

'Look, I don't want to rush things but the video's going to come to an end soon. It, er,' he hesitated, 'it sounds as if we've got things in common.'

'It does,' she said, giving him the reassurance he was clearly waiting for.

'Would you like to meet up? For a drink or something?'

'Good idea.'

They arranged an evening.

'I'll have to find a baby-sitter,' she said, as she rang off.

She thought for a moment, then rang Alix.

'Oh, Harriet, what a bore! I could have baby-sat for you myself but there's a thing on at the university that evening. I promised Tim I'd go. What a nuisance.'

'Never mind, I'll think of something.'

'No, listen, there's Caroline. She's a friend of our regular baby-sitter, Theresa. We use her when Theresa's unavailable. She's seventeen. Quite reliable. I'll give you her phone number.'

'Thanks, Alix. I'm just wondering how Nicky will cope, though. Since we moved back to Apple Burton, he's got out of the way of me going out in the evening.'

'High time he got used to it again then. Your first date! How exciting. What does he sound like?'

'A hassled father of two. His wife walked out about a year ago.'

'Sounds the perfect match.'

'Gee, thanks.'

She rang off, then rang Caroline.

'Sorry, Mrs Lee. I'm booked that evening. Any other time.'

Harriet put down the phone. She couldn't ask her father to come round. She'd never asked him to baby-sit before in the evenings and she couldn't face all the probing questions that were bound to follow. There was nothing for it. She dialled James's number.

'I'm sorry about this. I'm having trouble finding a baby-sitter. I'm afraid I won't be able to make it on Wednesday after all.'

'You've changed your mind.'

He sounded so hurt – what had his wife done to him? – that she said, after a moment's hesitation, 'Look, why don't you come round here? I'll cook us both supper. Something simple.'

'Great.'

'Are you vegetarian?'

'I eat anything nowadays so long as it's cooked by someone else. I get so sick of my own cooking.'

She laughed and put down the phone. She supposed it was safe. It was against the agency's advice to invite a man back home on your first date. But if she couldn't judge what someone was like at her age, what hope was there? She glanced at the last name on the list. Mick. She'd save that one for later. In case the evening with James turned out to be an absolute disaster.

Chapter Six

....

The next morning, when Harriet turned the corner into the road where St Cecilia's school was, she saw quite a flurry of activity around the school gate. Instead of standing quietly in groups, parents were dashing to and fro along the line. Several of the women were in tears. Peggy ran up to her.

'Harriet, have you had one?'

'One what?'

'A letter.'

Harriet's heart sank. 'No. Why? You don't mean there have been more?'

Peggy nodded. 'Several of the parents received them in this morning's post. And this time the tactic's changed. Instead of attacking the recipient of the letter, they accuse other people.'

'How horrible!'

'It is. It's like the tabloids. Everyone's ghastly little secrets being made known to everyone else.'

'And the worst of it is,' added Alix, 'it's not just the parents now. The writer's moved on to the teachers. Beverley Simons got one about Mrs Parker.'

'Which one's Beverley Simons?' enquired Harriet. 'I don't think I know her.'

Peggy pointed out a small dark woman surrounded by a group of chattering parents. She looked to Harriet as if she was enjoying being the centre of attention for the first time in her life.

'There can't be anything wicked in Mrs Parker's life. I don't believe it. What did the letter say?'

'That she's a lesbian and lives with a Miss Milsom.'

Harriet burst out laughing, caught sight of Alix's face and stopped. 'It isn't true, is it?'

Alix nodded. 'Some of us have known about it for a while. They were seen holding hands in the cinema.'

'But she's *Mrs* Parker.'

Alix shrugged. 'They always call teachers Mrs nowadays. It's simpler that way. Like on the labour ward. A kind of courtesy title.'

'Well it won't make any difference,' said Harriet stoutly. 'She's still brilliant at her job.'

'Let's hope it won't make any difference,' said Peggy. 'Some people are funny about that sort of thing. Lesbians in charge of small children. They think they're a bad influence.'

'How stupid!' exclaimed Harriet.

'It is,' agreed Peggy. 'Oh hello, Frances.'

'Frances, have any of the parents at the junior school received one of these letters?' asked Harriet.

Frances shook her head. 'Not that I've heard. And before you ask, Alix, I had a bowl of Alpen for breakfast.'

'Glad to hear it,' returned her sister. 'Now go home and have a piece of toast.'

Frances gave a snort of derision and moved away.

'So it really does seem to be the nursery school that's being targeted,' commented Peggy. 'I wonder why.'

They watched as Mrs Parker came out ringing her hand-bell. She looked as calm and confident as ever.

'It's going to be all right,' said Peggy with relief, bending to kiss Ben goodbye. 'She's taking it in her stride. I knew she would.'

'She doesn't know yet,' muttered Alix, kissing Imogen. 'I bet you anything you like she doesn't know yet.'

Peggy turned to her. 'All right. I bet you that new Nicole Farhi shirt you were wearing last Friday.'

'OK.' Alix nodded. 'You're on.'

Peggy grimaced. 'No, it's all right. I thought I'd like to give Frank a surprise, but you're safe. It'd never fit me in a thousand years.'

'We'll go shopping one day, Peggy, you and I,' promised Alix. 'Together we'll find something that will really knock Frank out.'

'With my figure?'

'Stop running yourself down,' said Alix, a little exasperated. 'There are plenty of wonderful clothes for women like you.'

Peggy flushed. Harriet, looking from one to the other, reflected that this was the first time any of the three of them had come even close to a quarrel. These letters were beginning to get on everyone's nerves.

The children disappeared round the corner into the school. The three women were about to move off when Brenda Barlow came up to them. She looked flustered.

'May I have a word with you? You see, I've had this letter. About Beverley Simons. I don't know what to do about it . . .'

'Burn it,' said Harriet quickly. 'Or give it to the police. Don't tell us about it. It wouldn't be fair to Beverley.' Never a fan of the tabloid school of journalism, Harriet felt she'd heard enough revelations about people's private lives over the last few days to last her a lifetime: Mrs Parker, Denise's Peter, Frank (though that was all made up, of course) and several others whispered about at the school gate.

Brenda Barlow hesitated. 'You see, I would burn it, but it doesn't only concern Beverley. It's her daughter, Charlene.'

Harriet attempted a quelling look, but Brenda Barlow wouldn't be stopped.

'The letter said Charlene's left by herself all afternoon while Beverley goes out to work. You do see, don't you?' Brenda's small dark eyes pleaded with Harriet. 'I can't simply ignore it. I can't help thinking about that poor little mite. Only three years old. Left all alone in the house . . .'

'Flat,' corrected Peggy. 'Beverley's a single mum. She lives in a council flat over the other side of Apple Burton.'

'Flat. All by herself. What would you do?' Brenda turned to Harriet.

Harriet hesitated. 'Look, I know it sounds terrible. But how do you know it's true? People are receiving letters all the time that are completely unfounded. Peggy here got one. Fiona got an e-mail about Julian. All a load of rubbish.'

A trace of disappointment flashed across Brenda's face. 'Some of them have been true, though, haven't they?' she persisted. 'Denise's was about Peter. He had been visiting prostitutes. And now there's Mrs Parker . . .'

'Yes, all right,' said Harriet hastily. 'Nevertheless, I should just ignore it. If it was true, social services or someone would have known about it by now, wouldn't they? She must have neighbours, after all.'

'Y-yes,' said Brenda doubtfully.

Harriet reflected that the writer – whoever it was – must be a pretty good judge of character. Brenda Barlow's naturally busybody nature made her just the recipient most likely to cause trouble for Beverley.

'I hope she does ignore it,' said Harriet to Alix as they walked home.

'I suppose so. I suppose you're right. On the other hand, if the kid really is being left on her own . . . ?'

Harriet looked shocked. 'Beverley wouldn't do that, would she? There are always childminders.'

'Expensive.'

'Neighbours, then. Or grandparents.'

'You're probably right. See you at one.' With a wave, Alix left

Harriet outside her house. She was off to the gym for one of her thrice-weekly sessions.

At lunch-time, Harriet was accosted by a reporter from the *Apple Burton Herald*.

'What are your views on lesbian nursery schoolteachers?'

Harriet flushed angrily. 'No comment.'

'How do you feel about having your child taught by a lesbian?'

'No comment.'

He went to plague another parent.

'I feel as if I'm living in some nightmare out of the *News of the World*,' remarked Harriet, joining Alix and Peggy.

It was Mrs Moss who led out the troupe of singing children. Most unusually, Mrs Parker was nowhere to be seen.

'You were right then, Alix.' Peggy sighed. 'She didn't know this morning.'

For a moment it crossed Harriet's mind that Mrs Moss might be the anonymous letter writer. Perhaps she'd always secretly coveted Mrs Parker's job? Then she saw how white and shaken Mrs Moss looked. Besides, Mrs Moss had always deferred to Mrs Parker. Most people did. Mrs Parker was a small, slight, determined-looking woman whereas Mrs Moss was tall and rather gangling, coltish almost, as if she still, in her forties, didn't quite have control of her limbs.

The children, trotting behind Mrs Moss, each carried a long brown envelope. Nicky waved his in front of Harriet's nose. She opened it at once. It was a notice about a meeting to be held in the main assembly hall of St Cecilia's school the following morning. Sergeant Staples and the rest of the school governors were going to be present.

'Things are getting serious,' said Alix.

'Whatever happened to that detecting you two were going to do?' asked Peggy.

'Let's see what comes out of the meeting,' suggested Harriet. 'After all, the police may already have come up with some ideas.'

Alix, always quick to pounce on a comforting platitude, snorted. 'Do you think so?'

Harriet returned home depressed. What was happening to their nice, friendly little school? The unnerving thing was that these letters made life so unpredictable for everyone. What devastating accusation would the anonymous writer come up with next? They could only wait and see. They were in his power. Was that the point of it all? Was he enjoying seeing them squirm as their shoddy little secrets came out one by one? And they weren't all true, that was the problem. It was this mixture of truth, falsehood and innuendo that was extremely damaging. The letters about Denise's husband, Peter, and about Mrs Parker had apparently been true. But the others – about Julian being gay or Frank bonking his secretary or Beverley Simons neglecting her child – there wasn't a shred of evidence for any of that.

There was a small piece in the evening paper about an anonymous letter writer at St Cecilia's. None of the allegations contained in the letters and e-mails were printed. Either the other parents, like Harriet, had kept their mouths shut, or the paper feared libel. Or perhaps the police had gagged them. Harriet went to the meeting the next day with a sense of foreboding, dropping Nicky off with Mrs Moss on the way.

The governors were already seated in the assembly hall facing the thirty or so parents from St Cecilia's nursery school. Harriet slipped into the seat Alix had saved for her. She looked round. There was an unnatural hush over the hall. No one felt like gossiping this morning. Gossip had become a dangerous and deadly pursuit. Reputations could be ruined in half a sentence.

Mrs Parker, looking pale but resolute, was sitting with the governors. Reverend Threlfall sat on the edge of his chair, gripping a sheaf of papers. He too looked anxious. Or was it guilt, Harriet wondered. A vicar must be privy to all sorts of secrets – and Reverend Threlfall was High Church, which meant confessions, Harriet believed. She wasn't entirely certain about this. Apart from last term's concert she'd never set foot inside St Cecilia's church. Her eye swept along the rest of the governors – Dr Wentworth, tall, lean and dapper in his grey three-piece suit, Sergeant Staples, Brenda Barlow, representing the parents.

When all the parents had taken their seats, Sergeant Staples cleared his throat and began to address the meeting. He had a round, red face and fairish hair. He looked more like a farmer than a policeman. He leaned forward in his chair, legs planted firmly apart, one elbow resting on his knee. In his hand he held a piece of paper which he consulted from time to time.

'I have called this meeting today because, as you probably know, there has been a series of anonymous letters and e-mails addressed to parents at the school. The accusations in these letters are extremely hurtful and in most cases –' he glanced at Julian Wilson-Smith, present in his capacity both as parent and local councillor – 'completely unfounded. The police are treating this matter very seriously indeed.'

'That makes a change,' whispered Peggy, from the other side of Alix.

'The letters have tended to come in typed brown envelopes. They've been written on a computer.'

The surly-looking man who was rumoured to be a writer put up his hand.

'Yes, Mr . . . ?'

'Osborne. Have the police any idea what sort of computer is being used?'

Sergeant Staples shook his head. 'It's a common typeface – probably IBM or Apple Mac. They're printed off by laser printer using the, er,' he consulted his piece of paper, 'font Times, Bill our computer expert down at the station says. Obviously this narrows our suspects down to someone who can use a computer.' He glanced round at them. 'But that's rather a lot of people these days.' He paused. 'I urge you all to be vigilant. If you do receive a letter, I'd advise you not to open it but to hand it straight in to Apple Burton police station.'

'Fat chance,' muttered Alix. 'Would you resist the temptation to take a peek inside?'

'In the case of e-mail, print it off, put it in an envelope and hand it in the same way. I assure you all the letters will be treated in the utmost confidence. And,' he looked round the room, 'if anyone has received a letter and not yet handed it over, I urge you to do so at once. I shall take charge of them. I'm personally supervising this investigation. They will be quite safe with me.'

Harriet watched with interest as several parents stood up and went over to hand in narrow brown envelopes. Among them was the bad-tempered-looking Mr Osborne. So he'd received a letter, had he? Or was this a pretence, to put the police off the scent? After all, who'd be most likely to have the imagination for this sort of thing but a writer? Harriet wondered again what kind of books Mr Osborne wrote. Thrillers? Detective fiction? Horror? Was he some kind of sadist? He'd seemed very interested to find out how much the police knew about computers. Harriet decided Mr Osborne might well be her prime suspect. She glanced at Brenda Barlow who'd remained glued to her seat. What had Brenda done with her letter about Beverley Simons? Had she burned it after all?

By the time all the parents had handed in their letters, Sergeant Staples had quite a pile of them in his lap. 'Thank you,' he said. 'Now I advise complete discretion on this matter. One or two of you have already been approached by local journalists – the nationals haven't got hold of it yet, but it can only be a matter of time – and I advise you to say nothing to any of them. Just say no comment.' He turned to the other governors. 'Would you like to add anything?'

Dr Wentworth nodded. He looked round at them all. Not for the first time, Harriet thought what an open, friendly face he had. It would be hard to distrust a man like that. 'I would just like to say that there is someone – someone very sick and unbalanced – out to poison and destroy our little community here at St Cecilia's. We mustn't let them. We must stand firm and pull together.'

The clichés seemed only to underline his honesty. Around the room, several heads nodded in agreement with what he'd said. Peggy put up her hand.

'Yes, Mrs Murray?' said Sergeant Staples.

Blushing at her own audacity, Peggy rose to her feet. 'Could you tell us, Sergeant Staples, is it just the nursery school that's being targeted? Or have any parents from the infant and junior schools received these letters?'

Sergeant Staples shook his head. 'Not that we are aware of, no.'

'So it is just the nursery?'

'Yes.'

A palpable shudder ran round the room. Parents avoided meeting one another's eyes.

The ginger-haired man, Tony Richards, got to his feet. His Alsatian, tethered outside, had been heard whining throughout most of the meeting. Harriet thought that, given the situation, it made suitably atmospheric background music.

'You haven't told us yet, Sergeant Staples, exactly what the police are doing about these letters,' demanded Tony Richards belligerently.

'Well, er, Mr Richards, isn't it?' Tony Richards nodded. 'We're pursuing several lines of enquiry. Our main hope, of course, is that the letter writer will become careless – about fingerprints, or in some other way – and give him- or herself away. So far, there has been no set of fingerprints common to the letters.'

'But what are you actually doing?' persisted Tony Richards. Harriet admired his stamina. Or was this a clever façade? Was Tony Richards in fact the letter writer? He must have plenty of time on his hands, being unemployed. And a grudge against Frank for sacking him. Perhaps in the months he'd had to brood, this had developed into a generalised grudge against society?

Sergeant Staples began to look flustered. 'You must understand, Mr Richards, it's a question of resources. Police in this area are already undermanned. We are doing our best but there are fifteen post-boxes in the Apple Burton area. You could hardly expect us to keep a watch on each of them twenty-four hours a day.'

'We could help. Why don't you ask some of us parents? We could get up a rota.'

'I hardly think amateurs . . .'

'Besides,' intervened Julian Wilson-Smith, in self-assured tones, 'in law, insult or vulgar abuse doesn't amount to defamation and isn't actionable. It's the publication, not the writing or circulation of a libel, that is actionable. And of course not all these letters have turned out to be libellous.'

Harriet nudged Alix. 'He's been doing his homework.'

Alix shrugged. 'I suppose he needs to know about libel, being on the council and all that.'

'Does it make him more or less of a suspect?'

'I'm not sure.'

'So when does it become ac – whatever it's called?' persisted Tony Richards.

'Actionable?' said Julian.

Tony Richards nodded.

'Well, let me see. If A writes to B a letter defamatory of B and B shows it to C, A is not liable because that was B's own act. But if A writes B a letter knowing it will be opened by, for example, B's secretary, then A is liable. Or if A knew B was blind or illiterate and would therefore have to pass the letter on to a third party, then A is liable. But of course such knowledge is hard to prove.'

By the time Julian had come to the end of this, Harriet's head was spinning. She glanced across at Tony Richards. He looked absolutely furious. He stared at Sergeant Staples.

'I don't think it's satisfactory. Not at all. You're trying to fob us off.'

'I'm not trying . . .' began Sergeant Staples.

But Tony Richards had left the room. Outside there was a brief cacophony of joyful barks as the Alsatian was reunited with his master.

Sergeant Staples looked harassed, Reverend Threlfall embarrassed, Dr Wentworth anxious. Harriet was just wondering whether they were all really above suspicion when Mr Osborne stood up.

'You've told us about the letters. What's happening about the e-mails? Isn't it possible to trace them to their source? It's quite difficult to send e-mail anonymously, isn't it?'

'It is, but it can be done. You send them to an e-mail address in Finland. There's a chap there who strips off the name and address and sends them on. The Feds have been trying to track him down for ages. You see, other than that he's somewhere in Finland, you can't tell his actual address from the heading on his e-mail.'

'Beyond your resources at Apple Burton, then?' responded Mr Osborne drily.

'It's even beyond Scotland Yard.' Sergeant Staples looked glum. Harriet felt a tinge of pity.

'What about DNA testing, then?' persisted Mr Osborne. 'Surely the saliva on the envelopes could be tested and matched with samples from the community? That would wrap up your investigation in no time.'

He must be a crime writer, thought Harriet.

Sergeant Staples, still reeling from Tony Richards' accusations, opened his eyes wide. 'You're surely not suggesting, are you, Mr Osborne, that we should DNA test the whole of Apple Burton?'

'No, but you could start with St Cecilia's school,' Mr Osborne suggested. 'With us parents, for instance.'

Sergeant Staples shook his head.

'DNA testing is extremely expensive, Mr Osborne. I couldn't justify allocating that amount of money to this case. Poison-pen writing is not a custodial crime. Besides which, not all of the parents might be willing to co-operate and that might throw suspicion on the wrong quarters.'

'Or the right,' muttered Mr Osborne, sitting down again.

Harriet wondered what his game was. Was he genuine in wanting DNA tests? Or was it a ruse to test the police? To see how far they were prepared to go in their investigations? Sergeant Staples did seem to be looking at him with suspicion.

'Any more questions?' he asked, in such a discouraging tone that no one dared raise their hand.

Mrs Parker leaned forward and touched Sergeant Staples' arm. 'I'd like to say something, Sergeant Staples, before the meeting closes, if I may.'

A hush fell on the hall.

'If you're sure, Mrs Parker.' He looked at her doubtfully.

She nodded. 'Quite sure.' She glanced at the expectant parents and pressed her hands together. 'I have never sought to hide my sexuality but equally, I have never sought to publicise it. I regard that side of my life as completely separate from my professional life – and as private.'

'Hear, hear!' murmured Dr Wentworth. Mrs Parker shot him a grateful look.

'However, I quite understand that some of you may now have reservations about . . . about sending your children here. I want you to know that I am, as always, available to discuss any worries you may have.'

There were several approving nods.

Mrs Parker paused and went red in the face as if she might burst into tears. Reverend Threlfall intervened. 'We held an impromptu governors' meeting last night and we want to reassure Mrs Parker of our unreserved support for the splendid work she is doing in the nursery.'

'Yes!' 'Indeed!' 'Quite right too!'

Many of the parents broke into spontaneous applause at this point but some, Harriet noticed, did not.

The meeting broke up.

'It's the books I'm worried about,' Harriet overheard Mrs Parsons say as they all trooped out of the hall. 'It's not Janet and John nowadays, you know. It's quite likely to be John and Jeff or Janet and Jane. We'll have to keep a careful eye on what our children are reading.'

'Quite,' agreed Brenda Barlow. 'Role models are so important at their age, aren't they? I want my little girl to grow up normal.'

Alix raised her eyebrows at Harriet. 'God! What's normal these days?' she muttered. 'Well, I don't know about you two, I'm off to the gym to put in an hour before it's time to collect Imogen.'

'I don't know where she gets the energy,' Peggy said, staring after her. 'I feel quite drained after that meeting.'

'So do I,' agreed Harriet. 'I can't face work this morning.'

They looked at each other. 'The Apple Burton Arms!' they said in unison. 'Alix's reaction to trouble is a session down at the gym, ours is to go and stuff ourselves,' added Peggy. 'No wonder I don't lose weight.'

'Never mind, there's something very comforting about the Arms,' said Harriet. 'It must be all those sofas.'

On the way there, they reviewed their list of suspects.

'Tony Richards – clearly under stress, storming out of the meeting like that – why?'

'That writer, Mr Osborne,' said Harriet. 'He seemed to know a bit about computers. It occurred to me he might be testing the police. Do you know what he writes?'

'Obscure history books, rumour has it.'

'Hm. Perhaps he's making the move into crime fiction?'

Peggy turned her freckled face to look at Harriet. 'You don't like him much, do you?'

'I don't know him. I just wish he'd smile once in a while.'

'Perhaps he has a lot on his mind.'

'Haven't we all?'

'Yes.' Peggy sighed.

'You're not still brooding over that letter, are you?'

'No, not really. It's just – oh, I don't know, something like that gives you a nasty shock.' Peggy ran her hand through her tousled, faded red hair. 'Of course I trust Frank, but . . .'

'Honestly, Peg, you've got to forget all about it. Otherwise, don't you see, you're playing right into the hands of the letter writer? You feel jumpy. That's exactly how he wants you to feel.'

'I know.'

They turned into the Apple Burton Arms where they ordered two coffees and two Danish pastries.

'I can't work up any guilt about this,' commented Peggy, biting into the pastry. 'I feel I deserve it. It's been a horrible time.'

'It has,' agreed Harriet. 'But you never know, that meeting may put a stop to the letters.'

'Do you think so?'

'Well, the writer knows the police are working on the case now and that we're all being vigilant.'

'You think the writer was at the meeting? Yes, I suppose he may have been. What a horrible thought!' Peggy gave a shiver.

Harriet nibbled on her pastry. 'Reverend Threlfall looked decidedly uneasy, I thought.'

'Didn't he? And Dr Wentworth.'

'He's such a nice man though, isn't he? I can't believe he'd write those letters.'

'Harriet! You fancy him!'

Harriet blushed.

'He's married,' Peggy pointed out.

'I know. To a very nice nurse. Unfortunately. I'm not ruling out Sergeant Staples.'

'No.'

Harriet sighed. 'But what's the motive in all this?'

'Perhaps there isn't any particular motive?' Peggy suggested. 'Perhaps it's just a generalised hostility against the world?'

'That would fit that Osborne bloke.'

'And Tony Richards. I bet he trains that Alsatian of his to bite.'

Chapter Seven

'Hello. I'm James Maugham.'

He was tall, with dishevelled brown hair and a slightly grubby anorak. Underneath the anorak he was wearing what appeared to be a home-knitted jumper. Bottle green. For someone who had described himself on the Sweethearts form as having masses of SA (sex appeal), it was all a little disillusioning.

Never mind, thought Harriet, swallowing her disappointment. I'm no oil painting either. A session bathing Nicky had left her red in the face. The humidity had made her hair go frizzy. She hadn't told Nicky she was expecting a visitor. She was keeping her fingers crossed that it wasn't going to be one of those evenings when he kept popping down every five minutes. He was used to finding her sitting alone in front of the television or reading a book. She didn't know how he'd take to having another male in the house after all this time.

She held out her hand.

'Hi. I'm Harriet Lee.'

'Pleased to meet you, Harriet.'

His handshake was firm and decisive. He gained a bonus mark for keeping his eyes fixed on her face rather than wandering all over her body, as Geoffrey's used to whenever he was introduced to a woman under forty. Harriet opened the door a bit wider.

'Well. Come in.'

In the narrow hallway James produced a bottle of wine from under his anorak.

'A contribution.'

'How kind of you.' Quite a decent Australian red, too.

'I didn't know what we were having. Should I have brought white?' He looked anxious.

'Pasta and salad.'

'Oh, then I should have brought white.' He looked agonised.

'It doesn't matter, really it doesn't.' Goodness, she thought, if he needs this much reassurance over a bottle of wine . . . 'Can I take your, er, coat?'

Embarrassment flashed across his face. 'Just bundle it away somewhere out of sight, would you?' he said, taking it off. 'It's my gardening anorak. I didn't mean to turn up in it but when I went for my jacket I remembered one of the girls had spilled Ribena down it. I'd meant to have it cleaned.'

She laughed and hung the offending anorak up in the cloakroom under the stairs. He'd gained another Brownie point.

'The sitting room's up here.' She led the way up to the first floor.

'Nice house. Lots of stairs, though.'

'Yes, that is a disadvantage. On the other hand, it means I can have a studio on the top floor.'

'Red walls!' he exclaimed, following her into the sitting room. 'How . . . extraordinary!' He wandered over to the window. 'Nice view. Reminds me of Paris. Those chestnut trees and the rain coming down and the lights shining on them. Trish and I went to Paris for our honeymoon.'

Harriet sat down on the sofa. 'Did you? I spent a year in Paris once, painting. That was before I had children, of course. It seems a lifetime away now. I wonder if I'll ever see Paris again?' And then, in case that sounded too much like a hint, she stood up again and said, 'Would you like a drink?'

He turned from the window. 'Glass of wine would be nice.'

'I'll go and open this downstairs.' She flapped an arm around. 'Make yourself at home.'

When she returned, he was kneeling on the floor going through her collection of CDs. Not that much at home, she thought, with a trace of irritation. She coughed. He sprang guiltily to his feet.

'Hope you don't mind?'

'Not at all,' she lied, handing him a glass of red wine.

'I see you've got Elkie Brooks' *Priceless*. She's Trish's favourite singer.'

'Oh?'

'Trish used to play her non-stop some days.'

'Really? Non-stop?'

Harriet frowned and took a gulp of red wine. Weren't they hearing just a bit too much about Trish? These dates were supposed to make her feel good about herself – at least that was what Alix had promised. Nothing less guaranteed to make a person feel sexy and desirable than someone going on about his ex-wife.

'I'll go and boil the pasta,' she said dully.

Over pasta and pesto sauce, which they ate balancing plates on their knees in the sitting room and listening to Elkie Brooks, James explained, 'Trish left me to go and live with a woman. Something like that doesn't half knock a hole in your confidence.' He twirled pasta inexpertly around his fork.

'So you decided to join Sweethearts,' Harriet prompted, in an effort to get him off the past.

'It was Trish's idea.'

'I see.' All his Brownie points flew out of the window. Didn't he have any initiative? 'Any luck so far?'

'This is the first date I've had.'

'I see.'

Harriet finished off her red wine and poured herself another. She thought that if things continued like this, there was a very real danger she might faint from boredom.

'All the women I've phoned sounded so bright and energetic. It's off-putting, somehow.'

'You prefer the quieter type?' Why don't I sound energetic and bright on the phone, she wondered. What *do* I sound like, then? Dull?

'You see, you said you were a painter and I thought, well, she's probably fond of peace and quiet too.'

'When I can get it.'

'How old are your children?'

'Nicky's three and Daniel's seven.'

'Asleep upstairs?'

'Nicky is. Daniel's away at school.'

'Is he? Isn't he rather young for that?'

She pressed her lips together. 'We thought it best.'

'You want him to be surrounded by male role models?'

'Something like that.' She declined to go into Daniel's problems with a man she'd only spent an hour with.

'But then I suppose they have their father?'

'Geoffrey? Good God, no!' She'd show him it was possible to be walked out on and still put the past behind you. 'Geoffrey's much too busy down in London. He coughs up maintenance, sends money for birthdays and Christmas and that's about it. Nicky's only seen him once since we moved up here.'

James shook his head. 'I don't understand some men. How can they walk away from their own kids? My arrangement with Trish suits me just fine. I can work late at the office during the week and the weekends are for my daughters. There's no one else I've met I'd rather spend my weekends with. Yet.' He gave her a sidelong glance.

'What do you work at?' she put in hastily.

'I'm an accountant.'

That brought the conversation shuddering to a halt. She tried a different tack.

'You've got two daughters?'

'Yes. Siobhan's ten and Fionnuala's eight.'

'Lovely names.'

'Oh good, do you think so? I'm glad. My wife calls them Susan and Frances.'

'Why?'

'I chose their names. My grandparents were Irish. Trish doesn't like me having that much influence over them.' He sighed. 'If it had come out in court that their mother's a lesbian I could probably have got custody of them. But somehow I couldn't do it. The girls need their mother.'

'It was a nice thing to do.'

A shade of self-pity passed over his face. 'So my friends tell me. It didn't get me any credit with Trish, though.'

Finding this unanswerable, Harriet cleared away the plates and refilled their glasses. In the kitchen she took stock of the situation. James Maugham was a good man but – it had to be admitted – boring. There was some vital spark missing. He'd let himself be kicked around by his wife. Probably he would always be kicked around by somebody. His only hope was to find some nice motherly soul to take care of him. Harriet switched on the kettle. She didn't feel in the least like mothering James. She had enough of that during the day with Nicky. And now there was the rest of the evening to be got through. She glanced at her watch. Half past nine. He was bound to stay another hour, at least.

When she got back upstairs with the coffee things she found he'd exchanged Elkie Brooks for *Lady in Red*. Goodness, she thought, I hope he's not in *that* sort of mood. She became very brisk and practical and rattled the coffee cups in a discouraging sort of way.

He took the cup she held out. 'You see, Harriet . . .'

She sat back, resigned. It was all going to come out. He had worked himself up to it. She was now about to hear James's life story. She took a sip of coffee and allowed her attention to wander. She wondered whether there was too much blue in the jug she'd been working on that morning.

'. . . and since Trish left, I've been dead inside. I'm looking for someone to wake me up. I want to get some feelings back.'

'Surely your daughters give you feelings?'

'It's not the same thing. You must know that.'

'No. I suppose it's not.'

He made a flapping movement with his hands. 'Shoot me down, Harriet, if I'm making a fool of myself, but I think we could make a go of it.'

'What?' She was so startled her cup shot out of her hands on to her lap. 'Oh Christ! Just a minute.' She dashed into the bathroom to dab at her skirt, found this was futile, tore it off and left it to soak in the basin. She put on a pair of jeans.

When she came back into the sitting room, she was tempted to ask him what he'd been saying, but he looked so crestfallen she hadn't the heart.

She sat down on the sofa. 'Er, when you said make a go of it, what exactly did you mean?' she asked cautiously.

'Well.' He hesitated and looked like a man about to backtrack. 'Perhaps we could see each other again?'

'Good idea!' she gasped, much relieved. 'We could have that drink.'

'We could.'

He looked disappointed but also somehow relieved. She hadn't turned him down flat. He was right. His confidence really had taken a battering over his wife's behaviour. His ego seemed in such a delicate condition that any kind of conversation with him was like treading on eggshells. Harriet wasn't sure how much more of it she could take and was quite relieved when presently he stood up and said he ought to be going.

Later that night, she woke up in bed, pain stabbing at her big toe. She opened her eyes wide in the dark. 'I don't believe this!' she muttered. She pushed aside the bedclothes and hobbled downstairs to find the medical dictionary she'd bought when she was expecting Daniel.

'Gout tends to be hereditary,' she read. 'It can be triggered off by certain foods or alcohol, particularly red wine. Avoid those foods, drinks and activities which have been found to trigger attacks. This condition rarely affects women.' That's all you know, she thought, closing the book with a bang.

She hobbled back upstairs to bed. Thirty-six and gout-ridden! It was like a warning. She wasn't going to be immortal after all, then. What a pity. It marked the end of her red-wine-drinking days, the end of her youth. Disease had taken up residence in her body. Thanks, Dad, she thought, shutting her eyes. Thanks a bunch for this. Then she remembered Daniel's rogue gene, which must have come from somewhere, and thought there were many worse diseases a parent can hand on to a child.

Chapter Eight

'Well? How did it go with James?' asked Alix the next morning at the school gate.

'All right. He didn't try to jump me, anyway.'

'Are you seeing him again?'

'Probably.'

'Probably! That doesn't sound very enthusiastic.'

'I don't feel particularly enthusiastic. I felt sorry for him.'

'Sorry! Harriet, this is supposed to be fun! If that's what you feel about him, I'd give it a miss.'

'I know, but . . .' She felt a tug on her sleeve. It was Tony Richards. And his dog.

'Um, could I speak to you for a moment, please? In private, like? You're Nicky's mum, aren't you? I'm sorry, I don't know your name.'

'Harriet. Harriet Lee.'

'Well, Mrs Lee, can I have a word?'

He looked so serious and concerned that Harriet thought, oh God, he's had one of those letters and there's something in it about me. Divorced mother of two's scandalous behaviour in joining dating agency. Invites strange men to her home with son asleep upstairs. Ignoring Alix's wink, she stepped to one side of the line of parents.

'Yes?'

His opening words confirmed Harriet's worst suspicions. 'You see, Mrs Lee, I've had one of these damned letters and I don't know what to do about it.'

'Well, you know what Sergeant Staples said. You must hand it over to the police.' She became conscious of Tony Richards' Alsatian sniffing round her ankles. She found it an unpleasant experience.

'Come here, Fred.' It would be Fred, she thought. 'The thing is, I was wondering if you'd mind reading it yourself, first?'

'Me?' Her voice shot up. 'Why me?' If it was something about herself, she didn't want to know. That sort of truth-telling could damage you for life. Even worse if it was lies, like Peggy's letter, and you began to wonder whether it was true. Anyway, what could it possibly be about? Only Alix knew about the dating agency. Perhaps it would be something about Geoffrey having found a new woman. That wouldn't surprise her. 'I don't think so, Mr Richards. I don't want to pry. I've had enough of these letters.' Then, against her better nature, the question popped out. 'What is it about?'

'I don't know,' he muttered.

'Don't know? Haven't you read it, then? Well done. We'd all be better off not reading these things. Not many people can exercise that amount of self-restraint, unfortunately. We all take a peep inside the tabloids occasionally to gloat. I think that's really admirable, Mr Richards.'

'Call me Tony.'

'Tony.'

He rolled a pebble around under his shoe. 'The reason I haven't read it isn't what you think, Mrs Lee,' he mumbled.

'Call me Harriet.'

'Harriet. You see, I can't.'

'Can't?'

'No.' His voice dropped even lower. 'I can't read.'

'Oh.' She flushed. How stupid she'd been. 'Oh, I see.' She paused. 'And you want me to read the letter so that you know what's in it before you hand it over to the police?'

'Exactly.'

'Of course I will.' She took the brown envelope from him and began unfolding the torn-off scrap of computer paper inside. 'Why did you pick on me, by the way?'

'You've got a kind face.'

'Kind? Have I? No one's ever said that before.' Harriet thought guiltily of all the unkind thoughts she'd had about him. She glanced at the letter and felt a perceptible sense of relief. It was neither about Tony Richards nor about herself. It was another one about Beverley Simons and her daughter, Charlene. *Did you know*, it read, *Beverley Simons leaves her daughter Charlene alone every day from two till five?*

She handed it back to him. 'It's the usual rubbish, I'm afraid. About Mrs Simons and her daughter. I'd hand it straight over to the police.'

'Thanks. I will.' He took the letter from her and shoved it into the back pocket of his jeans. 'I'm afraid it's true, though.'

'What is?'

'About Beverley Simons. She does leave her kid all alone in the afternoons.'

Harriet gazed at him with a sinking feeling. 'How do you know?'

'My sister lives in the same block of flats as Beverley.'

'Oh.'

What was she to do about this piece of information? Peggy had said Beverley Simons was a single mother. She must need every penny. On the other hand, how awful for her daughter to be left alone at her age. Harriet thought of Nicky. He was hardly left on his own even for five minutes. And what chaos a toddler could get herself into over the course of a whole afternoon. Spilling things, toilet accidents, scissors, knives, plugs – it didn't bear thinking of. She gave Tony Richards a despairing look.

He shrugged. 'Charlene's all right. Beverley leaves the telly on for her. She's always back by five. It's a small flat. She's quite safe.'

'Mm.' She waved as Nicky disappeared round the corner into school, preceded by Mrs Moss. 'Well, you must decide what to do with the letter.'

He looked at her. 'What would you do? Burn it?'

'I might,' she admitted.

'But that would be destroying evidence.'

'Yes.' She sighed. 'It's complicated, isn't it? I'm sorry, I'm not being very helpful, am I? It all seems suddenly beyond me.'

'Never mind.' He turned away and pulled on the lead. 'Come on, Fred.'

She felt she had let him down.

'But at least there's one thing,' she remarked to Alix on the way home. 'If Tony Richards can't read, that rules him out as our anonymous letter writer.'

'If you think he's telling the truth. It could all be an elaborate hoax, of course, to put us off the scent.'

'I believe him. He was so humble about it, and so ashamed.'

Alix gave a moan of exasperation. 'These people will hoard their illiteracy to themselves like a guilty little secret. Get it all out into the open, that's what I say. I've got the address of an adult literacy scheme left over from my days as a Citizens' Advisor. I'll dig it out for him.'

'Poor man. I wonder if that was why Frank sacked him?'

'Probably. You'd be surprised at the number of people who apply for the most unsuitable jobs, hoping to cover up their illiteracy. Some of them get quite far before they're found out.'

'Poor man.'

'Why did he latch on to you, anyway?'

'Don't laugh. He said I had a kind face.'

'So you have. You're quite a big softie at heart.'

'Naive, you mean?'

Alix swished at a bush with her hand as they walked past. 'That comes into it.'

'Gee, thanks.'

'Well, you are. Look at you dithering over Beverley Simons. You can't make up your mind about it, can you?'

'No,' admitted Harriet. 'Can you?'

'Yes,' said Alix calmly, swishing another bush. 'I'd get social services on to her. It's a crime leaving that child alone all afternoon.'

'If she is.'

It's not that simple, Harriet thought later, mixing colours on her palette. There are two sides. Beverley needs to earn money. Perhaps I should offer to look after Charlene in the afternoons? But would that be fair on Nicky? Perhaps we could organise a rota amongst the parents at St Cecilia's? But would that look like charity? Perhaps, she thought, starting to daub paint on to canvas, Tony Richards has got it wrong?

She became absorbed in a world of colour and shape and forgot all about Beverley Simons and Charlene, and when she arrived at the school gate at lunch-time she found the problem had been taken out of her hands.

'Have you heard?' Peggy's freckled face was pale and grim. 'Charlene's been taken into care.'

'So it *was* true that she was being left on her own?'

'Apparently. Sergeant Staples said that as several people had handed in letters about her, he felt duty bound to investigate the allegation. That little mite was left on her own every afternoon. I can hardly bear to think about it. She must have felt so lonely and frightened.' There were tears in Peggy's eyes. Harriet put an arm round her. 'I suppose Beverley thought it was for the best. She's proud about hand-outs. Charlene was always neatly turned out.'

'If only we'd known. Perhaps we could have helped.'

'That's what I said,' agreed Peggy. 'It's too late now. Beverley wouldn't accept help even if it was offered.'

'So what will happen?' asked Alix.

'Beverley says she's going to give up her job. If she does, she'll probably get Charlene back. And then they'll live on welfare, I suppose,' Peggy added.

'A real kick in the teeth for the single mother trying to get free of the system,' commented Harriet, wishing for a minute that Geoffrey was there so she could point out to him the havoc his party's policies were creating.

'I know. Free nursery school for all, that's what I say,' declared Peggy.

'Or perhaps people shouldn't have children if they can't afford them?' suggested Alix.

Harriet thought this statement was judgmental and out of character for Alix. 'Well,' she said, 'the letter writer's certainly making his power felt.' She glanced uneasily over her shoulder. 'First Denise's marriage falls apart, then Beverley's daughter is taken into care. What next?'

'Let's hope Sergeant Staples and his team find out who it is before any more damage is done,' murmured Peggy.

'There has been damage,' said Alix slowly, 'but perhaps it will lead to a healthier community in the long run. I mean, the letter writer's not entirely to blame, is he? He's just pointing out things we should have known. I expect Denise's marriage would have come unstuck sooner or later. And someone was bound to have blown the whistle on Beverley.'

'I don't know.' Harriet groaned. 'I think there are some things best not brought to light. I don't mean about Charlene being left on her own,' she added hastily, wondering what in fact she did mean.

'It's the atmosphere these letters are creating,' explained Peggy. 'Everyone's beginning to suspect everyone else.'

'Well, Alix,' said Harriet, 'at least you can't accuse us of being a safe and complacent little community any longer.'

'No, I can't accuse you of that,' agreed Alix.

'Hasn't Tim got any ideas about all this? He's into computers, isn't he?'

'Yes, he's becoming quite an expert.'

'So what does he think about these e-mail thingies?' asked Peggy.

'I haven't really had time to discuss it with him. He left at the weekend for Singapore. He's spending two months out there, drumming up overseas students. It's the only way universities can raise any money these days.'

'Alix! You didn't say! Two months! Won't you miss him terribly?' Peggy stared at Alix, round-eyed.

'Yes, in a way. But marriage can be very cramping, can't it? I can't tell you the number of widows or divorcees I've seen suddenly blossom in unexpected ways when they're left on their own. Marriage always requires you to damp down part of your personality, doesn't it?'

Peggy shook her head. 'I miss Frank even when he's only away for a night.'

Harriet asked, 'So which part of your personality is being released while Tim's away, Alix?'

Alix laughed and shook her head. 'That would be telling, wouldn't it? Enjoy your weekend, girls.'

On Saturday evening, Harriet looked at the last name on her list from the Sweethearts dating agency. Mick. Harriet's ill-fated union with Geoffrey had made her incline to Alix's view of marriage rather than Peggy's. Nevertheless, she missed the companionship of being able to sit down in the evening and talk over the day with someone who was more than three years old. Out of a sense of conscientiousness, she dialled Mick's number. Halfway through, she began to hope he would be out. Of course he wasn't.

'Mick here.'

'Hello. My name is Harriet. The agency, Sweethearts, I mean, gave me your number.'

'Great! Hang on a moment, Harriet.'

Harriet could hear some strange kind of chanting going on in the background. It was switched off.

'You caught me in the middle of my meditation.'

'Oh. Sorry.'

'It's all right. I was surfacing anyway. Otherwise I wouldn't have heard the phone. I've been getting into some really deep trances recently.'

'Oh.' She found herself unable to think of anything safe to say about this.

'Tell me about yourself, Harriet. Have you any other name, by the way?'

'Er, not that I know of. Why?'

'Harriet sounds a bit down to earth, a bit practical for me.'

What about Mick, she thought.

'Still, I dare say we could change it if the vibes between us turn out to be positive. What did you say you did?'

'I'm a painter. I . . .'

'Great! I steer well clear of nine to fivers.'

'What do you do then?'

'This and that. I'm a bit of a mixed media man myself.'

'You're an artist too?'

'You could say that.'

It all sounded a bit shady to Harriet. She changed tack. 'Why did you decide to join Sweethearts?'

'Oh, you know, I've played the field in my time. Now I want to settle down. Get a bit of depth into my life. I've tried in-depth Jungian analysis, acupuncture and colonic irrigation. Now I'm looking for a woman to share my life. What's your star sign?'

'Virgo.'

'Virgo.' He sounded disappointed. 'Date of birth?'

'August the twenty-fourth.'

'On the edge of Virgo then. It might be all right. I'll have to consult my personal astrologer on this one. Mind if I get back to you?'

'Not at all.'

Harriet rang off before he had time to ask for her number. Let him try contacting her by ESP. She drew a line through his name. It looked as though James Maugham was the best the computer was going to come up with. She wondered what life would be like – James and herself, with Trish as a shadowy third. It was not a terribly inviting prospect. Dating agencies – bad idea, Alix, she thought.

Chapter Nine

When Harriet arrived at the school gate on Monday morning she could have sworn that, despite the warmth of the June sunshine, there was a frost in the air. Parents seemed to turn their backs ever so slightly as she came up with Nicky. Peggy gave her a brief nod, then averted her eyes. Head bent, Harriet hurried Nicky past the line of backs – those of Brenda Barlow and Mrs Parsons seemed particularly rigid. The group of women was so tightly bunched together it was impossible to break in to it. Voices were lowered as she went past. After Nicky had given her a kiss and run off into the playground, Harriet stood miserably alone under a tree. Eventually, after what seemed like an eternity, she was joined by Alix, out of breath and hurrying Imogen along into the playground.

'Whew! Some mornings! Imogen insisted on eating three bowlfuls of Alpen. Normally she won't touch a thing.' Getting no response, she glanced at Harriet. 'What's the matter?'

'Something's up.' Harriet nodded over to the group of women still animatedly discussing something. 'I think they're not speaking to me.'

'Not speaking? Why ever not? Don't you become paranoid on me, Harriet.'

At that moment Peggy detached herself from the group and came over to where Harriet and Alix were standing under the chestnut tree.

'What's wrong with everyone this morning, Peggy? Why am I getting the cold shoulder? It's like being back in junior school and being sent to Coventry by the whole class. What's happening?'

Peggy shook her head and looked embarrassed. 'The thing is,' she hesitated, 'you haven't had one of these letters, have you, Harriet?'

'What?'

'Nearly everyone else has, you see.'

'Oh my God!' Harriet screeched. 'You don't mean I'm suspected of writing those horrible letters? And what about the e-mails? I'm computer-illiterate.'

'They don't know that, though.'

'Come to that, I haven't had a letter, either,' put in Alix.

'It's not only that. It's the drawings,' Peggy explained.

'But they're terrible,' Harriet protested. 'Scribbles. You don't need to be an artist to do them. A child could manage them.'

'I know, but . . . there's no logic in this, Harriet. These women are frightened. Denise's marriage has broken up, Beverley's had her kid taken away. What's going to happen next? Everyone's looking over their shoulder at everyone else.'

'Oh God! I can't sit back and be suspected like this. I've got to do something. What shall I do, Alix?'

'Time for a spot of detecting, I should think,' replied Alix.

'And I know just who to start with,' said Harriet firmly. 'That writer fellow. There's something fishy about our Mr Osborne. What do any of us know about him? He stands by himself and never seems to talk to the other parents.'

'No, he doesn't,' agreed Peggy. 'I don't even know his first name.'

'Humphrey,' stated Alix. 'I saw one of his books in a shop recently. Remaindered. Listen, I've got an appointment with Dr Wentworth this morning. I'll see if I can pump him for information,' she offered. 'We'll pool our findings at lunch-time.'

'I'll tell you what,' added Peggy, 'I could call on Joyce Threlfall. I need to arrange the time of the next mother and toddlers' group meeting in the parish hall. I'll see if they've had any letters. Or if Reverend Threlfall knows how to use a computer,' she added darkly. 'That should give us information on three of our male suspects.'

'Thanks,' said Harriet. 'I'm awfully grate –'

'Nonsense,' interrupted Alix briskly. 'Best foot forward, girls.'

Peggy grinned. 'As Miss Barnesley used to say.'

'The early bird catches the worm. It's no use crying over –'

'Yes, all right, Alix!'

'Imaginative lot, our teachers.'

'Come on, girls. To work!'

Harriet walked up the dark winding drive to Humphrey Osborne's house. It was a double-fronted yellow brick villa, very typical of East Yorkshire, though larger than most in the area. She reflected that writing must be more profitable than painting. Perhaps he wrote pot-boilers in his spare time? Romantic stories for Mills & Boon? No, with that sour expression, he could hardly be a romantic. It must be crime fiction. Yes, that would make him the ideal suspect.

After she'd rung for the third time (she knew there was someone in, she could see a light in one of the downstairs windows), Humphrey Osborne opened his front door. He was wearing a pair of shabby brown corduroys and an open-necked checked shirt. His silver-grey hair was dishevelled, as if he'd recently been running his fingers through it. He looked, as Harriet had anticipated he might, extremely cross.

'Yes?' he snapped.

Harriet turned on the charm.

'Hello, Mr Osborne. Sorry to disturb you. I'm Harriet Lee. My little boy goes to the same nursery as yours. You may have seen me at the school gate.'

Humphrey Osborne's eyebrows drew closer together. 'Well?'

She swallowed. 'Well – er – I need to talk to you for a few moments about arrangements for the summer fête. It's to raise funds for the school. I'm calling on all the parents. I wonder if you'd be interested in running a stall?'

He gave a sort of snort. 'No!' He made to shut the door.

Reflecting that he really was awfully rude, Harriet stuck her foot out. He glanced down, wondering why his door refused to close. He glowered. She smiled sweetly.

'Any contributions you could give us? Prizes? Donations?'

'Christ!' He rummaged in the back pocket of his cords and pulled out a crumpled five-pound note. 'Here. Will this do?'

'Great. Thanks.' She stuffed it into her pocket. She'd give it to Mrs Parker for general funds. 'Er – is your little boy enjoying nursery?'

He frowned. 'Yes,' he said shortly. 'Now, if you'd excuse me . . .'

'Let me see, what is his name? I've forgotten. Robert, isn't it?'

'Dominic.'

'Of course. How nice. We nearly chose Dominic for our elder son.'

He let out a groan of exasperation. If he'd been two years old, he would have stamped his foot.

'Mrs Lee, I have been working all morning on a particularly difficult paragraph. It was beginning to come right. Then the doorbell rang. I tried to ignore it, but it went on ringing. I thought it must be something urgent. I find it wasn't. I've given you what you came for. Now will you please go away before I lose the thread of my argument entirely? You may have time to waste in idle chit-chat, but I do not. Why not organise a coffee morning for other wives who have hours to waste? Or join the Mothers' Union? Good day.' He slammed the door shut.

Harriet walked slowly back down the drive, contemplating the situation. What a lousy detective she'd make, giving up like this at the first hurdle. What would Alix say? Pretty wet, wasn't it? Goodness knows, Humphrey Osborne had a foul enough temper to be the letter writer. Yes, she could just imagine him firing off his little explosions of misanthropy.

She retraced her steps and rang the bell again. The door opened.

'You still here?'

He looked positively thunderous. He was holding a mug of coffee. She supposed he'd been trying to work himself back into that paragraph. She took a deep breath.

'Look, I am sorry about this. I know what it's like to be interrupted in the middle of a piece of creative work –'

His sharp dark eyes looked fiercely at her from beneath the shaggy grey eyebrows. 'You do, do you?'

'Yes. I'm a painter. A professional one. No ladylike daubs. No painting by numbers. I wouldn't take up any more of your time but I really need to speak to you.'

'Not about the summer fête, I hope?'

'No about these horrible letters.'

He sighed and opened the door an inch wider. 'You'd better come in, then. I've completely lost my train of thought anyway.'

'Sorry.' She stepped meekly over the threshold and into Humphrey Osborne's dark panelled entrance hall.

'This way.'

He led her across the hall to a door on the right. She followed him in and blinked in the gloom. The small, square, smoke-filled room was painted dark brown and lined with books. There was a plain wooden desk by the window. Right in the middle of it, surrounded by books and papers, was a computer. She noted the apple logo, familiar even to someone who'd never used a computer in her life. An Apple Macintosh. It flashed a series of images at her. Beside it she counted three unwashed mugs. Humphrey Osborne pointed to a sagging armchair, and she sat down. He sat on his grey office chair, picked up a pipe from his desk and swivelled round to face her. He brought out a leather pouch and began stuffing tobacco into the bowl of his pipe.

'I hope you don't object? If you do, it won't make any difference. This is my territory. Few enough places I can smoke these days.'

'I know.'

'He raised an eyebrow. 'You're a smoker?'

'Only when I'm working. It helps me concentrate.'

'Hm. Do you really believe that?' He sniffed, packed his tobacco down with the end of a dead match and lit it. 'Well now, about these letters. Have you had one?'

'No, that's the trouble. Because I haven't had one, people are beginning to suspect me.'

He looked at her. 'I wouldn't let it get to you. People are stupid.'

'There're the drawings as well. They think it's the sort of thing a painter would do. Not only words but sketches.'

'Mine didn't have any sketches.'

'Oh?' Harriet feigned surprise, as if she hadn't seen him hand a brown envelope to Sergeant Staples at the governors' meeting. 'So you've received a letter?'

'I have.' He pulled on his pipe. 'And, like a good citizen, I handed it straight over to Sergeant Staples.'

'Without reading it?'

'No. I – er – I read it.'

'Was it another one about Mrs Parker?'

'No.'

'About Beverley and Charlene?'

'No.'

She hesitated. 'Was it about yourself?'

He took his pipe out of his mouth. 'I'm not going to tell you. You have no right to ask that.'

'I know, but . . .' She leaned forward in her chair and spread out her hands in a gesture of what she hoped looked like charming helplessness. 'The police are dragging their heels on this. All Sergeant Staples' talk about limited resources. They're not taking it seriously. But Beverley Simons had her daughter taken away from her and at least one marriage has broken up over this.'

'Has it?'

He tapped his pipe several times against the fender. A sign of guilt, she wondered.

'I'm afraid I don't have time to listen to gossip at the school gate.'

She frowned. 'This isn't gossip. This is serious.'

'Yes. It is. So you've decided to do a spot of detecting, is that it?'

She nodded.

He sat back in his chair. 'I'd be careful if I were you. It could be dangerous. If the writer found out, who knows how he or she might react?'

A shiver ran down Harriet's back. Was this a threat? The expression in those small dark eyes was inscrutable.

'I'm not alone. There are others helping me.' She wanted to make that quite clear. She had back-up.

'So there are several of you in it, are there?'

'Yes.'

'Well, I've told you as much as I'm going to tell you, Mrs Lee. I received a letter and I handed it over to Sergeant Staples.'

'But have you any idea who the writer could possibly be? You see,' she plunged in recklessly, 'we wondered, with you being a writer, whether you might have some knowledge about this sort of thing? Poison-pen letters, I mean.'

He frowned across at her. 'I'm not a writer of fiction, Mrs Lee. Still less of lurid crime fiction. I'm an historian. I write history books – slowly, painstakingly and accurately. I do not make things up.'

'Oh.'

They sat for several moments in silence. Humphrey Osborne puffed on his pipe.

'Well, er, you must be busy.'

'I am.'

'I'd better go.' She half-rose from her chair.

'I'll tell you one thing.'

She sat down again.

'I had a good look at the typeface on my letter before I handed it over. You remember Sergeant Staples saying the letters are printed by laser printer using the font Times?'

'Er, I don't really know much about computers.'

'Don't you? Vital if you want to get anywhere with this case, I should have thought. Anyway, the typeface on my letter was actually a particular version of the Times font, slightly narrower than the Microsoft Windows version which is Times New Roman. That means the letters – or mine, at any rate – were printed from an Apple Macintosh.'

She frowned in an effort to understand. 'If the writer of these letters uses an Apple Mac computer, that narrows down the field. Doesn't it?'

'Not really. It's a common computer. I use one myself.'

'I noticed.'

He gave her a look. 'If I were you, Mrs Lee, I'd exclude no one from my list of suspects. No one.'

Again a shiver ran down her back. Was he playing games with her? She stood up.

'I'd better go. I've taken up enough of your time.'

'Quite so. It has, however, been an interesting conversation.'

What did that mean?

He accompanied her to the front door.

'Sorry about being in a grump when you called. Normally Mrs Towers answers the door, but it's her day off.'

'Oh, yes.' Now she remembered. There was a stout fair-haired woman in her fifties who often collected his little boy from nursery. Alix had said she was Humphrey Osborne's housekeeper.

'And by the way, I'll have my five pounds back.'

'What? Oh, yes, of course.' Harriet fumbled in her pocket and handed him back the crumpled note. 'Sorry. Goodbye.' She stumbled over the doorstep and heard the door close behind her.

Had it been a successful interview? Harriet made her way back down the yew-lined drive. How would Miss Marple have conducted it? She wouldn't have known anything about computers either. She'd have gone on her instinct about human nature. The trouble was, Harriet wasn't sure what her instinct was about Humphrey Osborne. Had he been feeding her a lot of nonsense about computers, or had he genuinely wanted to be helpful? There'd been flashes during their conversation of a real human being. But what had happened to his wife? Was he divorced, or a widower? Had his wife perhaps died in mysterious circumstances? She must ask Alix.

Harriet shut the high front gate behind her. She'd not got out of him what was in his letter. What was he hiding? It was true that he wasn't a fiction writer but then neither, entirely, was the letter writer, for some of the letters had turned out to be true, which implied an ability to ferret out facts on the part of the writer. What had Humphrey Osborne said? 'I write history books – slowly, painstakingly and accurately.' No, he couldn't be ruled out. And what a gloomy house for a little boy to live in, she thought.

Chapter Ten

....

When Harriet arrived at the school gate that lunch-time, she found Alix and Peggy deep in conversation with Fiona Wilson-Smith. Fiona looked dashing in a rich crimson satin shift dress, the kind of dress that would make anyone else look like a lump of dough but which on Fiona looked subtly sexy and alluring. Not fair, thought Harriet who was dressed, as usual, in jeans.

'How did your visit to the elusive Humphrey Osborne go?' asked Alix.

Harriet stared at her.

'It's all right,' said Alix. 'Fiona's in on this with us.'

Harriet wondered whether this was wise. 'It was inconclusive. He's not a crime writer. He sticks to history, so he says. He's not really as sour as he first appears. On the other hand, he seems to know an awful lot about computers but I don't know enough to know whether he was telling me a load of rubbish. He's got an Apple Macintosh, though, and he seems convinced the letters were written on one of those.'

'The computer the secretary was using in Dr Wentworth's surgery was an Apple Mac,' said Alix.

'And Martin Threlfall has one,' put in Peggy. 'He was given it by St Cecilia's parishioners for his sermons and the parish accounts.'

'It's a very common computer,' explained Fiona. 'Julian and I both have one at home. In the office I use an IBM.'

'Humphrey Osborne told me he'd received a letter.'

'Did he?' Alix turned to her. 'What was in it?'

'He wouldn't say. Alix, what happened to his wife?'

'Suicide, I think, about eighteen months ago.'

'Was there anything suspicious about it?'

Alix flicked her plait over her shoulder. 'I don't think so. She overdosed on sleeping pills, as far as I can remember.'

'Well that could be suspicious. He could have given them to her.'

Fiona looked at her. 'What are you trying to say, Harriet?'

'Nothing, really. Only I'm not ruling out Humphrey Osborne. That gloomy old house gave me the shivers. What did you get out of Dr Wentworth, Alix?'

Alix shrugged. 'Nothing much. He was polite, but evasive. He did admit he'd received one e-mail, though, at the surgery. It was about some diagnosis he'd made three years ago. Turned out to be a mistake. The patient was admitted to hospital too late and died. Dr Wentworth said he got his knuckles rapped for the first time in his career.'

'I suppose a doctor's allowed one mistake,' said Peggy. 'Now you mention it, I do remember reading something about it in the local papers at the time.'

'Odd, though, that he should have come out with it all to you, Alix,' remarked Fiona. 'After all, he's supposed to be in a professional relationship with you.'

'Oh, I've known him for years on and off, what with my mother and everything,' replied Alix vaguely.

'Besides, he was admitting something that's already common knowledge,' said Peggy slowly. 'The letter could be simply a ruse, to put us off the scent.'

'Like Humphrey Osborne's,' added Harriet. 'What did you find out from Joyce Threlfall, Peggy?'

'She was a bit weepy at first, but after I'd told her what had been written about Frank, she opened up. It turns out they have received a couple of e-mails messages. They printed them out and handed them over to Sergeant Staples, of course, so I didn't see them.'

'Did she tell you what was in them?' asked Fiona.

'It seems Martin Threlfall got into a bit of a mess at his last parish. Left its finances in chaos. Nothing underhand, just inefficiency. Hence the Apple Mac. He's getting on much better now, Joyce says.'

'Who would know about that?' asked Harriet. 'I imagine it's not common knowledge?'

'No,' agreed Peggy. 'The only people who'd know would be people who were around at the time he was interviewed for

St Cecilia's. That is, the churchwardens. The PCC possibly. It didn't reach the ordinary congregation. At least I've never heard anything about it, and St Cecilia's isn't a parish that's bashful about gossiping.'

'Who was on the PCC at the time who's also connected with the nursery school?' asked Alix.

'I don't know,' replied Peggy. 'I could find out.'

'I can save you the trouble, Peggy,' put in Fiona drily. 'I was on the PCC two years ago. In fact I was churchwarden. Julian had just resigned due to pressure of work and I'd been elected to replace him. Dr Wentworth was on it, he was the other churchwarden. Sergeant Staples. Mrs Parker. Brenda Barlow. Mrs Parsons. Oh yes, and Humphrey Osborne.'

'I shouldn't have thought it was his cup of tea,' remarked Harriet.

'He's a regular attender at church and this was before his wife died,' Fiona explained. 'He was much more sociable then.'

'But again,' said Alix, 'the accusation in Martin Threlfall's letter is well known to some people – in fact, wasn't there something in the *Herald* about it at the time? It didn't stop him being appointed, though, so it can't really damage him now, can it? We can't rule him out as the letter writer, I think.'

'Whoever it is must have a very good memory,' said Fiona. 'I was churchwarden and I'd forgotten all about this until now.'

'Yes,' agreed Harriet. 'And who better than a trained historian for remembering small details that other people forget?'

'The fact is,' Alix concluded, 'it's been a pretty inconclusive morning. We started out with three suspects and we can't rule out any of them.'

'It's the minor but highly significant details that are escaping us.' Harriet sighed. 'It's never like this in novels.'

'Of course, it may not be a man,' said Fiona. 'Why are you all assuming it is? In fiction, it's usually a woman who writes these kind of letters.'

'Some obscure elderly spinster sat upon for years who suddenly discovers a way of exercising power,' said Alix. 'The trouble is, times have changed. There are no thwarted spinsters any more.

The thwarted are the young, all these unemployed young fathers separated from their families and with no stake in society.'

'There's no one here who fits that category.' Harriet sighed again. 'Except possibly Tony Richards. By definition, such young men don't appear at the school gate.'

'What if it's an elderly woman?' Peggy suggested. 'One of those grandmothers who pick their grandchildren up and feed them their tea while their parents are at work.'

'Yes, some sour middle-aged gran who sacrificed her own career for her children,' said Harriet, borne along on a wave of fantasy. 'And is eaten up with envy and resentment that she has to pick up the pieces so that her daughter or daughter-in-law can go on working.'

'And who thinks we're setting our children a dreadful example and keeps firing off missives about it,' added Peggy.

All four looked at each other.

'Mrs Parsons!' they shouted.

They burst into laughter. Mrs Parsons was well known for handing out pieces of advice to mothers at the school gate. According to Mrs Parsons, her two daughters had regularly slept through the night from the age of two weeks, had been out of nappies before they were one year old and could read by the time they were three. According to Mrs Parsons, girls were easier than boys until adolescence, when the position was reversed.

'Oh God,' groaned Peggy. 'I'd love to pin it on her. She once told me that Ben walked funny and I should get him seen by the doctor.'

'She told me Angelica needed a brace for her teeth,' Fiona said.

'She told me Imogen was going to grow up round-shouldered.'

'She told me Nicky squinted. Well he does. But she needn't have mentioned it.'

'How I'm longing,' said Peggy, 'to be a wicked old woman myself. I shall thoroughly enjoy handing out advice to nervous young mothers and keeping them awake half the night with worry and inferiority complexes.'

They dissolved into giggles again. Out of the corner of her eye,

Harriet noticed Humphrey Osborne walking towards them. When he heard their laughter, he turned on his heel, went back along the waiting line of parents and resumed his solitary position on the margins of everyone else's groups. Harriet hoped he hadn't thought they were laughing at him. She would have rather regretted that.

Her attention was distracted by Brenda Barlow who came across at that moment and waved a sheet of A4 paper under their noses.

'Will you all sign this? We're going to send it to the school governors.'

'What's it about?' Fiona took the piece of paper and read through it. 'No, certainly not. I'm not going to sign that. No way.'

She handed the paper back to Brenda, who held it out to Harriet.

With Alix and Peggy looking over her shoulder, Harriet read that some parents at St Cecilia's were expressing concern that an avowed lesbian like Mrs Parker was in charge of the daily care of very young children, especially in view of the fact that St Cecilia's was a Church of England school. Harriet handed the sheet back to Brenda.

'I never go to church,' she remarked, 'but I would have thought that, especially in a Church of England school, tolerance and understanding should come first.'

'We *are* tolerant,' Brenda replied. 'What she gets up to in the bedroom is her own business, we're just uneasy about her teaching our children. Aren't you?'

'No.' The women shook their heads.

Offended, Brenda Barlow moved away.

'That paper was printed using an Apple Mac,' muttered Fiona. 'It's exactly the same typeface as mine.'

'You said Brenda was on the PCC at the time of Martin Threlfall's appointment,' Alix added.

'Nothing like a church-goer for knowing everyone else's business,' commented Harriet. 'Sorry, Peggy.'

'No, I agree with you. The letter writer could easily belong to the church. I wouldn't be surprised at all.'

'There is quite an overlap between parents at St Cecilia's school and the congregation at St Cecilia's church,' began Fiona, then broke off. 'Here they come.'

The children came out singing 'Twinkle, twinkle little star', led by Mrs Moss.

'Mrs Parker's still keeping a low profile,' murmured Alix.

'I'm not surprised, with petitions flying around.' Peggy frowned in Brenda's direction.

Harriet sighed. 'I hope this won't drive her away. Nicky's really fond of her.'

'So's Ben.'

They collected their children and dispersed. Alix took Imogen off in the car to her first dentist's appointment, so Harriet and Nicky walked home on their own.

'Mummy.' Nicky hopped along beside her. 'I have a proposition to make. First we'll go home. Then we'll have a drink of juice. Then we'll watch cartoons. Then we'll go to the playground. All right?'

'All right,' she agreed, wondering whether other parents allowed their three-year-olds to organise their lives like this. 'If that's what you want to do.'

'I do. I most certainly do.' He gave a little skip and blew her a kiss.

Harriet became aware of the steady tread of footsteps behind her. They'd been going on for quite some time, all the while Nicky had been organising their afternoon. She turned round, thinking it might be Alix after all, and encountered James Maugham. He was dressed in a brown suit and carried a briefcase.

'Hello. This is a bit off your beaten track, isn't it?' she said. James had told her he worked in Driffield, a town about the size of Apple Burton ten miles away.

He looked tense, and he gripped his briefcase. 'I was doing a spot of work in the area. Why haven't you rung?'

She was taken aback. 'I – I've been busy. You know what it's like with a child.' And poison-pen letters to investigate. Nicky stared up at James with interest.

James frowned. A petulant expression appeared on his face that hardly matched the adult status represented by his suit and briefcase. 'I thought we were going to keep in touch?' There was more than a hint of reproach in his voice.

Goodness me, thought Harriet, exasperated, it's only been four days. 'Look, I'll sort out a baby-sitter and ring you very soon. OK?'

This seemed to satisfy him. He nodded and moved off.

Nicky screwed up his eyes and gazed after him. He put his head on one side, considering. 'Was that my daddy?' he asked.

'Daddy? No. Certainly not.'

'I thought he looked a bit like him.'

'Does he? I don't think so.' Daddy was much more handsome than James and possessed an air of self-confidence James definitely didn't have.

She bent down to Nicky. 'You know what Daddy looks like. Shall we go back and get out the photographs?'

Nicky squashed a ladybird under his sandal. Then he ran his sandal backwards and forwards over it.

'Don't do that, Nicky,' she said, distressed.

'I want to watch cartoons. You said I could.'

'OK, we won't look at the photographs. It was only an idea.' She straightened up.

'That's naughty, Mummy! I'll exterminate you! You said I could watch cartoons.' He stamped his foot. 'I need to watch cartoons! I need to!'

'Nicky, you *can* watch cartoons.'

Chapter Eleven

Early next morning, Harriet looked carefully through her mail. In view of the other parents' suspicions about her, she half-hoped she might have received a letter from the anonymous writer. But there were no long brown envelopes. Instead there was another list of names from Sweethearts. She glanced down it – Edward, Jack, William, Geoffrey. She'd give that last one a miss. No matter how nice he was, she'd always be prejudiced against him. Anyway, she figured that if James was already turning out to be awkward (had he really been in Apple Burton because of work, or was he spying on her?), she couldn't cope with getting involved with any more of Sweethearts' suggestions. She had enough on her plate trying to track down this mysterious letter writer.

She laid the list aside and opened a letter from Daniel's school. A drawing fell out. She bent to pick it up. Rows and rows of carefully shaded-in squares. Don't think about what he might have achieved, be content with what he *has* achieved, she repeated to herself, like a mantra. It must have taken him hours to do. She pictured him – head bent, tongue slightly sticking out, absorbed in a world of his own. Her heart gave a wrench inside her, and her eyes filled with tears. She went to stand at the window.

The headmistress had written that Daniel was learning to dress himself. He had quite settled down into the school routine. He was sleeping regularly between ten and six. That's a blessing, at any rate, thought Harriet. At home, Daniel rarely went to bed before midnight. He was simply never tired. He was looking forward to his visit home, the headmistress added. Her words, not Daniel's. Harriet was under no illusion that Daniel was actually missing her.

She heard a cough at her elbow and turned round. Nicky was standing there in his pyjamas, trailing his ragged pink towel behind him.

'Mummy, I have an important message for you. You're invited to my party.'

He dropped a kiss on her hand. She bent down and hugged him.

'Mummy, is my party soon?'

'Yes. Next weekend. Four days. We can make a calendar and cross them off.'

'Is Daniel coming to my party?'

'Yes.'

'Goody!' He spun round, clapping his hands. 'And Imogen and Ben and Scott and Lucinda and Angelica?'

'Yes. Yes, they've all said they'll come.' And fingers crossed they still would, despite the cloud of suspicion his mother was under.

'Can we have a cake?'

'Of course. What kind of cake would you like?'

'Power Rangers.'

'Oh. I was thinking of Snow White with the seven dwarfs tucked up sweetly in bed, like Angelica had.'

'That's for girls. I want Power Rangers,' he said firmly.

'Boys can have Snow White cakes too, you know.'

'No they can't.'

'Well, we'll see.' She resorted to evasion.

He gazed up at her through his smeary glasses. 'Mummy, I miss Daniel.'

'So do I.' She sighed. Then looked at the clock. 'Hurry up and eat your Coco Pops, Nicky. We'll be late for school. You've got to get dressed yet.'

He pulled a face. 'Don't like Coco Pops any more.'

'You've got to eat something, Nicky. It's a long time until lunch. Shall I make you some toast?'

'Yes.'

'Yes what?'

'Yes please. Oh please. Oh please.'

She brought him the toast. He took one look at it and burst into tears.

'*Now* what's the matter?'

'I didn't want it cut in two.'

Harriet ground her teeth. 'OK. I'll eat this and I'll make you some more.'

She buttered a fresh slice. 'Now, you don't want this cut, do you?'

He stamped his foot. 'Don't ask that! Just do it!'

She gazed at him in despair. What had happened to the days when children were nice, repressed little things and never answered back? Would her father have put up with this sort of behaviour for one moment?

'I'm not your slave, Nicky.'

He cocked his head on one side. 'Why not?'

She sighed. 'Here's your toast. Now hurry up and eat it.'

He gave a shriek. 'I didn't want brown!' He spat out the words as if she had presented him with something absolutely disgusting.

'Nicky, there's no more white bread. You'll have to make do with brown.'

'No!' He howled in rage, and swept the plate off the table so that the toast landed buttery side down on the kitchen floor. 'No! No! No! No!'

She felt like giving him a good shake. Instead she put him outside the kitchen door. He lay on the carpet in the hall, biting his towel and drumming his heels against the door. She tugged it open.

'Stop that!'

He ignored her and went on howling, lost in a world of rage and grief. Harriet took a deep breath and turned her back on him. She walked to the far end of the kitchen and looked out at their small garden, focusing very hard on a rose bush that was just coming into bloom. And she thought, as she usually thought at times like these, that if this relationship with Nicky failed, she'd have nothing. Daniel felt little real emotion for her. Her father judged her. Geoffrey had left her. All these failures placed too great a burden on both Nicky and her, she sometimes thought.

A few moments later, she heard the patter of small feet behind her and a little voice said, 'Want a cuddle.'

She lifted Nicky up and rested her cheek against his. The rage went out of her. Out of Nicky too – he was limp in her arms. They were both exhausted. Very quietly they went through the process of dressing.

'I'm sorry.'

'I know.'

They walked quietly to school and, at the gate, Harriet gave him a big hug. She walked home quickly, avoiding the company of the other mothers. She felt like a wrung-out rag. She had a thumping headache. How to go from this to standing calmly in front of a canvas, selecting colours and organising shapes?

She went up to her studio and lit a cigarette.

In London once, drinking with a group of painters (all male) in a Soho bar, the conversation had gone like this:

'I never embark on a new painting until I can be sure it will push against the limits of the genre.'

'I like to paint at night and sleep in till two in the afternoon. It's the only way.'

'I have to have absolute silence, my dear. But absolute. Not a floorboard must creak or a tap drip. Gina brings me a pot of black coffee at eight and then leaves the house and doesn't get back till seven in the evening.'

'I've just bought a studio in Battersea. I need to be able to shut myself away from the family.'

'I'm planning to move to the country. I can't work in towns any more.'

They'd turned to Harriet. 'Where do you paint?'

'At home in the mornings,' she'd replied, in quiet desperation. 'After I've got Daniel breakfast, dressed him, taken him to nursery school, filled the dishwasher, filled the washing machine and Hoovered. I have three hours then before I need to collect Daniel.'

The men had exchanged glances, as if to say, that accounts for it.

Nothing much had changed since then, Harriet reflected, except that she now had two children instead of one and she no longer had a dishwasher. Geoffrey had hung on to it, claiming accurately, but meanly, that he'd been the one who'd forked out for it in the first place. And nothing much was likely to change. She earned enough money from her painting to live on; but *her* paintings were never seen at the major exhibitions, *her* paintings were never mentioned in the Sunday papers. It was as much as she could do to keep turning out the kind of professional pictures – poppies in a jug, an empty chair in a room – which sold; she hadn't time to think about stretching the boundaries of art.

She stubbed out her cigarette on the lid of a paint tin. Perhaps when the children were older. She set up a canvas on the easel. When they'd left home. But Daniel would never be able to leave home. Not completely. She stared at the canvas. If only she had time to think! She picked up a brush. Think! Think! She began mixing colours. 'Stupid daubs!' Her father had said that once, storming in from work and finding her painting at the kitchen table. 'Haven't you any school work to be getting on with?' For he'd never, to this day, counted painting as work.

Harriet sighed and laid down her brush. No use going on like this. Nicky's tantrum, coming on top of the headmistress's letter (though it had been all right, quite encouraging in fact) had unsettled her.

She went out for a walk and sat for a long while in the park, contemplating the wreckage of her life.

'Are you all right?'

She looked up. It was Humphrey Osborne, with his pipe in his hand.

She pushed her hair back from her face. 'Yes. Yes, I'm all right.'

'Good.' He nodded curtly and walked on.

She hesitated, stood up and hurried after him.

'Are you going to collect Dominic? If so, we could walk together.'

He nodded again, without taking his pipe out of his mouth.

'Or am I interrupting your train of thought?'

'No.' His shoulders relaxed. 'It's just that I've got out of the habit of walking with anyone.' He gave what she supposed he supposed was a smile. It looked more like a grimace to her.

'No, you never really talk to anyone much at the school gate, do you?' she risked.

He stopped, took his pipe out of his mouth and stared at her. 'Have you any idea how unnerving it is to stand day after day at the school gate surrounded by a pack of gossiping females?'

'There's Dr Wentworth,' she objected. 'And Reverend Threlfall puts in an occasional appearance.'

'They come in cars. In and out in a flash. Busy men, both of them.'

'Well anyway,' she remarked as they walked on, 'join the club. Half the women on the gate aren't speaking to me at the moment.'

'Because of these letters? How ridiculous.'

'Yes. But unnerving. And it's Nicky's party next weekend. I'm wondering whether they're going to let their children come.' She hesitated. 'Would . . . er . . . would Dominic like to come?'

'Dominic doesn't go out much since his mother died. He's a nervous child. We sent him to nursery because Mrs Towers thought he wasn't seeing enough children. But I'm wondering whether it's right for him, mixing with all the different kinds of children who go to St Cecilia's.'

Harriet stared at him. I was right, she thought angrily, you *are* a misanthropist. And a snob into the bargain. She said goodbye as quickly as she could and went off to join Alix and Peggy at the gate. Let him stand by himself, she thought. Serve him right.

That night, after she'd put Nicky to bed, her depression returned. These letters, this frosty silence at the school gate, were getting her down. If only she had another adult to talk to, someone who was outside all this. She even for a moment, though only for a moment, contemplated ringing Geoffrey. But he'd be no help, might even be slightly embarrassed after all these months. Anyway, at this time of night he'd probably be in the House. Harriet fingered the list Sweethearts had sent her. She dialled Edward's number.

'Hi! Eddie Baker here. I'm not in at the moment, but if you'd like to leave your name and number, I'll get back to you.'

Nice voice, she thought. Deep. Southern accent.

'Hello. This is Harriet. I've been given your number by Sweethearts. If you feel like getting in touch, my number is –'

'Hello?'

'Hello?'

'Eddie here. I mean really here.'

'Oh,' she replied, momentarily confused. 'I thought you were out.'

'No. I often leave the answering machine on. I like to filter calls. So, Harriet, you joined Sweethearts. Why?'

She was a bit taken aback. Usually she was the one who asked that question. She'd found it useful for vetting people – filtering, as Eddie called it.

'Well I – I wanted to meet some new people. We've only recently moved back up here and –'

'We? You're married?'

'Divorced.'

'Just wanted to get things clear.'

'Surely married women wouldn't –'

'You'd be surprised.'

'Oh. Well. I'm a painter, so I don't get to meet many people.'

'No, I don't suppose you do. I lived with a potter once. Sloped off to her studio in the mornings and I never saw her again till the evening.'

At last, she thought, someone who has some idea about artists. Eddie's voice was rather nice, she decided. Calm and low and reassuring. She could do with some reassurance with all this nastiness over the letters.

'What do you do?' she asked.

'Me? I live out in the wilds of the Yorkshire Wolds with nothing but a few sheep to disturb me. I used to work in advertising down in London till a few months ago. Took the golden handshake, rented out my house and ran. If I'm careful, the money'll last two, maybe three, years. Then I suppose it'll be back to the Big Smoke and eight-mile tailbacks on the M25. At the moment I'm enjoying getting fresh air back into my lungs and doing up this cottage. If you're an artist, you might be able to paint me a few murals or something.'

'Murals aren't really my line –'

'Only joking, darling. You'll have to get used to my sense of humour.'

Why, she wondered. 'So why did you join Sweethearts?'

'Like you, I was moving into a new area. I wanted to meet new people.' This tripped off Eddie's tongue so neatly it sounded almost implausible. 'I've done the scene – climbing the greasy pole to success, working late, clubbing, babe watching. I want the simple things in life now – walking in the country, good food, good wine, listening to good music, talking. I want to find a few like-minded women to do these things with.'

It sounded like the perfect answer. Perhaps it was.

'Any children, Harriet?'

'Two. One's away at school.'

'Shall we meet at your place, then? Save baby-sitter money?'

'You want to meet?'

'Yes. I've been in this game a while now, Harriet. I can make up my mind pretty quickly about people on the phone. I'm an immediate person. I feel comfortable talking to you. Come on now, Harriet, don't say you don't feel it too. There's a telephone chemistry between us.' He laughed. It was a nice laugh. Low and gentle. 'Day after tomorrow?'

'All right, then. Come round to my place and I'll cook us supper. Something simple.'

'To go with my simple tastes. Good. I like the sound of you, Harriet. I like a woman who can make up her mind quickly and who's prepared to take a risk. You're an artist. I like a woman who's a bit of a rebel, a little bit wild.'

Wild? After she'd put the phone down, Harriet went to look at herself in the mirror. Denim shorts, loose paint-spotted T-shirt. Grubby hands. Chewed fingernails. Untidy hair. Wild? She was a mother of two. She couldn't afford to be wild. Eddie Baker was in for a big disappointment. Which was a pity, because she'd rather liked the sound of his voice. And with one thing and another it would be a relief to have someone to lean on for a change.

At lunch-time the next day, Harriet was waylaid at the school gate by Humphrey Osborne appearing out of nowhere and blocking her path.

'Oh, hello,' she said.

He took his pipe out of his mouth, hesitated, banged it against the heel of his shoe, straightened up, hesitated again.

'Er, I was wondering if you'd care to have supper with me tomorrow evening at my place?'

'Well, um –'

'I could send Mrs Towers round to baby-sit your son, if you like,' he continued in a rush, quite unlike his usual monosyllabic self. 'She's very dependable, able to deal with any crisis, and it would save you having to fork out for a baby-sitter.'

'But –'

'I cook a mean boeuf stroganoff . . .' He tailed off and looked at her severely.

She took a deep breath. 'Look, it's kind of you but I . . . um . . . well I have someone coming round tomorrow evening, but –'

'Very well.'

She could practically see the porcupine bristles standing up on his back. '– any other time,' she finished, and found herself addressing thin air. Humphrey Osborne had turned on his heel and walked off.

She went over to join Alix, Peggy and Fiona.

'What's the matter, Peggy?' she asked, as she drew near and saw that Peggy looked distinctly red about the eyes.

'She's had another letter,' Alix explained. 'It said Frank was seen out on Monday night with his secretary.'

'The thing is,' Peggy turned to Harriet, 'Frank *was* out on Monday night. Rotary business, he said.'

'That would be easy enough to check,' put in Alix.

'I'd leave it,' advised Fiona. 'Once you start even half-believing these things you'll go mad.' Harriet wondered whether she was speaking from personal experience. Had Fiona, despite appearances, been shaken by those e-mails about Julian? 'Hand it over to the police and forget all about it.'

'But other letters have turned out to be true,' wailed Peggy. 'The ones about Mrs Parker and Beverley Simons and about Denise's Peter.'

'I know,' said Harriet. 'But plenty of others have been just plain ridiculous.'

'Julian visiting gay clubs,' put in Fiona, tweaking down her short blue skirt.

At that moment, Muriel Winter came along and accidentally banged into the back of Peggy's legs with her buggy.

'Bloody hell! That hurt, Muriel! What the fuck did you think you were doing?' yelled Peggy, with an anger so unlike her usual gentle self that it brought home to Harriet how deeply upset her friend must be about the letters.

'Fiona's right. Try to forget it, Peggy,' she urged. 'We mustn't let the writer of this filth, whoever he is, win.'

'You're right. I know you're right,' Peggy said tearfully. 'It's just I can't help wondering . . . I mean, I trust Frank, but you know what men are like.'

'Yes,' sighed Harriet.

'I know,' muttered Fiona.

'Mm,' agreed Alix.

The four women stood in dejected silence.

'What did Humphrey Osborne want with you, Harriet?' asked Alix eventually. 'I saw him waylay you.'

'Oh, it was nothing. I mean, he asked me to supper.'

'Harriet! Did he really? Perhaps he fancies you?'

'The only person Humphrey Osborne fancies is Humphrey Osborne. No. I think there's some other reason. I think he wanted to talk to me about something. That's the impression he gave.'

'Perhaps he *is* the letter writer,' said Peggy. 'Perhaps he wants to confess?'

'Or perhaps he's got the jitters and wants to keep tabs on our investigations?' suggested Fiona.

'It could be dangerous,' Peggy added. 'Be careful, Harriet.'

'I'm not going. I can't. I've, er −' she glanced sheepishly at Peggy and Fiona, 'got someone coming round.'

'Another of your blind dates?' Alix grinned. 'What's this one called?'

'Edward − Eddie. Perhaps I should have put him off, though. I might have learned something important about the letters from Humphrey Osborne.'

'Never mind,' said Alix. 'You enjoy yourself with this Eddie. Let's hope he turns out to be more exciting than the last one.'

Harriet winced. What was this going to do to her reputation at the school gate? Alix was making it sound as if she had endless streams of strange men traipsing in and out of her house. Fiona looked extremely interested and Peggy was staring at her in amazement.

'What did he sound like?' Alix enquired.

Harriet shrugged. She would have liked to have got off this topic. 'Difficult to tell. Nice voice. Sounded reliable. Respectable,' she lied, for the benefit of Fiona and Peggy.

'Respectable!' Alix looked disappointed.

The children came out. Nicky ran up to his mother, arms outstretched. 'Mummy, I'm a bungle bee!'

'A what?'

'A bungle bee.'

'Oh I see. A bumble bee.'

He looked at her as if she was exceedingly dim. 'No, a bungle bee!'

'Right. What does a bungle bee do?'

'Flies.' Nicky flapped his arms up and down. 'And buzzes.'

They walked home to the steady accompaniment of a low buzz.

Chapter Twelve

He stood on the doorstep, smiling.

'Hi. I'm Eddie.'

He was shortish, about the same height as herself. Heavy jowled, with a hint of stubble on his cheeks, he looked like a cross between a labourer and an artisan. His thick blonde hair was tied back in a ponytail. His jeans were faded but clean and newly pressed, and he was wearing a pale blue cotton shirt. Harriet caught a faint whiff of after-shave.

She opened the door wider. 'Come in,' she said, wondering what it was she was letting in.

'An offering.' He produced a bottle of red wine from behind his back with a flourish.

Oh dear, she thought. Gout. She took the bottle from him. 'Great. Thanks. The sitting room's up here.' She led the way up the stairs.

He looked round at her red walls. 'Amazing colour!' He walked over to the window. 'Nice view. Reminds me of Paris.'

She thought she'd heard that one before. Hadn't James . . . ?

'The one bad thing about the simple life is that I've had to give up the travelling,' he remarked over his shoulder as he stood looking out of her window. 'No more hopping over to France for the weekend on Eurostar.'

He turned to face her, gave her a very quick once-over, then smiled and swaggered a little.

It struck her that he was the most sex-conscious human being she'd ever come across. She'd thought Geoffrey was bad enough – always that extra gleam in his eye when he spoke to a woman under forty, a general straightening up and standing to attention if an attractive woman walked into the room. He'd left her with a permanent distrust of handsome men. But this man outdid even Geoffrey. Sexuality fairly crackled in the air around him. Harriet found it hard to believe she was entirely the cause of it.

'Pasta and salad all right?' she said briskly and prosaically, to cut through the something that was beginning to build up in the atmosphere.

He cocked his head on one side. 'Well, I do like a bit of red meat, but I dare say veggies will be good for me, once in a while. Pasta's fresh, is it?'

'Yes. Can I fix you a drink?'

'A glass of wine. Not red, I think, if it's pasta. Or – wait a minute – you don't have any rosé, do you?'

She shook her head.

'Not many people do. Never mind. A glass of white will be fine. Dry, of course, and chilled. Chablis, if you have it.'

She went back downstairs wondering if Eddie really thought this was the simple life. And if so, what had his life been like before?

She put on the water to boil for the pasta and came back upstairs with a glass of chilled (thankfully), dry (thankfully) white wine. It wasn't Chablis. She wondered whether he'd notice.

'Cheers.' He took a sip. 'Mm. A Chardonnay, if I'm not mistaken. Not bad though.'

She felt she'd passed some sort of test.

'I've got to go and see about the pasta. Make yourself at home. Put on some music or something.'

'Thanks. I will.' He smiled boldly at her. 'But first I want to have a good look at these paintings of yours. Are they all yours?'

She looked round at the oil paintings and the sketches of her children. 'Yes, they're all mine.' She awarded him a Brownie point for at least simulating interest. James had not so much as glanced at her pictures all evening.

Downstairs in the kitchen she wondered whether, in view of Eddie's stated preference for red meat, she ought to add some frozen mince to the pasta. She decided this would probably be just too unsophisticated. It was a long time since she'd given one of those interminable-seeming dinner parties for Geoffrey's cronies, and her culinary skills had degenerated into what suited the palate of a three-year-old. Fish fingers, baked beans and Angel Delight, mainly. She wondered if Humphrey Osborne's boeuf stroganoff was really as good as he'd made out. She'd probably never know now.

She carried up the plates. Eddie was sitting in an armchair, one leg crossed over the other, nursing his empty glass of wine and listening to Dire Straits. He was already halfway through the first side. She deducted the Brownie point. He couldn't have spent that long looking at her pictures then. She went back downstairs to bring up the wine.

'What you need in this house is a lift,' he joked. Or perhaps it wasn't a joke. 'Any way of keeping this cool up here? An ice bucket or something?'

'I'm afraid not.'

'The rustic life.' He grinned. 'What you'd expect from a painter. Other-worldly. Like that potter I lived with.' He started on his pasta, displaying considerably more dexterity with a fork than James had done. 'I like your style, Harriet. I like the bright, bold colours you use. Like sunshine or holidays. You must have been happy when you painted these pictures, were you?'

'Happy?'

She looked at the picture hanging opposite of crimson poppies in a blue vase. She'd painted it during Daniel's first year when she'd been exhausted, depressed, scared of the future, longing to get away from it all, longing to spend a day, or even a few hours, wandering down a dusty road somewhere in the sun, not having to make endless trips back and forth to the hospital for Daniel's check-ups.

'I painted them mainly to cheer myself up. And because they're cheerful, they're in the sitting room. The ones upstairs in my studio are quite different. Quieter, greyer.'

'Perhaps another day?' he suggested smoothly.

She flushed. It hadn't been a hint for him to express further interest. In fact she disliked anyone, apart from her children, going into her studio. It was the most intimate part of the house for her, more intimate even than her bedroom.

'So you're going to go on painting flowers in vases for the rest of your life?'

'Yes.' She tilted her chin. 'That's what I do. It may not sound much, but there it is.'

Creating beauty where there was none, it was her life's work. Never quite being able to do what she always had to go on trying to do. A lot of what she did was mess and failure. But people still seemed to want to buy it.

'Don't be so defensive. It wasn't a criticism. I admire anybody who can make things. So many people these days dash around with a busyness that makes them feel good but doesn't actually achieve anything. God knows I saw enough of that when I was in advertising. I came up here looking for something else.'

'What?' she prompted, pouring them both another glass of wine.

'I don't know. I fancied that if I slowed down I might actually begin to learn something again. It's amazing,' he went on, 'how many talented women I've met through this dating business. Not desperate women as you might think. Working, professional women. Well educated mostly. Women who're getting on with their lives even if they do feel a bit lonely at times. Mind you, a lot of them get a bit samey after a while.' He glanced at her. 'I'm looking for someone a bit different. A bit crazy. A bit intense. I'd say you were intense.'

'Would you? Perhaps I am. I'm intense about my painting.'

'Yes. It shows.'

'And about my children.'

'Were you intense about your husband?'

'Geoffrey?' She bent down to clear away the plates. 'Not really. He wasn't the sort of person you could be intense about. He wouldn't have liked it. He likes things light and bright, does Geoffrey.'

'Not very satisfactory for you.' He gazed up at her. His eyes were rinsed-out blue.

'You get used to it.' She turned away with the plates. 'Coffee?' she called over her shoulder.

'Decaff?'

'Yes,' she lied. Anyway, how could you tell the difference? Except in the middle of the night, of course.

Downstairs, she took a bottle of brandy out of a cupboard and put it on the tray beside the coffee mugs, thinking it might raise her status a bit.

When she arrived back upstairs, she found Eddie had changed position. He was now sitting on the floor by her chair. That gave her three options – to change chairs, to sit in the same chair and let him sit at her feet or to squat down on the floor beside him. To give herself time to think she put on a tape by Enya. Then she sat down on the same chair she'd been sitting on earlier. She leaned forward to pour out the caffeinated coffee.

'Brandy with your coffee?'

'Let's have a look at it. Oh yes, I'll have some of that.'

Eddie glanced at her with a touch of respect. It was an old bottle left behind by her father. He still kept a cupboard full of drink – his cellar as he called it – over at this house. There wasn't room for it in his flat. It was the first time Harriet had touched any of it. She supposed it had better be the last time, too. Her father had a sharp eye for that kind of thing.

Eddie leaned back against her chair, sipping his brandy and just not touching her legs, bare under the long cotton skirt she was wearing.

'This is cosy, isn't it?' After a few moments he added, 'Are you comfortable there?'

'Yes.'

He patted the rug. 'Come and sit here beside me. I'm not going to jump you, Harriet. That's not my style.'

She began to feel unnecessarily prim. She sat down beside Eddie on the rug, sticking the brandy bottle between them.

He laughed. 'Like a sword. Don't you trust me, Harriet?'

'I don't know you.'

'I trust you. I told you, I make up my mind quickly about people. I'm intuitive – goes well with being an artist, I should think.' He grinned. 'I can tell pretty soon into a phone call who's a bore, who's a whinger and who's only after one thing.'

'What category do I come in?'

'None of those, darling.'

She couldn't help smiling. 'So what kind of women do you like?'

'I've an open mind. So long as there's some spark there – you know? Most of the women I've been out with recently have been between thirty and forty. I'm not a babe magnet, I don't go for younger than that any more. Like you, they're size ten, or between ten and twelve, at the outside. Women who look after themselves.'

Harriet, who was size twelve edging up to size fourteen, decided to keep quiet.

Eddie reached across and removed the brandy bottle. He took her hand in his and began gently weaving his fingers in and out of hers. Harriet closed her eyes and leaned back against the chair. She felt the tenderness coming off him. Tenderness she hadn't experienced from another grown-up since her mother had died.

'All right, darling?'

'Marvellous.' She opened her eyes. 'Wonderful. I haven't –'

'It's been a long time, hasn't it?'

She looked down at her bare feet (she'd kicked off her sandals). 'Yes. Yes, it has.' She didn't dare ask how long it had been for him. She suspected she wouldn't like the answer.

'We'll take it slowly. I believe in taking things slowly. It's part of my new philosophy of life.'

She shifted round on the floor so that she could see his face, but kept her hand resting in his. 'It's a friend I'm looking for, more than anything.'

He nodded. 'So am I. A friend to bring out my feelings. You don't know how hard that is to find.'

'Oh yes, I do.'

Eddie covered his hand with hers, brought it up to his lips and kissed it, looking at her all the while. Then he patted her hand and let it go.

'I'll give you a ring.'

He'd risen to his feet and was smoothing down his jeans almost before Harriet had registered his change of mood.

'Right. Good.' She scrambled to her feet, a little startled.

She stood at the downstairs window and watched Eddie walk to his car (a battered Maestro, possibly part of his simple life) and drive off. Feeling a tinge of regret that he hadn't looked back, she turned away from the window and wondered what she was getting herself into as far as Eddie was concerned.

Chapter Thirteen

'So?' said Alix, the next morning. 'How did it go with Eddie?'

'I'm not sure.'

'What do you mean? Not another one you feel sorry for?'

'Oh no. I don't feel *sorry* for him.'

'Well?'

'I don't know what I feel.'

Alix screwed up her mouth. 'Sounds promising. You're looking very nice this morning, if I may say so. Not so grubby.'

'It's my hands. I cleaned them up for Eddie.'

'You see, I knew this dating lark would do you good. Sometimes, Harriet, I think I know you better than you know yourself.'

'Where's Peggy?' asked Harriet, anxious to get Alix off the subject of Eddie.

'Isn't she here?' Alix glanced along the line of parents. 'No, it doesn't look as if she is.'

'I hope nothing's wrong.'

'Probably one of the children is ill.'

Mrs Moss came out to gather in the nursery school children. There was still no sign of Peggy. Harriet and Alix started back home.

'It's not like her to miss a morning.' Harriet bit her lip.

Alix glanced at her. 'Look, if it'll set your mind at rest, I'll give Peggy a ring when I get back home. I've got her number somewhere.'

'It might be a good idea. I can't help wondering if she's had another letter and can't face us.'

'I'm sure it's nothing. See you at one,' said Alix, leaving Harriet at her gate.

At one o'clock Alix arrived at the school gate with the news that Peggy had discovered something. She'd rung Frank's office shortly after he'd left for work that morning to remind him to pick up some strawberries on the way home and found herself speaking to a different secretary, a much younger-sounding one than Shirley.

'So?' said Harriet.

'So Frank's got a new secretary. A younger woman. And he never even told Peggy that Shirley had left. She'd been with him eight years. Peggy knows her quite well. You'd think he'd have mentioned it at least.'

'Yes. Yes, you would.' Harriet sighed. 'I knew there was something wrong. Was she upset?'

'She tried to laugh it off, but she sounded on the verge of tears to me.'

'Poor Peggy. Has she spoken to Frank about it?'

'Not yet.'

'It might be nothing.'

'It might.'

'I mean just because Frank's got a new secretary and hasn't told Peggy doesn't necessarily mean there's anything suspicious going on.'

'Not necessarily,' said Alix, in the sort of tone that suggested she very much had her doubts about this.

'The thing is, we'd never have even thought there was anything suspicious if it wasn't for those wretched letters,' said Harriet. 'Oh God, I wish the police would hurry up and find whoever it is who's writing them. Hello, darling,' she added, as Nicky rushed headlong into her knees.

Saying goodbye to Alix, who was taking Imogen into town, they started to walk home. After a while, Harriet heard a cough behind her. She turned round. It was Humphrey Osborne, with a whey-faced Dominic trailing after him, kicking up stones.

She stopped. 'Hello.'

Humphrey Osborne took his pipe out of his mouth and cleared his throat again. 'Um, I thought – how about this Saturday?'

'What?' she said, confused. At the same time, she couldn't help thinking that he must be a bit of an egotist, expecting people automatically to be on his wavelength like this.

'For supper. If you're not doing anything, that is,' he added, somewhat drily.

She stared at him. This was agonising. It was the kind of thing that drove her up the wall. Life was so slovenly sometimes about the way it organised things.

'I'd love to, really I would,' she said, putting as much sincerity into her voice as she could muster, 'but –'

'But?' He glared at her.

'You see, Daniel's coming home.'

'Daniel?' For the first time in their brief acquaintance, Humphrey Osborne looked unsure of himself.

'My other son.'

'I didn't know you had two children,' he said, surprised.

'Yes. Daniel's the elder one. He's seven.'

'Seven. And you send him away to school?' He stood facing her on the pavement, the atmosphere between them heavy with his disapproval.

She felt a sudden rush of anger. 'Yes, I send him away.' She grabbed hold of Nicky's hand and dragged him off.

'Hey, Mummy! I was watching that little fly.'

'I'll find you another one.'

She let go of his hand and strode along the street.

'Wait for me!'

She slowed down, without looking back. Nicky caught up with her.

'That was Dominic's daddy, wasn't it?'

'Yes.'

'Were you cross with him?' He stared earnestly at her through his glasses.

'Yes.'

'Why?'

'He said something.'

'What?'

'Oh, Nicky!'

'What? Tell me.' He stamped his foot.

She looked down at him. 'He said – he wondered where Daniel's school was.'

'Oh.' He digested this. 'Why did that make you cross?'

'I don't like nosy people.'

'Oh.' He bent down to watch some ants scurrying across the pavement. 'Dominic cried at school today,' he said casually.

'Did he?'

'Yes.' He straightened up. 'He misses his mummy, Mrs Parker said. We must all be nice to him, Mrs Parker said.'

'I'm sure that's right.' And nice to his daddy, too? Harriet began to feel a little guilty. What if Humphrey Osborne wasn't the letter writer at all, just a lonely old widower?

Nicky bent down to inspect the pavement again.

'Come on, Nicky. At this rate, we won't be home before tomorrow morning.'

'What would happen then?' he asked, hopping along on one foot.

'Then we wouldn't get any sleep.'

'What would happen then?'

'Then you'd be tired at school and Mrs Parker would wonder what was the matter with you.'

'Mummy, what's a lesbian?'

She came to a halt. 'Where did you hear that word?'

'Scott shouted it at Mrs Parker.'

'It means a woman who loves other women.'

'Oh good.' He sounded relieved. 'I thought it might be something bad.'

She bent down till her face was on a level with his. 'Mrs Parker would never do anything bad, would she, Nicky? You love Mrs Parker, don't you?'

He nodded his head vigorously.

She straightened up and took his hand. These letters, she thought. They're beginning to poison all our lives. Her guilt over Humphrey Osborne receded a little. She thought of Peggy and wondered how she was feeling and whether she'd be asking Frank about his new secretary that evening.

The next day was taken up in preparing for Daniel's homecoming and Nicky's party. In the morning, she baked buns. In the afternoon, Nicky helped her dust and Hoover Daniel's room. She carefully checked that everything was exactly as he'd left it on his last visit. Daniel's room was out of bounds for Nicky, but all the same she had to make sure that nothing had been moved or touched. Otherwise disaster would strike.

Nicky opened the wardrobe door and poked his head in. 'His tins!' he shrieked. 'Where are his tins?'

She hesitated. 'I – I took them away. I want Daniel to play with his other toys this weekend.'

Nicky screwed up his mouth. 'Daniel likes his tins.'

'I know he does, but it's silly and we shouldn't encourage him.'

'Daniel's not silly!' He launched himself at her legs and began pummelling them. 'He's not silly! You're silly, Mummy.'

'Nicky, calm down.'

She tried to seize his shoulders, but he wriggled out of her grasp and ran out of the room, crying. She sighed and sat down on the bed.

Daniel liked to collect empty tins. Baked beans, sliced peaches, cocoa, he wasn't interested in what had been inside them. He always tore the labels off. What he wanted to do was to count them into neat little rows on the kitchen floor. He must have over thirty of them by now. He gloated over them and cherished them like a miser with his pot of gold. Sometimes he even tried to steal tins from the supermarket. Left to himself, Daniel would expend more time and energy this weekend playing with those tins than with his brother. Or his mother, come to that. She felt it was time to dig her heels in and break him of this fixation.

'Want a cuddle,' said a small voice by her elbow.

She lifted Nicky on to her knee.

'You'll be able to show Daniel all your birthday presents. There'll be plenty of new things to play with. Will you let him?'

Nicky nodded. Already, at three, he was beginning to see that his elder brother would need his protection. It's hard on him, she thought. It isn't normal. Having a brother like Daniel is making Nicky grow up too quickly.

'Now, let's go down and finish the washing-up and then we'll go to the shops to buy things for your party.'

It had been such a busy day that she'd hardly had time to think about the letters, or Peggy. Just noted, with Alix, that she'd not turned up at the school gate again. Harriet wondered what it meant.

She was pushing Nicky round the supermarket in his special child trolley (heavier and more awkward than an ordinary trolley) when she came face to face with James.

'Well, this is a coincidence,' he said jovially. He was back to his off-duty clothes. The anorak had put in an appearance again, she observed. 'Thought I'd give the shops in Apple Burton a try for a change. You get sick of your local, don't you?'

'I don't know. Do you? Don't you have a Tesco's in Driffield?'

'They vary,' he said vaguely. 'When are we going to have that drink?'

She flushed, guiltily. 'You see, my elder son's home this weekend and I have a birthday party to organise.'

'I'm going to be four,' announced a voice from the trolley.

James bent forward. 'Are you? That's very old.'

'It is, isn't it?'

'And what are you hoping to get for your birthday?'

'I'm having a Robin dressing-up suit,' shrieked Nicky, in a tone that admitted no doubt in the matter. Little does he know, thought his mother, that I had to scour about twenty shops to find one.

'Well that's very nice. I'm sure you'll look splendid.' James straightened up and caught Harriet's eye. 'I'll wait for you to give me that ring then.'

The suspicion of hurt in his voice, the extra stiffness in his back as he walked off, increased Harriet's sense of guilt. He was understanding about children. She wondered what Eddie was like with children. When talking about her paintings, Eddie hadn't mentioned the sketches of her children that hung in her sitting room; in fact, he hadn't mentioned her children at all. Harriet realised dimly that beneath all the bustle of getting ready for Daniel, she'd been waiting for Eddie to call. She wondered whether the fact he hadn't done so was significant one way or the other.

'Bother!' she said crossly. Her encounters with James always seemed to have the effect of leaving her vaguely uneasy.

When she arrived home, the phone was ringing. Dumping her bags in the hall, she ran into the kitchen to answer it. It was Eddie.

'I wanted to say – I loved your house. It has style. I don't mean the kind of style you see in magazines – the kind you pay other people to organise for you. I mean your own style. I like the way you use the space. Nothing cluttered, but unexpected little things popping up in various corners. It was nice.'

The little spots of resentment she'd been working up against him melted away. 'Thanks.'

'I loved your paintings, too. I forgot to say, I loved those sketches of your children. Who's the one with the drop-dead gorgeous eyes?'

'That's Daniel.'

'Beautiful face.'

'Yes.' Beautiful, unawakened face. In her drawings, her elder son resembled an unearthly spirit, a Puck, an Ariel, not of this world.

'Will you paint me some time, Harriet?'

She laughed. 'Perhaps. I can't see you yet.'

'I must give you the chance to study me then. What about coming round to my place Saturday evening?'

'I can't. Daniel's home for the weekend.'

'He's at boarding school?'

'Yes.' She waited for Eddie to pronounce judgment on her, the way Humphrey Osborne had done, but all he said was, 'You'll want to spend your time with him, then. I understand. I'll give you a ring after the weekend.'

As Harriet put down the phone, she reflected that she had now turned down invitations from three men to go out on Saturday night. Perhaps there was something in belonging to a dating agency after all. You might not get to go out more often, but turning down dates certainly gave your self-esteem a hell of a boost.

She felt a tug on her jeans.

'Mummy, when will Daniel be here?'

She looked at her watch. Half past four. In quarter of an hour, Daniel was due. Her stomach started turning somersaults with excitement. 'Soon. Very soon, Nicky,' she promised.

To occupy them both, she brought the bags in from the hall and began unpacking them. Nicky darted to and fro between her legs, opening and shutting drawers, arranging packets and tins in places where she didn't want them to go. As they finished, they heard a horn blow outside. She dashed along the hall and opened the front door.

There was the school minibus. And there was Daniel, coming down the steps carefully, left foot first, with that slightly limping gait of his, clutching his satchel in one hand and a tin in the other. There he was. Three foot eight in his yellow anorak and blue jeans. Her son. Harriet moved forward to hug him. All the fears and anxieties of the past few weeks dissolved in the evening air. Her elder son was home and that was all that mattered. She took him in her arms and he put his arms around her, as he had been taught to do.

Chapter Fourteen

Later that evening, when Nicky was in bed, Harriet and Daniel sat in the kitchen. It was nearly eleven o'clock. Daniel showed no signs of tiredness. He was eating some toast. All of a sudden, he picked up his mother's arm as if it was an object, not part of her, and threw it towards the fridge.

She stood up immediately. 'What is it, Daniel? Do you want some juice or some milk?'

'Milk,' he answered.

'Milk or orange?' she said, testing. Daniel had a habit of repeating her last words.

'Orange.'

Harriet brought both cartons over to the table. Daniel looked inside both of them, then took up the carton of orange juice. He did not glance at his mother, or say thank you. Nor did she expect him to.

While he was drinking his juice, Harriet drew a map of their weekend. Pictures were always easier for Daniel to grasp than words. When she was younger, people, her father especially, had accused Harriet of using her painting as a substitute for a normal relationship with the world. (Since she'd started to earn her living

108

by her painting, that particular criticism had fallen by the wayside.) But she couldn't help wondering, as she'd wondered a hundred times in the past, whether that rogue gene had come from her. She remembered the doctor's words. 'It's nobody's fault, Mrs Lee. Put it down to a random and quite unpredictable combination of DNA molecules at the moment of conception.' Random and unpredictable, like life. Sometimes, though, Harriet wished there *was* somebody to blame.

She'd seen a programme once on television. 'We live in a world where perfection's an impossible dream,' the scientist had said. 'For perfect symmetry you have to go back to the first nanoseconds of the big bang, when the entire universe was concentrated into one point.' They lived in a world of broken symmetries and Daniel was living proof of that, a broken, imperfect human being.

'Look.' She thrust the paper she had been drawing on over to Daniel. He stared, unblinking, at the pictures. The first one was of Nicky sitting on the floor of the playroom, surrounded by parcels. 'It's Nicky's birthday tomorrow.'

'Fifteenth of June.' Daniel interrupted her in his flat monotone. He understood about dates but not the emotions aroused in Nicky by the prospect of his birthday.

She explained carefully. 'In the morning, Nicky will open his presents and play with them. Then we'll have lunch. Then in the afternoon it's Nicky's party. All his friends from school will be coming.'

'Go centre, go centre,' Daniel said urgently, bouncing up and down in his chair.

Harriet felt her stomach tighten with anxiety. 'No, listen Daniel, we won't have time to go to the garden centre tomorrow. It's Nicky's party.'

He grunted. Angrily, he took the pencil out of her hand. He scribbled furiously over her pictures until they were obliterated. Then he smiled at her, his open, trusting, meaningless smile. 'Saturdays go shops, go centre,' he said firmly.

Harriet sighed. Their lives became congealed when Daniel was home. He lived within the confines of a limited and repetitive routine. He loved ritual and order. He rejoiced in patterns and diagrams. After every time away, she hoped he might have become more flexible. But it was clear he was not yet ready to tolerate the slightest deviation from their Saturday routine.

'Go centre,' he repeated.

'We'll see,' she said. These words, spoken by an adult to any normal child, invariably mean no. But you couldn't just say no to Daniel. The damage would be too great. She had to think of Nicky as well. She didn't want his day spoiled.

She went to phone her father.

'Dad, you said you were coming round tomorrow morning with a present for Nicky. Could you stay for a bit while I quickly take Daniel to the shops and the garden centre? It's what he expects, you see.' She was aware she'd adopted a pleading tone.

'Certainly I'll stay. If you can't get Daniel to change his plans.'

Her father thought she gave in too easily to Daniel. He didn't understand the rigidity that lay behind Daniel's open face.

'Daniel, Daniel.' She ran a hand down his cheek. 'What am I going to do with you?'

He grabbed her hand and rubbed his face in her palm. 'Pencil,' he murmured ecstatically.

Harriet stroked her son's head. If only her mother was still alive. She'd have known what to do about Daniel. She'd have understood.

The phone rang, startling Harriet out of her thoughts. As she picked up the receiver, she glanced at the clock. Half past eleven. Who on earth could be ringing at this late hour?

It was Peggy. She sounded very strange.

'Harriet? I'm at my mother's with the children. I had to come. I mean I had to get away.' She was gabbling so fast Harriet could hardly make out the words. 'It's Frank, you see. Or Frank and Gemma, as I should now say. Quite an item. I knew he wouldn't stay with me. Why would he? As mother says, I'm nothing much to look at, now I've got so fat.'

'Peggy, wait. Slow down. I can hardly keep up with you. What's the matter?'

'I told you. Those letters turned out to be true after all. You were sure they wouldn't be,' she added accusingly. 'Frank's confessed. Said he'd been wondering for months how to break it to me. I suppose everyone at the office knew. Makes me feel a right fool. You didn't know, did you?'

'Of course not.'

'No, I don't suppose you did. Look Harriet, I can't talk long now. Suddenly nothing makes sense any more. I just phoned to say Ben won't be coming to Nicky's party, I'm afraid. We're at sixes and sevens here. I don't know what my movements are going to be over the next few days.'

'Is your mother there with you?'

'Yes, she's here.' In the background, Harriet heard a voice call Peggy's name. 'Look, I have to go now. I just wanted to say – oh, Harriet, please catch this letter writer before he does any more harm.'

'I'll try but –'

'I've been thinking and thinking, trying to work out who it could be. Someone who knows where Frank works, who knows all about us. It's really creepy. Listen, Harriet, will you do something for me? Will you go to church on Sunday?'

'Church?'

For one wild moment, Harriet wondered whether Peggy was going to ask her to pray for her. She hadn't set foot in a church since Nicky's christening.

'Yes. I can't help thinking that the writer must be someone connected with the church. So many of the parents at St Cecilia's are also involved with the church, you see – Dr Wentworth, Sergeant Staples, Brenda Barlow, Mrs Parsons, the vicar, of course. You never know what you might find out. People let slip the most astonishing things after a service. They let down their guard a bit. Please go. I think you might find out something.'

'Of course I'll go,' Harriet assured her. Anything to calm Peggy down. 'Don't you worry about it. We'll find the letter writer. You concentrate on coming through this. You've enough to worry about.'

'I know. I –' Again the clipped, high-pitched voice called Peggy's name. Peggy's mother? 'Sorry, Harriet, got to go.'

'Take care,' said Harriet, but Peggy had already rung off.

Harriet looked at the clock again and wondered whether it was too late to call Alix. Then she remembered that Tim was away and Alix, who suffered from insomnia, never went to bed before midnight. She dialled Alix's number. At first she thought the number was engaged, then it gave a funny sort of click and Alix came on the line.

'Hello?'

'Alix, it's me, Harriet. Is there something wrong with your phone?'

'I don't think so. I can hear you perfectly. Can you hear me?'

'Yes. Alix, I've just had the most awful phone call from Peggy. She sounded absolutely at the end of her tether –'

'Why? Oh no, you don't mean the letters have turned out to be true after all?'

'Yes. Frank's having an affair. Peggy sounded distraught.'

'Where is she?'

'She's gone with the children to her mother's.'

At the other end of the phone, Alix clicked her tongue in exasperation. 'Just the worst place for her to be. She ought to have gone somewhere on her own. Or come to one of us.'

'Why? What's wrong with her mother?'

'Don't you remember her? She's a perfectionist. Has high stand-ards about everything. House proud. Bakes her own cakes. Has rules about everything. She'll make Peggy feel a complete failure.'

'Now you mention it, I do remember her house was awfully clean. It made me nervous. When I went for tea as a child, I was always afraid of dropping things on the carpet. And of course I always did.'

'Exactly. Peggy's mother is the sort of person who makes everyone behave much worse than they normally would. It's her gimlet eye. Rivals Miss Barnesley's. I'll leave it over the weekend. Then I'll go round on Monday and see if I can persuade Peggy to go home. After all, it's Frank who should move out, not her.'

'Peggy wants me to go to church on Sunday. She thinks I might find out something about the letter writer, though why she's bothering about that now –'

'It's not a bad idea, though. See what you can find out. Do you want me to look after the children?'

'No, it's all right. Daniel will probably enjoy it.'

Harriet had read somewhere, in one of the numerous medical books she'd pored over in the first year after Daniel's birth, that children like him often enjoyed the order and ritual of church services.

'Let me know how you get on.'

'I will,' she promised and put down the phone.

She looked at Daniel. Church. That would certainly be a new experience. If he liked it, would they have to go every Sunday? She could imagine what her father would have to say about that. Her father had trained originally as a scientist. Though what Harriet knew about science could be written on a molecule, living with a scientist and an atheist all those years had taught her to be clear in her thinking, to reason things out, to scorn superstition. For which she was grateful. It had helped her cut through all the myths that surround a child like Daniel. The Wild Boy of Aveyron, the mysterious visitor from another planet.

Harriet watched her son draw square after square on the paper in front of him. He'd learned to hug her. That was something. It had been a slow process, had taken nearly a year, but at least he'd learned that – to put his arms around her and stand still while she kissed him. The day he'd first done that had been one of the sweetest of her life. As a baby he'd not even looked at her, had lain stiff and unsmiling in her arms, his head turned away from her. Yes, whatever her father said, there had been progress. But what an effort it took. He'd had to be taught the least little thing – even how to blow out the candles on his birthday cake – slowly, painstakingly, over and over again. In comparison with Daniel, Nicky had practically brought himself up. Parents whose children were healthy didn't know how lucky they were.

She laid a hand gently on Daniel's thick blonde hair. He stayed perfectly still, not responding, but not moving away either. Which was also progress.

Chapter Fifteen

Daniel came down for breakfast the next morning with his hands and face washed, his hair neatly combed, his teeth brushed and the buttons of his shirt done up unevenly so that one end flapped outside his jeans.

'Hello, darling.' She caught him as he went past and gave him a kiss.

'Darling,' he repeated, without a trace of emotion. He glanced round. 'Three for breakfast? Three minus two equal one. Nicky! Nicky!' His voice was sharp with anxiety.

'Leave him, Daniel. He's still asleep. He'll be here quite soon.'

'Soon?'

'Thirty minutes.'

'Thirty minutes,' Daniel repeated. He checked the table to see that everything was in its correct place. He moved a knife and spoon a few inches to the right and put his blue mug on the left of his cereal bowl.

'Let's button your shirt, Daniel.'

Harriet unfastened his shirt, then stood behind him, moving his hands with hers as, very slowly, she did up the buttons again. She remained silent as she did this. Words would only confuse him. Sometimes she had nightmares that Daniel was drawing her into his silence; that they would end up, the two of them, cut off from the outside world, walled in by their silence. Then she had to fight to use words.

She shook some Rice Krispies into his bowl. Rice Krispies were the only cereal Daniel would eat. God help her if they ever went out of production. Daniel pulled out his chair, circled it three times (the number three was very important to him, a magical number) and sat down. After a couple of mouthfuls, he glanced up. 'Thirty minutes?'

Harriet shook her head.

Fortunately, before Daniel had time to enquire again, Nicky could be heard through the monitor stirring in his bed. She went upstairs and brought him down in his pyjamas.

'Three,' muttered Daniel, then studied his cereal bowl. Nicky dropped a kiss on his arm in passing.

'Let's sing "Happy Birthday".'

Obediently, Daniel joined in the singing, as he had been taught.

Nicky plunged excitedly into his presents. Soon the room looked like a bomb-site of wrapping paper, string, boxes half-opened then laid aside as he hurried to open the next one. Daniel began to grow distressed. He hated disorder. Harriet glanced at him.

'Daniel, do you want to go and listen to some music?'

'Music!' he repeated, not looking at her but giving a little shiver of excitement.

He got down from the table and ran next door into the playroom. Soon strains of Mozart's *Requiem* could be heard. Daniel couldn't do his shoes up – didn't see the point of it – but he'd mastered the workings of her old record player by the age of two and a half. He could barely read but had been capable, from twelve months, of humming complicated passages from Tchaikovsky. Luckily it was classical music he liked for he had a habit of playing the same piece over and over again.

Harriet sighed. Her changeling child. This queer little stranger in their midst who barely acknowledged their existence. He'd made her strong. She'd had to learn to stand up to people, to stand up for her child against those who couldn't understand him, against those who said he was impossible to teach and would never amount to anything. She'd even had to defend him against his own father, who shrugged his shoulders and went off to the House whenever things got difficult. Despite everything, she'd persevered and now he could read 'cat', 'car' and 'dog'. And even if he couldn't speak in a way that was comprehensible to outsiders, he was a marvel at his sums and loved music. But all the other things that made life so wonderful – friendships, conversation, books – would never mean anything to Daniel.

At ten her father came round with a Teach Yourself To Read game for Nicky. Nicky, dressed in his green and red Robin suit with black cape, accepted it dutifully. Daniel was still in the playroom listening to Mozart. Suddenly he appeared in the doorway.

'Hello, Daniel,' said her father, awkwardly as usual. He'd never got used to his elder grandson. He persisted in treating him just like any other child. 'Are you looking forward to Nicky's party?'

For Daniel this question was perfectly meaningless. He didn't deal in emotions. Ignoring his grandfather, indeed not looking at any of them, he said, very distinctly, 'My tins.'

Harriet felt herself tense up. A worried expression flitted across Nicky's face. Her father was watching too. She forced herself to relax. If she didn't remain calm, her anxiety would communicate itself to Daniel and that would be fatal. I will show you, Daniel, she thought, that the world will not fall apart if you cannot play with your tins.

'Go shops, Daniel?' she suggested. Her father disapproved of her speaking in this pidgin English but she had to start with what he could understand. Too many words confused him. 'Daniel eat banana in shop?' This was to deflect his attention from his tins.

It seemed to work.

'Go shops, goody!'

He flapped his arms in excitement and ran into the hall to fetch his shoes. Out of the corner of her eye, Harriet saw Nicky sigh in relief and turn back to his game.

'We won't be long,' she said, bending down to fasten Daniel's shoes. 'Thanks, Dad.'

Daniel nudged her. ''Brella.' He went to get it.

Harriet was puzzled for a moment. Then she remembered that the last time Daniel had been home, it had rained. Now, though the sky outside was blue, the umbrella would have to be taken with them. Watching her put it into her bag, Daniel gave a sigh of contentment. There was no risk. Everything was going to be exactly the same as all the other Saturdays.

They could never vary their route, Daniel was insistent on that. He walked along beside her, ignoring passers-by, but taking great care not to step on the cracks between the paving-stones and edging close to his mother whenever they passed a dog. He had an intense and apparently incurable terror of dogs.

As always, they went first to the vegetable shop, though there was nothing she really wanted to buy there, and then to the supermarket. She felt Daniel tense up as he caught sight of the people milling around the entrance. Until last year, she hadn't been able to take him shopping since a visit to the supermarket invariably produced a tantrum. People moving around, from Daniel's point of view, were a disorderly muddle. Recently, however, he'd begun to enjoy shopping. The people remained upsetting but that was outweighed by his fascination with the cartons of juice and milk, the packets and tins arranged in orderly rows on the shelves.

'Monosodium glutamate. Bad,' he muttered, as they made their way through the crowds, pushing their trolley. Not that they needed a trolley but that was also part of their routine. Overhearing Daniel's statement about monosodium glutamate, a woman looked round in amazement, then pursed her lips. Harriet could see she was putting Daniel down as another precocious middle-class kid. Whereas what he was doing was simply repeating parrot-fashion a phrase he'd heard on television. It had no meaning for him.

'Daniel, banana?'

Daniel's eyes gleamed. She unpeeled the banana and handed it to him. He followed behind her, nibbling away at it contentedly as she pushed the trolley rapidly up and down the aisles. Suddenly there was an almighty crash behind her. She looked round. Daniel, the empty banana skin discarded on the floor, was standing surrounded by tin cans, a huge grin on his face. Abandoning her trolley, Harriet rushed over as a smart-suited man descended on Daniel from the other side.

'I'm so sorry. He was probably reaching for a tin and pulled them all down by mistake,' she gasped, scrabbling about on the floor, picking up tins.

'Well, madam, perhaps you could teach your child not to touch the food on the shelves,' replied the assistant manager frostily, as he too bent down to pick up tins. 'He's old enough to know better.'

'Yes. I'm sorry. Daniel's er . . . well, he's not quite a normal child,' she whispered reluctantly.

The assistant manager looked at Daniel's handsome face, wide-eyed and grinning, with an expression of disbelief.

Daniel's grin began to fade as he saw the tins disappearing back on to the shelves. He stamped his foot in distress. 'Ti! Ti! Ti!' The eerie wailing stopped other shoppers in their tracks.

'Here. Daniel's tins.' She thrust two tins into his hands. The crying stopped as suddenly as it had begun. 'Sorry,' she muttered again. Head down, cheeks burning, Harriet pushed the trolley towards the nearest checkout. Daniel trotted beside her, smiling from ear to ear, a tin in each hand.

'Food for Nicky's party.' He nodded approvingly as she placed her few bits of shopping on the checkout counter. 'Nicky's friends.'

'Yes,' she replied, getting out her purse. Daniel knew the word friend, but not what it meant.

'Mummy,' he said in a too-loud voice, as they were leaving the shop, 'the girl on the checkout smiled at me. She's my friend. Can she come to my party?'

'We'll see.'

They made their way to the garden centre. It not only had flowers and plants but small animals as well, and birds and fish and a parrot. Daniel flapped his arms in excitement as they went in through the gate. Harriet was not deceived. It was the cages Daniel enjoyed, not the animals. He was indifferent to the shuffling of the gerbil, the munching of the rabbits, the antics of the white mouse running up and down its wheel; anything, in short, which would have delighted an ordinary child. It was the orderly arrangements Daniel liked. Each species of animal in its own separate cage. He would put us all in cages if he could, she thought.

'One – hamsters. No, zero. Zero – hamsters,' he stated with precision as they passed through the barrier. He'd remembered the order of the cages exactly.

So they went first to watch the hamsters. At least she watched the hamsters. They were ignored by Daniel who was busy running his fingers along the wire netting of the cage, a look of intense concentration on his face. Harriet glanced across at two little girls who were oohing and aahing and pointing to the rabbits. Daniel hardly ever pointed at anything. He did not welcome the world. He never even looked at the girls, though they were standing close by. He is alone, she thought, totally and permanently alone. When she thought about it like that, it made her feel dizzy, even slightly panic-stricken. She took his hand.

'Come along, Daniel. Zero – hamsters. One . . . ?' All she could do was try to enter his world, however odd it was, so that he would not, quite, be alone.

'One – mice. Two – rabbits. Three – fish. Four – parrot.' His face shone as they moved past the cages in orderly fashion. They stood watching the brightly coloured parrot scrabble around for seeds. 'Greedy,' murmured Daniel, chuckling with satisfaction.

As they watched, the parrot lifted up his beak, fluttered his wings and gave a great squawk. Daniel burst into tears. He was unpredictable about noises. Some, like car horns, for instance, he totally ignored, others, even quite soft noises, made him weep. She knelt down beside him, but resisted the tempta-tion to put her arms round him. That would only make it worse.

'Ssh, Daniel. Ssh.' He was screaming now. People were staring. 'Ssh! It's all right, Daniel. Look, the parrot isn't crying. Parrots don't cry.'

'Parrots don't cry,' he repeated in between screams, his body rigid.

She became aware of a pair of cord-trousered legs standing beside her.

'Can I help? Is he frightened?'

She looked up. It was Humphrey Osborne, the last person she wanted to see at that moment. He was holding a wide-eyed Dominic by the hand.

'No, it's all right, thanks. There's nothing to be done. The parrot squawked. Sudden noises sometimes frighten him.'

'Parrots don't cry! Parrots don't cry!' shrieked Daniel.

Harriet saw understanding flash into Humphrey Osborne's eyes. 'Is this Daniel?' he said.

'Yes,' she replied defiantly, with a little tilt of her chin.

A dull flush came into his cheeks. 'I'm sorry,' he began, 'you must have thought me –'

Suddenly, as if a tap had been turned off, the screaming ceased. Daniel untwisted his face and began darting rapid glances at

Humphrey Osborne. People stopped staring and started going about their business again. Harriet got up off her knees.

'Age?' asked Daniel, in his strange voice which was a little too loud and went up and down in the wrong places. 'You seven.'

'He means he's seven,' explained Harriet. 'He has difficulty with "I".'

'Age?' repeated Daniel.

'I'm sorry –'

Humphrey Osborne interrupted her. 'Fifty-five.'

'Fifty-five plus thirty-six plus seven equal ninety-eight,' came the swift response.

Humphrey Osborne looked startled. 'He's good at sums.'

'Yes, Daniel loves sums.' Would do them all day if she let him, that and nothing else.

'Logarithms,' Daniel confirmed, then lost interest and began running his finger up and down the wire meshing again.

Humphrey Osborne looked confused. 'Does maths run in the family?'

'No. I'm hopeless and so is his father.'

There were children like Daniel who took degrees in mathematics, yet could barely read. She was reluctant to push him too far in the direction of his obsessions. She wanted him to learn as many words as possible, learn to feel his way among the meaningless sounds, as if it was a foreign language he was learning, not his own.

Bored, Dominic tugged on his father's hand. Humphrey Osborne smiled apologetically. 'We'd better go. I've promised Dominic I'd have a look at those very expensive children's playhouses they have out the back. He's been nagging me for weeks to come and see them. Goodbye, Daniel.'

There was no response. Daniel ran his finger up and down the wire, absorbed in the pattern, smiling radiantly, lost in his own world, very far from human beings.

'He's not being rude,' Harriet explained. 'He loves patterns. Patterns and diagrams and numbers. He prefers them to people.'

There was an expression of sympathy on Humphrey Osborne's face as he walked off. I can do without that, she thought angrily.

I don't want your pity. You and your gloomy house – no wonder your son wants to move out into a playhouse.

Back home, Daniel went straight upstairs, ignoring his brother and grandfather. He was going to add his two new tins to the collection in his wardrobe. Only they weren't in his wardrobe any longer. Harriet dumped her shopping on the table in the kitchen and waited. From upstairs came an unearthly wail. 'Ti! Ti! Ti!' It welled up from some strange and secret place, as if the very life was being torn from him.

Nicky ran through from the playroom covering his ears with his hands. His grandfather followed. Then Daniel appeared in the doorway, his face twisted with grief.

'Ti! Ti! Ti!' he shouted.

'Two tins, Daniel,' she said, pointing to the tins in his hands.

There was a momentary pause. He looked down at the tins. 'Thirty-three plus two equal thirty-five.' The wailing started up again. 'Your ti! Your ti!'

'No, Daniel. Two. That's enough tins for Daniel.'

He began running round in circles in the kitchen, round and round, obsessively. Harriet was aware of her father's silent disapproval.

'All right! Bed!'

She picked him up and carried him up to his bedroom, took off his shoes and laid him down on the bed, rigid, resisting, screaming all the while. She put a Mozart tape into his cassette recorder and closed the door. The screaming continued.

'I'm glad to see you're taking a firm line,' commented her father when she came back down to the kitchen. 'At last.'

From behind his glasses, Nicky gazed at her reproachfully. She knelt down.

'It's all right, Nicky. It will be all right.'

'I want my pink towel.'

Silently she handed him the towel. He stuffed the end of it into his mouth for comfort. Her father watched with an expression of distaste.

'Can't you cure him of that?'

'No.'

Having made the point that she was bringing up her children all wrong, her father went home. Harriet and Nicky made sandwiches for his party, Nicky standing on a chair, her apron tied round him, spreading the margarine carefully and precisely on the bread. Gradually, the screams from upstairs faded. She laid down her knife.

'I'll go and get him now.'

Nicky followed her upstairs. Daniel was sitting on the edge of his bed, rocking backwards and forwards, senselessly.

'Daniel! Daniel!'

His head was bent. He would not look at her. He'd retreated. She saw that he'd bitten his arm. The skin was broken and bleeding. With difficulty, she lifted him off the bed and carried him, still stiff in her arms, downstairs. He sat on the kitchen floor, motionless. She got a tube of cream and began dabbing it on his arm. He shook her off. She and Nicky stood staring helplessly at him. Nicky picked up his pink towel. Finally Daniel raised his head.

'Daniel, thirty-five tins? No?'

'No' with a question mark was the nearest Daniel ever came to 'yes', his refusal to say yes being part of his refusal of life.

She shook her head.

Daniel stood up. His body went rigid. He opened his mouth. He screamed. He peed all over the kitchen floor. Nicky looked distressed.

'Stop it!' she shouted. 'Stop it! Stop it! Stop it!' Tears came into her eyes. Would it always be like this? Would it never get any better? Nicky stood silently observing them, hugging his pink towel for comfort. She laid a hand on his shoulder. 'It's all right, Nicky.'

With a sense of defeat, she went to retrieve Daniel's tins from the cupboard where she'd hidden them. He clapped his hands and grinned when he saw them.

'Don't tell your grandfather,' she muttered to Nicky.

She fetched Daniel clean trousers and pants and mopped up the kitchen floor.

Watching her, Nicky smiled. 'Daniel's all right now. He's got his tins.'

'Yes. He has his tins.'

She sighed as she watched her elder son bend over the shiny

metal objects, arranging them neatly in rows on the floor. Daniel loved those old tins more than he loved his mother or his brother. Stupid, she told herself, you can't possibly envy a *tin*.

Chapter Sixteen

Nicky's party was not the absolute disaster she'd feared it might be. All the children invited from St Cecilia's, apart from Peggy's Ben, of course, turned up. And even if the atmosphere as their parents dropped them off was distinctly chilly, that all went over Nicky's head as he dashed around in his Robin suit, opening presents and handing round crisps. Daniel enjoyed getting all the children to line up to play musical chairs. He enjoyed watching them play pass the parcel and pin the tail on the donkey. But after tea, when the children began to mill around, he started to became distressed. Making little grunting noises, he ran backwards and forwards trying to get them to stand in a straight line. Harriet bore him off to his bedroom and left him contentedly rearranging his tins in his wardrobe.

Later, long after Nicky had gone to bed, Daniel sat watching a quiz programme on television. He didn't understand the questions, but he squealed with delight every time the buzzer went off. Harriet sketched him watching, trying to catch that look of utter absorption on his face.

When the programme ended, she laid aside her sketch pad and said, 'Bath, Daniel?'

He didn't so much as glance at her, but his whole body shivered with excitement. He loved water, had driven her nuts when he was younger by splashing it all over the bathroom floor. Now he'd learned to control his excitement. A bit. He ran upstairs to the bathroom, turned on the taps and would have got in fully clothed if she hadn't caught him in time.

While Daniel sat in the bath, Harriet fetched her sketch pad and began to draw a map of their day. It was pointless telling him a bedtime story. Stories never interested him. He couldn't empathise with the characters.

'. . . then we went to the shops.' She drew a shop. 'What did we buy, do you remember, Daniel?'

'Tins.'

'And what else?'

'Tins and tins and tins.'

'Tins of what?'

'Tins of what?' he repeated.

'Tins of soup.'

'Soap?' He giggled and rolled his large brown eyes.

'Not soap, soup,' she said gently.

He frowned and splashed a leg in the water. 'Daniel know.'

'Yes,' she said hastily, 'of course you do. And then we went to the garden centre.' She drew a cage with a hamster inside.

'Zero – hamsters. One – mice. Two – rabbits.' He splashed his hands excitedly in the water.

'And?' She waited to see if he would remember anything else. Meeting Humphrey and Dominic Osborne, for instance. She sketched a man and a boy beside the cage. He frowned and began to look sulky. Then his face cleared.

'Parrots don't cry!' he shouted, bursting with pride.

She was thrilled. For once he'd remembered something that wasn't to do with numbers or objects but feelings. 'Very good, Daniel!' She would have hugged him except that, for Daniel, a hug was not a treat. She had to reward him in a way he would appreciate. She went downstairs to the kitchen and took out a tin.

'A new tin for Daniel,' she said, lifting him out of the bath. The tin distracted his attention from the fact she had let out the water. Usually he screamed and bit and tried to get back in.

Harriet left him playing happily in bed with the tin, holding it close to his face, turning it round and round so that it glittered in the light. From time to time he chuckled. He was lost again, lost in that odd world of his that had numbers and objects in it, but no people.

Harriet went across to her studio for a moment and stood in the dark looking out at the chestnut trees. Daniel will always be like this, the doctor had said, getting nearer to people then withdrawing again. It was as if a sheet of glass separated her elder son from the rest of the world. Sometimes, like this evening, you could see him come up close to the glass, almost press his nose against it, but he always retreated.

She watched a dark cloud scud across the sky. 'I know I'm behaving badly,' Geoffrey had said, 'leaving you to cope on your own with Daniel, but I can't help it. I'm not cut out to be the parent of a handicapped child.' 'Neither am I,' she'd retorted. But it wasn't optional for her as it seemed to be for Geoffrey. She'd have Daniel for the rest of her days, long after Nicky had left home. Or perhaps not that long. Children like Daniel wear out quickly, the doctor had said. They often die in their late twenties.

She glanced at the unfinished canvas propped up against the easel. As long as she could go on with her painting, she could take whatever else life threw at her. Just about. And she was beginning to make some good friends up here. Alix. Peggy (she wondered how Peggy was). Perhaps even Eddie. He'd been friendly on the phone yesterday, friendly and caring. But she'd better not think too much about him yet. Not until she knew for certain whether she could trust him.

The next morning, Harriet set off for church with Daniel and Nicky. They arrived early and lingered on the path outside. She recognised several parents from St Cecilia's. Sergeant Staples went past, holding his daughter by the hand. Mrs Parsons with the twins, Fiona and Julian and Angelica, Dr Wentworth, Brenda Barlow, Mrs Moss, but not Mrs Parker. The sun beat down on them as they stood outside the ancient church with the square tower. The red and yellow roses made a splash of colour against the smoke-darkened brick. Nicky skipped around, enjoying being out in the fresh air. Daniel knelt down and began arranging pebbles into rows. It seemed a waste of a beautiful morning to go inside the dark and gloomy church but Harriet felt she owed it to Peggy.

'I want to go in,' said Nicky suddenly.

'Come on then, Daniel.'

She held out her hand. Looking sullen, Daniel remained crouched over his pebbles. Please not a tantrum, she thought, not here. Then the organ began playing. Daniel raised his head. His eyes sparkled.

He scrambled to his feet and, grabbing her hand, led her, almost dragged her into the church.

Harriet chose a pew by the door so that they could make a quick exit if necessary. Nicky stood up on the pew while Daniel stood beside her, looking down the aisle. The music changed to a hymn. The priests and servers processed in from a door at the side. At the head of them was a teenage boy carrying the cross. Dirty scuffed trainers showed beneath his robes. Then came two small girls carrying candles, then Reverend Martin Threlfall, then a priest she didn't recognise. Daniel watched wide-eyed as the procession moved towards the altar. When everyone knelt as the choir started to sing the *Kyrie*, he gave a small shiver of excitement. He forgot to kneel and sit with everyone else but stood staring down the aisle, as if hypnotised by the singing and the lights flickering on the altar.

Nicky was a different matter. He wriggled and sighed and began a running commentary on the proceedings, his clear, precise voice seeming to ring out across the church.

'Mummy, why are they wearing those clothes?' 'Mummy, they're funny men, aren't they?' 'Mummy, can we blow out the candles later?'

A few rows forward she saw a man turn in his pew. It was Humphrey Osborne. He slipped out of his pew and came noiselessly back down the aisle to where she was standing struggling to control Nicky. She frowned at him. He wasn't going to tell her to leave, was he?

'There's a crèche for younger children in the crypt,' he said in a low voice. 'Do you think Nicky would like to join it? Dominic's there and several of the other children from St Cecilia's nursery.'

She took Nicky down, then raced back up, but Daniel had hardly moved a muscle. Harriet sat back in her pew and let the service wash over her, the chanting, the words dimly remembered from her schooldays when Miss Barnesley had insisted on every girl attending morning assembly. She thought it amazing that it all still went on unchanged, regardless of what scientists were discovering about the world. Beside her, Daniel suddenly drew in his breath. She braced herself for a scream. Then he sniffed and a beam appeared on his face. He was enjoying the incense. She disliked the smell herself.

The sermon was given by the priest she hadn't seen before but who, according to her service sheet, was Keith Graham, the curate. He was a large dark-haired man, given to theatrical gestures. In his white robes, he towered over the congregation in the pulpit. Daniel stared, fascinated.

'Punishment,' he boomed. 'We're not supposed to speak about that these days. We talk about socialising into the community or curing people or, more sinisterly, reprogramming them. Perhaps this is where we've gone wrong.' His penetrating gaze swept in a wide arc over the congregation. 'Take these anonymous letters people have been receiving. I've heard the writer described as sick. Probably he is. But is it not also permissible to wonder whether the hand of God is at work among us? Ferreting out our shameful little secrets. The secrets we've told no one. The secrets that lie festering on our consciences. The secrets that we've never confessed because we don't go to confession.' He drew himself up. 'And yet confession is one of the Church's sacraments. Perhaps this is our chance to come clean, to rid ourselves of our burden and be forgiven in the confessional.'

He went on in the same vein. Harriet tried hard not to listen. All the same, she couldn't help catching a sentence here and there. It made her absolutely furious. She sat in her pew tearing a paper handkerchief to shreds in her lap. It was like her father always said: science had given men and women their freedom and the Church kept pushing them down on their knees. She wondered whether Keith Graham had received an anonymous letter. Was he married? He looked about forty-five. A late vocation. Could he possibly be the letter writer? Had he perhaps been seized by an evangelical fervour to clean up the community by bringing its secrets out into the open?

They didn't go up to the altar. It would have been hypocritical on her part, Harriet felt, and Daniel was content to watch the orderly procession of people line up in two neat rows by the side of the pews. It would suit Daniel if human beings always moved up and down in straight lines, she thought. She was beginning to find the atmosphere oppressive and longed for the service to be over. If it went on much longer it would be she, not Daniel, who broke out into screams.

Then, thankfully, the final prayer was said, the final hymn was sung and Nicky came trotting up from the crypt with the other children.

'Harriet!' Brenda Barlow stopped by her pew. 'I didn't know you were a church-goer.'

'I'm not really but –'

'Perhaps Father Graham's right. Perhaps this letter writer *is* having a good effect on the community,' bubbled Brenda.

Harriet stared at her. Didn't Brenda sound just a little too enthusiastic? Could it possibly be that Brenda herself was the writer? She'd always exhibited an intense busybodiness and an absolute moral certainty on any question you cared to bring up. She took the *Daily Mail* and was a firm supporter of Mary Kenny, two things that should make her a suspect in Harriet's book.

Brenda bustled away to greet someone else. Fiona came past, with Angelica.

'I can guess why you're here,' she said. 'Come over to the church hall for coffee. That's the place for gossip.'

Feeling her cover had been well and truly blown (would Miss Marple have been so careless?), Harriet grabbed her sons by the hand and followed the general exodus over to the hall.

'Good to see you again, Sally!'

Martin Threlfall, standing in the doorway of the church hall, pressed her hand warmly and radiated such delight over Sally's reappearance among the faithful that Harriet hadn't the heart to disillusion him. It was incidents like these that put a question mark beside Martin Threlfall's name on the list of suspects. Surely the letter writer would be more on the ball about names and faces than Reverend Threlfall seemed to be. Or was this a bluff? A persona he'd adopted? Was Martin Threlfall capable of adopting a persona? Would he even know what one was?

Nicky tugged at her hand, interrupting her flight of fancy. 'Juice, please.'

She went over to the table and purchased two glasses of orange for her sons and a cup of coffee for herself.

'Are you planning on becoming a regular or is this a one-off?'

asked Humphrey Osborne, coffee cup in one hand, unlit pipe in the other.

'Definitely a one-off.' She searched around for a plausible excuse for being there. 'I wanted to see what Daniel would make of it.'

'And?'

'He loved it.'

Out of the corner of her eye, she watched Nicky drift over to a group of children. Daniel followed at his heels.

'Good. Pity you hit Father Graham's turn to give the sermon. He's relatively new here. Used to be in the civil service. Pretty dreadful sermon. I expect he'll get rapped over the knuckles by Father Threlfall. It's not at all the sort of thing he approves of.'

'What? Punishment?'

'No. Frightening people. That was what he was trying to do. Never works.'

'Doesn't it?' We're all pretty frightened of the letter writer, she thought.

'Nice chap, Martin Threlfall. Rotten judge of character though. This is the second dud curate we've had. Still, they don't stay long.'

Harriet was staring at Humphrey Osborne and wondering whether he counted himself a good judge of character (the letter writer, whatever other traits he might have, was surely that) when her attention was distracted by a mutter arising from the group of children. Hurriedly she put down her cup.

'Excuse me.'

'Mummy! Mummy!' It was Nicky calling her.

Another child's voice – was it Dominic's? – rang out. 'Ugh! He's being sick!' 'Yeuck!' cried another voice. The children were edging away. There in the middle of them stood Daniel, being sick in his usual uninhibited fashion. There was an expression of acute embarrassment on Nicky's face. The grown-ups in the room stopped chatting and stared. Several of them tut-tutted.

'I'm so sorry,' muttered Harriet. 'The excitement. Nervous digestion. Not an entirely normal child.'

The atmosphere, which had been tense, suddenly warmed at these words. The child wasn't spoilt, but ill. They could handle that. Someone tore off a wad of kitchen paper and handed it to Harriet to wipe Daniel's face. Someone else went to fetch a bucket and mop. That vague feeling of benevolence towards one's fellow beings engendered by a church service, instead of being dissipated as it usually is, for once found a positive outlet.

'Who is normal?' muttered a man standing near Harriet. 'I'm not quite normal myself.'

She could have hugged him. She cleaned up Daniel as best she could, then hurried her children away. She noticed that Humphrey and Dominic Osborne had already disappeared. At the first sign of trouble, she wondered.

At lunch-time Alix rang up.

'Well? What did you find out?'

'Not much. I had to leave early. The children were a bit of a liability. I can see why Miss Marple remained a spinster. I'm putting Brenda Barlow down on the suspect list, though. She's much too pleased about these letters. They're giving her the chance to say I told you so to a lot of people.'

'Yes, I'd noticed that.' Alix hesitated. 'Harriet, what about Fiona?'

'Fiona?'

'I've been thinking. All the letters and e-mails we know about so far have turned out to be true. Fiona's is the only one that hasn't.'

'That's true. And the accusation in it − that Julian is gay − is so wildly off the mark that no one would believe it anyway.'

'Exactly.'

'It's worth thinking about, isn't it?'

'Yes. What about your Humphrey Osborne?'

'He isn't my anything, Alix. And he's certainly still on the list.'

'When Daniel's gone back to school, we must put our heads together.'

'For Peggy's sake.'

'Yes. Harriet, let's work on her tomorrow to get her to leave her mother's. I'm convinced it's the worst possible place for her to be right now.'

'OK, we'll work on it. Always assuming Peggy turns up at the school gate tomorrow.'

'She's bound to. She can't keep the children off school for ever.'

'No. See you tomorrow then, Alix.'

'Bye.'

In the afternoon, Harriet, Daniel and Nicky went to the playground. It was a nice place, where everything was made of wood. Wooden horses, wooden climbing frames, a wooden house to play in, wooden tunnels to crawl through. Nicky sprang into action. Daniel sat beside Harriet on the bench, ignoring the other children and turning a tin round and round in his hands. She watched Nicky crawl through a tunnel, helped him on the climbing frame and then sat down again as he went to join some children in the wooden house.

'Nicky's friends,' commented Daniel, his eyes fixed on his tin.

'I don't know about friends. I don't think he's ever met them before.'

'The girl at the supermarket's my friend.'

'I know.'

Suddenly he gave a grunt and dropped his tin. She bent down to pick it up for him. He ignored it. He was watching two children squeal in delight on the slide.

'Daniel play too?' she asked, hardly daring to hope.

He didn't reply but sat staring at the children, completely absorbed.

'Mum, how can Daniel make friends?'

He wanted some rules. As Harriet looked at him, an expression of wistfulness stole over his face. She could see he was wondering why he couldn't join in these children's games. Why couldn't he learn the rules? But there were no rules for this messy running to and fro. Watching the children made him confused. He lacked the vital clue to their games.

Her heart turned over for him. It was the first time her elder son had shown even a glimmer of awareness that he was different from other people. Such awareness was more than Harriet could bear. She tugged at his hand and called to Nicky.

'Come on. We're going home.' Her voice sounded harsher than she'd intended and several of the other parents stared.

She walked them very fast along the pavement. At the traffic lights they were halted. Daniel looked up at her anxiously.

'God made Daniel, made mistake, no?'

'There is no God, Daniel,' she replied savagely, rushing them both across the road as the lights changed.

Her haste frightened Daniel, and he began to weep. Nicky started crying in sympathy. She walked home clutching two howling children by the hand. By the time she reached the front door, she was in tears herself. She calmed them down, poured them both a drink of juice and sank down on to the sofa, tears rolling down her face. She didn't notice Daniel leave his juice and shuffle over to her till she felt his arms around her neck and his lips pressed against her cheek.

'Mum, parrots don't cry.'

He dabbed a finger in the tears on her face. She looked at him. And Daniel looked back, with eyes that were full of concern.

Later that afternoon, Harriet scribbled a note to Daniel's head-mistress. 'This afternoon there was a breakthrough for a couple of minutes. Daniel responded to my feelings.' She glanced over at him. He was crouched on the kitchen floor aimlessly tipping water from one jug to another. On and on he went, seeming never to get bored with his monotonous, self-imposed task. 'Daniel,' she called, but he wasn't looking at her now. He'd retreated into that lonely world of his that contained objects and numbers and diagrams, but no people and no emotions.

She smiled a little sadly. She'd learned, over the years, that Daniel's time scale was different from other children's. He would pick up a word, use it once and then forget it for months. But she could wait. Now that it had happened once. Now that she'd proved what she'd always believed, that Daniel had it in him to respond to another human being. She must wait for him to sort it all out in his mind, to uncover the language that would help him comprehend at least a little of the complex world of human relations. She would wait a lifetime if necessary.

That evening, after Nicky had gone to bed, she watched her

elder son walk carefully, one foot at a time, back up the steps of the minibus. At the top, he turned and waved at her, as he had been taught. Then the door closed behind him.

Going back into the house, the silence hit her like a stone. She went up to Daniel's bedroom, began tidying up and then suddenly had to pick up a jumper of his and hold it against her face. It smelled of him, that slightly sour smell of dried saliva. She rocked to and fro on the bed, clutching his jumper. How long would it take for her to get used to Daniel going away from her? To stop feeling numb every time the minibus drew up outside the house? She lay back on his bed, cradling his jumper in her arms, feeling limp and exhausted. Eventually, she fell asleep. It was three in the morning when she awoke, cramped and stiff, and went downstairs to her own bed.

Chapter Seventeen

The next morning Harriet found a long brown envelope lying on her mat. It had a local postmark and her name and address were typed on the front. Of course, it might be anything – a bill, a cheque from Douglas from the art gallery, a circular from one of the political parties. All the same, she couldn't help having a funny feeling about it. Gingerly she picked it up and turned it over. What horrid perverted fantasy did it contain? Or what home truth? Something about Geoffrey, perhaps?

Harriet carried it into the kitchen and laid it down on the table. The proper thing to do would be to hand it over to Sergeant Staples unopened. She poured out Coco Pops for Nicky, made herself a cup of tea then, knowing she'd never do the proper thing and unable to bear the suspense any longer, she sat down and tore open the envelope.

Printed on the same kind of computer paper as the other letters, this one said *You sent your son away because you couldn't cope with him.* She put it down. Who would write a thing like that? Though it was true. In a way. Her hands began to tremble. She felt shaky inside.

How many people knew about Daniel? A few of the mothers like Alix and Peggy. Dr Wentworth, of course. He supplied Daniel's medication. Mrs Parker and Mrs Moss (she'd wanted to explain Nicky's background). Then all those people who had been at church. She glanced at the postmark again. Saturday. So that ruled out people like Reverend Threlfall, Fiona, Brenda Barlow – or did it? They could have heard about Daniel from other sources. After all, his existence was hardly a secret. She'd never sought to hide him away. Harriet thought for a moment. Of course, there was somebody who'd met Daniel for the first time on Saturday. Humphrey Osborne. She remembered his angry reaction when he'd first learned that she sent her elder son away to school. Was that why he'd looked so guilty when he met Daniel? Had he already posted the letter that morning?

Had Humphrey Osborne written that letter? The question spun round in her mind all the time she was getting Nicky ready for school.

'Hurry up, Nicky.'

'I'm putting on my pencils as fast as I can,' he said, in an injured tone. 'I'm a good boy.'

She gave him a kiss. 'Sorry, Nicky, I was thinking about something. Of course you're a good boy.'

He looked up at her. 'Were you thinking about Daniel?'

'Sort of.' Who could have written that letter?

'Will we see Daniel again soon?'

'Yes, in four weeks.' What a long time it seemed. What would have happened in another four weeks? Would they have found the letter writer by then? Or would the horrible process be continuing?

At the school gate they met a white-faced and strained-looking Peggy holding Ben by the hand.

'How are you?' murmured Harriet.

'Coping. I think. I have to, for the children's sake.'

'I've had a letter. At last. I hope people will stop suspecting me now.'

Peggy hesitated. 'Was it about yourself or – or someone else?'

Harriet saw she was thinking about Frank and wondering what

fresh allegations there might be. Damn that letter writer, she thought angrily.

'It was about Daniel. It said I'd sent him away because I couldn't cope.'

'How disgusting.' Peggy's lips quivered.

Alix came up. 'I've had a letter.'

'Join the club,' said Harriet.

Mrs Moss came out to collect the children. Alix kissed Imogen and waved her off and then said, 'You too?'

'Yes, it was about Daniel.'

'Mine said, *Your mother's a nutter.* Which is quite true. She's a certified paranoid. I suppose the letter writer thought I'd be ashamed. But I'm not,' she added defiantly.

So that's what's wrong with her mother, thought Harriet. Poor Alix. I wonder where she is now? In some home, I expect. Aloud, she said, 'So that's another two letters which are true. The writer certainly does his homework.'

'Doesn't he?' agreed Alix. 'And it makes you wonder about Fiona, doesn't it?' She glanced down the line to where Fiona was standing, in high heels and designer shorts, chatting to a group of mothers. 'We're all agreed that the accusation of Julian being gay is nonsense, so why is her letter the only one that isn't true?'

Peggy burst into tears. 'I'm sorry,' she sobbed. 'It's all getting on top of me. These horrible letters. I suppose I should be strong and liberated about it, but the thought of Frank with another woman just makes me feel sick and as if the world's collapsing. I keep thinking of them in bed together or watching a film and going for a Chinese. He can do that sort of thing, now that he hasn't got baby-sitters to worry about. Mum thinks I should file for divorce.'

'Bit hasty,' murmured Harriet. 'Why not try to patch things up? Perhaps Frank will mend his ways?'

'It's too late for that.' Peggy blew her nose. 'He says I'm no fun any more. He's set on staying with this Gemma person.'

'You should get him out of the house immediately,' said Alix firmly. 'Then you could move back in and start a new life. You're better off without him if he's like that.'

Peggy stared at her. 'It's not as simple as that. I've depended on

Frank. I'm not as strong as you, Alix. I've never been strong.' She started crying again.

'Come on, old thing.' Harriet put an arm round her. 'Let's get you home.'

'I'm still staying with Mum.'

'We'll go there then. You're crying so much you'll never find the way back by yourself.'

Peggy smiled shakily. 'Thanks, Harriet.'

'I'm taking my letter round to the police station after I've seen Peggy home. Shall I take yours, Alix?' offered Harriet.

'Good idea. Anything to get rid of the horrid thing.' Alix dropped a brown envelope into Harriet's hand.

'This is really nice of you,' said Peggy. 'I feel so pathetic having to be walked home.'

'Nonsense. I remember what it felt like when me and Geoffrey finally broke up. I felt like death.'

'At least you don't make me feel inadequate. There's Alix telling me to start a new life. And my mother telling me to buck myself up and how she never thought Frank was good enough for me anyway.' Peggy smiled wanly. 'It doesn't help.'

'I know. But you'll come through, in time, Peggy. I know it's easy to say. But I did. The children kept me going.'

'Harriet, who do you think wrote those letters?'

'Well, despite what Alix said about Fiona, my money's on Humphrey Osborne.'

Peggy turned and looked at her. 'You still think it's a man, then?'

'Yes, I do. Don't you?'

'I don't know. Men aren't usually that observant – about relationships and things. I'm beginning to think it must be a woman.'

Harriet gave a shiver. 'Does that make it better or worse, do you think?'

'Worse, somehow.'

'I agree.'

They stopped outside a semi-detached house with a neat front garden and net curtains at the windows. The front door opened.

A tall, slim woman with tightly permed hair whom Harriet dimly remembered from childhood said harshly, 'Come inside quickly, Margaret, and don't show everyone you've been crying again.'

Hunching her shoulders, Peggy walked miserably up the drive and into the house. Her mother gave Harriet a brief nod then firmly shut the front door.

Alix is right, thought Harriet, turning in the direction of the police station, we must get Peggy out of there.

At the station, she handed the two letters over to Sergeant Staples.

'The accusations in them are both true, Sergeant. In a way. My elder son is handicapped. He needs to be in a special environment. And Alix's mother is mentally ill.'

The Sergeant sighed. 'I don't like this at all. One by one these letters are all turning out to be true. I've been talking to some of the parents. The situation is getting explosive. Everyone's under stress wondering what the letter writer's going to reveal next. I'm afraid someone will do something silly.'

'What do you mean?'

'Take the law into their own hands. Think they know who it is and take their revenge. Probably on the wrong person.'

A shiver ran down Harriet's spine. She'd been high on many people's list of suspects. Did that mean she was in danger?

'What kind of person writes these letters, do you think, Sergeant?'

'Someone with a grudge against society, or perhaps this particular community, and with too much time on their hands. We've come round to the view that the writer may not actually be a parent at the school. Perhaps it's some childless woman who envies you all? That's what behind this – envy, concealed resentment, suppressed desires. Someone who finds these letters give him, or her, a sense of power and importance. Look how many lives the letters have affected. Marriages have broken up, children have been taken into care. It's all been quite devastating. Watch out for yourself, Mrs Lee, and let us have any more letters the moment they arrive.'

Harriet left the police station wondering whether Sergeant Staples could possibly be right – was the writer someone unconnected with the school? It seemed unlikely. The writer knew so much about all their lives, seemed so close to them somehow. Sergeant Staples might have had his own reasons for suggesting an outsider. Perhaps he secretly suspected one of the parents and wanted to catch them off guard? Perhaps he suspected her? She shivered and walked on.

As she walked, Harriet began to have an uneasy feeling that she was being followed. She glanced back over her shoulder once or twice but could see no one. The street was deserted. She felt herself tense up. What had Sergeant Staples said about parents taking revenge into their own hands? She realised that she was walking very fast, practically running. She forced herself to slow down and take several deep breaths. How stupid, she told herself. What are you afraid of? This is broad daylight. Then she saw James Maugham, staring at her from across the road. Harriet put her head down and began walking fast. She heard footsteps behind her. He'd crossed the road. He was catching her up. She felt so frightened she thought she might faint. This wasn't the way to do it. Taking a deep breath, she turned round and faced him.

'Hello, James. It's that drink, isn't it?' she gabbled. 'I was about to phone you. Then I discovered I'd lost your number.'

He said nothing. Just went on staring at Harriet till she felt thoroughly unnerved. What was the matter with him? She hadn't done anything wrong. He was treating her like a criminal, whereas *he* was the one in the wrong, following her about like this.

'What do you want?' she asked at length, feeling she couldn't stand being stared at a moment longer.

James looked at her coldly. 'I thought you were a nice woman. A good woman. But it's been nearly two weeks now and you haven't bothered to pick up the phone. You're just like all the rest.'

His icy blue eyes seemed to bore into her. She felt paralysed, unable to speak. Then he turned on his heel and walked away.

Harriet stood on the pavement in the sunshine, trembling and sweating. James was stalking her. There was no doubt about it. He hadn't even bothered to make up an excuse for his appearance in Apple Burton this time. She'd read in the papers about men who stalked women, sent them abusive letters and made sinister phone calls. She should report him to the police. But then it would all come out about how she'd joined a dating agency. There'd be knowing winks down at the station. They might even say she was asking for it.

Harriet began to walk slowly home, glancing over her shoulder every now and then. A car backfired in front of her and she jumped. James had made her afraid. And also a little bit cross. How had she managed to allow him to get under her skin like this? What was eerie was the way he always seemed to know exactly where she'd be. Had there been other times when he'd followed her without her knowing? She wished he didn't know her address. What if he harmed Nicky? When she got home, even though it was the middle of the morning, she double locked the front door behind her and went to check that the back door was securely fastened.

She went up to her studio and lit a cigarette. She switched on the small radio she sometimes listened to while she worked. Another body had been found in Gloucester. Bit by bit, things buried for years were coming to light. Like these letters revealing all our secrets, she thought. She switched the radio off.

What on earth was she going to do? It crossed her mind that James might be the anonymous letter writer. Sergeant Staples thought it was an outsider. And James was clearly unbalanced. His wife had gone off with another woman. He possessed the kind of generalised grudge against women that might lead him to do anything. He might have selected St Cecilia's at random, thinking he'd never be suspected since he lived in a different town.

The more she thought about it, the more Harriet became convinced James was a suspect. All these appearances in Apple Burton would have given him plenty of opportunity to post the letters. It may have been just a dreadful coincidence that the dating agency's computer had matched him with a parent from St Cecilia's, but was that why he was so keen to keep in touch with her? Was he trying to keep tabs on reactions to his letters? But then how would he have known all those things about them? About Daniel, for instance? Or Alix's mother?

With these questions spinning round in her mind, Harriet found it impossible to concentrate on her painting. After quarter of an hour, she gave it up, lit another cigarette and went downstairs.

There was one person she did trust. More or less. One person totally unconnected with St Cecilia's. She rang Eddie.

Chapter Eighteen

Eddie's cottage was small and sparsely furnished. The ceilings were low and the windows small. Originally, it had been a labourer's cottage. It was on the edge of a farmyard, near some outbuildings. The taxi driver had had difficulty finding his way down the narrow country lane, and in the end she'd got out and walked.

'What?' said Eddie, opening the door. 'You haven't walked all the way here, have you?'

He was wearing jeans, a white cotton shirt and his corn-coloured hair, which looked newly washed, was loose around his shoulders.

'Of course not. I came by taxi. I don't have a car any more. I sold it when I moved up here.'

'Good for you, sweetheart. I'm all in favour of the simple life, as you know. But I don't think even I could do without a car.'

The front door opened directly into the living room. Eddie had done it up himself, he told her. The walls were deep blue with, here and there, gold stars and suns which gave it a vaguely zodiac feel. The star and sun motif was continued in the couple of rugs scattered over the highly polished wooden floor. The furniture was black and minimal. White linen curtains hung at the window. She had to admit Eddie had an eye for design.

'I thought this was supposed to be the simple life,' she said.

'It is. Look.' He took her by the shoulder and spun her round. 'No telly, no video. I'm cleaning out my mind.'

A soft miaowing by the stove made Harriet turn round. A small tortoiseshell cat lay on the rug in front of the stove, watching her.

'You didn't tell me you had a cat. Isn't she sweet?' She went over and knelt down beside it.

'He. And I don't. It's a stray. Found it on my doorstep this morning. I checked at the farm and at the other cottage. Nobody knows who it belongs to. I think there's something wrong with it – it walks strangely. It may have been hit by a car. I've given it some milk and some tuna. It's been asleep most of the day.'

'Poor cat.'

As Harriet watched, the tiny creature scrambled painfully to his feet and walked over to her, dragging one of his hind legs. He was so thin she could see the outline of his ribs.

'We ought to get him to a vet.'

Eddie shrugged. 'I rang the RSPCA. They said leave it till tomorrow. See how he is. As long as it's eating it's all right, they said.'

'He doesn't look all right to me, poor little thing.'

Shivering, he'd lain down again on the rug. Harriet knelt watching him. It wasn't that she was particularly fond of cats but for some reason, lying there so small and vulnerable on Eddie's rug, he reminded her of Nicky.

'Drink?'

She looked up. 'Yes, that's one of the advantages of using taxis.'

'What would you like?'

'Have you got any wine?'

'Come and see.' He took her by the hand and led her into his tiny dark green kitchen. On the wall was a wine rack full of bottles. 'My cellar. I'm doing a curry. Red suit you?'

She thought of her big toe and gout. 'Could I have white?'

'White now. Red with the curry,' he said firmly.

He poured them both a glass and then showed her the rest of the cottage. Two bedrooms and a shower room. His bedroom was painted deep yellow. There was a red rug on the floor and red curtains at the windows. The other bedroom was undecorated.

'Small, but it has everything I need.'

'It's lovely. Where did you live in London?'

'Converted warehouse in Docklands. I've let it.' He began tying back his hair in a ponytail. 'I'd better get down to cooking.'

He left her in the living room. Harriet sat sipping her wine and watching the cat. He'd fallen asleep again. Every now and then in his sleep he gave a little shiver and a moan.

'He doesn't look very well to me,' she commented as Eddie appeared from the kitchen bearing two plates of curry. 'Don't you think we should take him to the vet?'

Eddie shrugged. 'The nearest vet is fifteen miles away. I looked it up. Come and eat. Cat will be all right. Don't you worry. If he isn't, I'll take him in first thing tomorrow.'

She came and sat at the table (black, with spindly steel legs).

'Sorry,' she said, taking up her fork, 'I'm a bit on edge. This is the first time I've left Nicky with a baby-sitter since we came up here.'

'I understand.' He refilled her glass with red wine.

What the hell, she thought, taking a swig. It's only gout. 'And there've been horrible things happening at Nicky's school. There seems to be a poison-pen letter writer at work.'

'Really? I thought those only happened in novels?'

'And I think I'm being stalked.'

'Are you?' He leaned forward, interested. 'Who by?'

'Someone I met through the dating agency.'

He shook his head. 'What a creep. I should go to the police.' He looked up. 'You needn't worry about me. Even if things go wrong between a woman and me, that's not my style.'

'I didn't think it was.' She glanced over at the cat.

'Eat your curry, babe. Don't you like it?'

'It's great.' Harriet gave herself a mental shake. She was hardly being very entertaining, moaning on about anonymous letter writers and stalkers.

As if to confirm her lack of conversational skills, Eddie grinned and said, 'Think the conversation will stretch to another bottle?'

She flushed. 'What? Oh, yes. Could it be white?'

'Rather odd with curry, darling.'

He came back with red.

Feigning an appetite she didn't have, Harriet dug into her curry with alacrity and sought around for a change of subject. 'I'm glad you liked my paintings.'

'I do like them. A lot. Are you going to be famous? Am I going to be known as the friend of a famous painter?'

'I doubt it. I'm not that out of the ordinary. I might be if I had more time to spend on it.'

'Shouldn't you live in London? Be in the swing of things?'

'I've had enough of London. It's too expensive and it's no place to bring up children.'

'I like the way you care about your children. Even if it does mean you're less successful as a painter.'

'I do my best,' she muttered.

'I wonder what it's like to feel dedicated about something,' mused Eddie as he waited for her to finish her curry. 'Advertising was only a way of making money for me. And now I've made my life completely free.' He fingered the stem of his wine glass. 'I have nothing. No wife. No child. No social standing. I'm out in the wilderness.' He glanced at her. 'And looking for a woman to share it with.'

She looked at him, laid down her fork, glanced at the sleeping cat and said, 'What kind of woman?'

'Someone with whom there's a bit of chemistry. You know, Harriet, there're hundreds of nice women out there. I've met some of them through the agency. We go out for a meal, or a drink if I'm less sure about them. We spend a perfectly pleasant evening together. But they do nothing for me. There's no bloody feeling there. It's a tragedy. Then I meet someone like you. A bit mysterious, a bit out of the ordinary, a bit wild.'

She bent her head over her plate. 'I'm not wild,' she muttered. 'I can't afford to be. I've two children to bring up.'

He leaned across the table and put a hand over hers. 'I sense something in you, Harriet. Something not quite buried. After all, you're an artist.' Abruptly, just as she was getting used to the idea of physical contact with a grown male again, Eddie released her hand and began clearing away the plates. 'Coffee?'

She nodded. While he was out in the kitchen, she went over to inspect the cat. He was sleeping peacefully, but every now and then there was a little rattle in his throat she didn't quite like.

'I could get jealous of that cat.' Eddie came back into the room bearing coffee on a tray. 'I give it a home and it thanks me by taking up my friend's attention all evening.'

The words were said with a smile, nevertheless she sensed an edge to them. She rose from her knees. 'Sorry. I guess I'm just an over-anxious mother.' She took a cup of coffee from the tray.

'Let's have some music.' He put on a soul compilation. The simple life apparently didn't extend to doing without a compact disc player.

'I —'

He held up a finger. 'Ssh.' He sat down in a chair. 'Listen.'

They sat in silence listening to Wilson Pickett thump out 'In The Midnight Hour'. Harriet felt as if she was back in her art college days when they'd all sat around in each other's rooms solemnly listening to rock. The fact that Eddie seemed to take music so seriously was a mark in his favour. Perhaps he'd even get on with Daniel.

'Nostalgia,' he said when the song was over. 'Reminds me of a girl I once knew in Berlin.'

She felt a bit let down. 'You've known a lot of women, haven't you?'

He put his head on one side. 'A fair number. I tend to think of them in groups. So and so belonged to that period of my life. You know.' He held out a hand. 'Come here. You look sad. Let's dance.'

He took her in his arms and they danced slowly and carefully to Otis Redding. Eddie was a good dancer. His body leaned softly into hers. Most men, most Englishmen anyway, didn't know what to do with their bodies, held them rigid and apart.

'You're a good dancer,' she said.

'So are you.' He held her close. 'Our bodies fit nicely together, don't they?' He kissed her slowly on the mouth. Then he took her by the hand, switched off the player and said, 'Come on. Let's go to bed.'

Harriet cast a backward glance at the cat sleeping beside the stove.

'It'll be all right. Don't worry.'

He led her down the corridor to his yellow bedroom. He laid her down on his bed and drew the red curtains. He switched on a bedside lamp. The room became bathed in a glow of yellow and red. He undid his ponytail so that his hair swung loose about his shoulders again. He lay down on top of her, kissing her and stroking

144

her hair. His body felt warm and soft and heavy on top of hers. His hair smelled as clean and soft as a woman's. She felt drugged by the power his body apparently had over hers. It was such a long time since she'd slept with anyone, years and years since she'd slept with anyone except Geoffrey. Slowly and expertly, he began to undress her.

'Beautiful breasts.'

His fingers touched her clitoris. She grew damp at his touch.

'Nice wet pussy. That's a nice pussy, girl. Come on, baby, you know you want it. Come on, baby, this pussy needs attention,' he murmured. His fingers worked their way gently inside her, much more gently than she remembered Geoffrey . . . She closed her eyes and came with a groan.

'That's my girl. That's my baby,' he whispered.

She reached down. His penis felt small and soft between her fingers. Harriet felt it was somehow an indictment of herself.

'Take me in your mouth.'

'What?'

'Take me in your mouth.'

She shifted round and bent over him. Gently she sucked him and felt him begin to harden in her mouth.

'That's it. Go on, baby. I want to fill your tummy with my spunk.'

She pulled away.

'Go *on* . . .'

He forced her head back down. His sperm filled her mouth, making her gag. There was a pubic hair caught on her lip. She sat up and brushed it off.

'Swallow it. Swallow it,' he hissed.

She shook her head. She ran into his bathroom and spat the globule of sperm into the basin. She turned on the cold water and scooped up handfuls into her mouth, trying to rinse away the horrible gluey mess of his spunk. She took one of the toothbrushes standing in the mug above the basin, squeezed out a large dollop of toothpaste and brushed her teeth vigorously for several minutes. Then she went back into the bedroom.

Eddie was sitting on the edge of the bed looking sulky.

'Why did you do that? Why didn't you swallow my spunk?'

'I – I couldn't. I felt sick.' She hesitated. 'It's nothing personal. It's always been like that.'

He shook his head. 'I don't know.' He slid off the bed and began putting on his jeans. 'You need to loosen up a bit, you do.'

Harriet went over and gazed at herself in his wardrobe mirror. Her hair was in need of a cut. Lines were beginning to appear on her forehead. Her funny bumpy nose. She pressed it against the glass.

'What are you doing?'

'I don't know.'

'Silly.' Eddie came up behind her and rested his hands on her waist. She felt her body respond, even now. He nuzzled into her hair. 'You've got a really nice waist, you know. Most women nowadays don't have waists. You should flaunt it, not cover it up.' (She'd come wearing a loose navy T-shirt over her cotton skirt. She always wore a loose top to disguise what she thought of as her enormous stomach.)

'I'm not much of a one for flaunting.' She turned round and faced him. 'I'm sorry, Eddie. I'll do better next time.' She bit her lip. After all, he hadn't yet mentioned whether there'd be a next time. To hide her confusion, she bent down to pick her skirt off the floor.

He kissed her lightly on the mouth. 'Don't worry about it, sweetheart.'

Something in the way he said this made her stop in the act of fastening her skirt and say, 'We are going to see each other again, aren't we?' She paused. 'Or aren't we?'

He brushed the back of his hand across his eyes. 'Of course, darling. Of course.' He sat in a chair and watched her dress. Conscious of her stomach, she wished he wouldn't. 'A woman like you, Harriet – a clean, decent, honest woman – could really help me.' He glanced down at his fingernails. 'The fact is, I've been a bit of a bastard with women in the past. I'm trying to change.'

It was true. She'd known it from the beginning. She could almost smell the other women on him. He felt used up, drained, slightly jaded with the whole process of lovemaking. No wonder he had difficulty getting an erection. Harriet sighed quietly to herself. A woman of her age – she'd have to get used to that, the leftovers from other women. She finished dressing. Even now, the memory of his fingers caressing her inside sent a flame leaping through her veins. Was it just lust, or was Eddie right, was there something deeper between them? A special sort of empathy between outsiders? She watched as he bent over the bed to straighten his duvet. How could you ever tell? How could one ever know whether passion was love? Give it time, she thought.

He straightened up. 'Another coffee before you go?'

She glanced at her watch. 'Please.'

He padded down the corridor into the kitchen. Harriet went into the living room. It was very still. Her stomach turned over in fear. Trembling, she crept over to the rug by the stove and bent down. Then she gave a scream. Eddie came through from the kitchen.

'For God's sake! What's the matter?'

'The cat! The cat!' she screamed.

Eddie took one look at her, stepped forward and slapped her cheek. She stopped screaming. They both stood looking down at the cat. Tears rolled down Harriet's face.

Eddie sighed. 'It's a pity. But after all, it was only a stray.'

'It's a sign. Nicky!' Her hand flew to her throat. 'Something's happened to Nicky! I must phone home.'

Seized with terror, Harriet sprang towards the phone and dialled her number. Caroline answered on the second ring. Nicky was in bed, sleeping soundly. She'd just looked in on him.

'Thanks, Caroline. I'll be home in a little while.'

Feeling foolish, she replaced the receiver and glanced sheepishly across at Eddie.

'Sorry. I don't know why I reacted like that. I sometimes get in a panic about the children. That cat reminded me of Nicky somehow. It's so small and vulnerable. Was.'

'Here, drink your coffee.' He shoved the cup into her hands. 'Hey! Cheer up.' He put an arm round her shoulder. 'I'll give it a decent burial. Say a few words.' He looked into her face with a smile.

Harriet saw that Eddie didn't feel responsible for the cat's death.

He'd given the cat milk and shelter and that was enough. He couldn't carry his caring through. Very few men could. He'd never be any good with her children. He'd play with them a bit and then forget about them. Get jealous of them if they took up too much of her time.

'I'll phone for a taxi,' she said.

As she waited for the taxi to come, she sat sipping her coffee. Gradually the trembling in her limbs stopped. She watched Eddie wrap the cat in an old piece of blanket and carry him outside. 'I'll sort it out in the morning,' he said, coming back in. He stood warming his hands at the stove and in a couple of minutes they heard the taxi pull up in the yard. She stood up.

'I'll have to go.'

'Take care.' His lips brushed hers. 'Take care of yourself, my beautiful, anxious Harriet.'

Even now, even after the terrible thing that had happened with the cat, her body ached to stay the night with him. She got into the tax feeling absolutely furious with herself.

When she arrived back home, she paid Caroline, checked on Nicky, and then wandered up to her studio. She lit a cigarette and sat looking out of the window at the chestnut trees. She expected too much, that was her trouble. When her mother died, Harriet had known that a particular kind of tenderness had gone from her life for ever, the kind that knew you through and through and accepted you for what you were and didn't want you to be other than yourself. Men, at least the men she seemed to meet, could never quite achieve that sort of tenderness. It was unfair of her to expect them to. The closest she'd come to recreating that relationship with her mother had been in mothering her own children, in giving back to them what she'd got from her mother. And Daniel didn't even need it. Or perhaps he did. Perhaps he needed it more. Well. She stubbed out her cigarette, yawned, stretched and stood up. She mustn't expect too much from Eddie. She'd gone into this with her eyes open. Her last thought on getting into bed was to wonder how Peggy was.

Chapter Nineteen

The next morning Harriet woke up feeling itchy and sore. She washed herself very carefully with cold water and put on some cream. Her cunt felt as if it was on fire. She could hardly bear the feel of her knickers. She abandoned any idea of wearing jeans and put on a loose cotton skirt instead.

She went downstairs to make breakfast, picking up the *Apple Burton Herald* on her way. In the kitchen, her eye was caught by a headline. 'Local councillor in sex scandal.' She opened up the paper. Splashed all over page two were photographs of Fiona's husband, Julian, and, separately, photographs of several good-looking young men. She ran her eye down the page. In bold type it informed her, 'Local councillor forced to resign over rent-boy scandal.'

Harriet put down the paper. So even this accusation had turned out to be true. Poor Fiona. That surely meant Alix had been wrong about her being the anonymous letter writer. How did the writer do it? How had he found out so much about them all?

At the school gate, parents were subdued. They stood around in groups of twos and threes discussing this latest crisis in hushed tones. There was no sign of Fiona or Angelica.

'Isn't it terrible?' Alix joined her. 'I was obviously wrong about Fiona.'

'Yes. That leaves Humphrey Osborne as our strongest suspect. How's Peggy? Have you phoned her?'

'So so. Depressed, actually. She's still at her mother's, which is making her more depressed, but she says she can't face going home and seeing the house without Frank in it. I offered to bring Ben to school this morning, but she said no, she wanted him with her, to take her mind off things.'

'This is just awful,' said Harriet, as Mrs Moss appeared in the playground to bring in the children. 'Peggy was always so cheerful.'

'I know.' Alix hesitated. 'But maybe, just maybe, if she can get over this, it will make her a stronger person, don't you think? I mean she'll have to stand on her own two feet from now on, like the rest of us, instead of leaning on Frank all the time.'

'I know but . . .'

'Excuse me, Mrs Lee. Could I have a word?'

It was Humphrey Osborne. Alix winked at Harriet and stood tactfully to one side.

He came straight to the point. 'Can we arrange that supper?'

Harriet looked at him uncertainly. She didn't feel much like trusting anyone this morning.

He continued, 'I've seen the *Herald*. Things can't go on like this. Something has to be done. The police are dragging their heels. I thought if you and I put our heads together . . .'

'All right,' she replied, thinking maybe she would find out something, some small clue. Maybe Humphrey Osborne would give himself away. Maybe pigs would fly.

'Tomorrow evening then? About eight?'

'It'll depend on whether I can get a baby-sitter. It's rather short notice.'

'Give it a try. Please.' He began to move away, then glanced back at her and said, rather oddly, 'Take care of yourself, Mrs Lee. There's someone rather dangerous around.'

Who did he mean? The letter writer? James? Eddie? Himself?

Harriet rejoined Alix and they began to walk home.

'Dinner?'

'Supper, he called it. What's the difference, do you suppose?'

'Less food? Less formal? A cosy tête-à-tête?'

'That's what worries me. I don't trust any man at the moment.' Harriet thought of Eddie and was conscious of her itching private parts. She was going to have to go to the doctor's if this didn't clear up pretty soon.

'I would offer to come with you to Humphrey Osborne's,' said Alix, 'but I don't know how we'd go about suggesting it.'

'I'll be all right. I want to go. You never know what I might find out.'

By the time Harriet arrived home, she felt shivery and feverish. What on earth had she got? There was no point going up to her studio this morning. She made herself a cup of coffee and dialled Eddie's number.

'Harriet! What a nice surprise!' He sounded as if he had just woken up. 'How are you this morning?'

'Not too good actually,' she said coldly. 'I seem to have picked up an infection.'

He groaned. 'Sorry, babe. I thought it had gone. I picked it up years ago from a woman in Italy. It comes and goes. You'll have to go to your GP and get a prescription.'

'Great! What's Dr Wentworth going to think of me? His daughter goes to the same school as my son.'

'Don't be so middle-class. This doesn't sound like my wild Harriet. He won't think anything. People get infections all the time.'

'I feel lousy.'

'It'll go in a few days. Don't worry.'

'Mm.'

She put down the phone, feeling faintly angry with Eddie. All right for him to say don't worry. Her clitoris was red-raw and swollen. There was a nasty-smelling discharge in her knickers and every time she went to the loo a horrid burning sensation shot through her. She phoned the surgery. The only appointment they could give her was for twelve-thirty. She phoned Alix and asked if she would collect Nicky for her if she was late.

'Of course. It's nothing serious, I hope?'

'No, just a check-up,' she said vaguely. 'Listen, you pass our house on the way back from school. Nicky may make a fuss and want to get some toy or something. Since you pass our house anyway, you may as well have a key. I'll drop it off on my way to the surgery.'

'OK. And keep your eyes peeled while you're there. Wentworth's one of our suspects, don't forget.'

'Mm,' said Harriet and rang off. She hardly felt like a normal human being any more. It was Alix who had got her into all this in the first place, by suggesting she join a dating agency. So far she'd had one stalker and one sexually transmitted disease. Surely there were easier, and safer, ways of meeting new people?

She waited sheepishly in the surgery's reception. What would

Dr Wentworth think? Perhaps she should have gone to some anonymous STD clinic. If she hadn't been in total agony, she'd have walked right out the door again. She watched a child waiting with his parents. He was about Nicky's age. Funny how tedious other people's children were. The child was prancing about, showing off, knocking a lid off a tin and saying 'Silly Billy' in a way which she would have found totally entrancing if it had been Nicky but in someone else's child seemed simply futile.

Harriet picked up a newspaper. Idly leafing through it, her eye was caught by a picture of a tall, fair-haired man. Geoffrey. There was a long article suggesting he was being strongly tipped for a seat in Cabinet in the next reshuffle. So all his hard work was finally paying off. If only he'd given a fraction of that energy to his sons. She put down the paper. What made men so driven? That hard, thrusting ambition that men seemed to have so much more of than women. Were women too easily distracted? Did they lack the necessary ego?

'Mrs Lee?' the receptionist called out. Harriet stood up. 'Dr Wentworth will see you now.'

He was writing something as she came in. She noticed the Apple Macintosh standing to one side on his desk. He looked up and smiled.

'Now Mrs Lee, what can I do for you?'

I've got the flu, she thought, an innocent little flu. 'Er, I think I've got an . . . er . . . infection,' she said, flushing bright red and biting her lip.

'Pants off, hop up on the bed and we'll have a look at you,' he said cheerfully when she'd explained.

She took her knickers off behind the screen and lay on the bed with her legs apart. Her insides felt so raw and tender that she flinched as he touched her. He whistled.

'Sore?'

'Yes,' she gasped.

'This may hurt a bit then. Legs a bit wider. That's it.' He felt inside her. 'Well, that's it. You've got an infection all right.' He peeled off his gloves and threw them in the bin. 'Get dressed again and I'll give you a prescription. It should clear up in a day or two.'

She swung off the bed, put on her knickers and came back round the screen feeling like some prostitute in a Zola novel.

Dr Wentworth wrote out the prescription. 'And tell your – er – partner to get himself examined too.'

Harriet flushed again. Dr Wentworth was a school governor. He would know she was divorced. What must his opinion of her be now? If she were to tell him about her gout as well would he think she was utterly debauched?

'Antibiotics. Take them three times a day. Finish the course.' He handed her the prescription. He looked so clean and handsome and fresh-looking. She bet he didn't give his wife nasty infections. He stood up. 'How's Nicky getting on at St Cecilia's?'

'He loves it. Idolises Mrs Parker.'

'I noticed you didn't sign that petition to have her removed. Neither did I. She's a splendid teacher. We want to hang on to her.'

'Do you think we will?'

'All the governors are behind her. But if the parents were really to make a fuss things might get difficult. Nasty business, these letters.' He looked at her. 'I'd take care of yourself, Mrs Lee.'

As she left the surgery, Harriet reflected that that was the second time today someone involved with St Cecilia's had told her to take care of herself. Did she look so vulnerable? Was she in danger? She shivered. Did Dr Wentworth know something? He must know everyone's intimate secrets. He knew hers. Knew that, though she appeared to live the respectable life of a mother of two, she had another, murkier, life which involved STDs and sleeping with strangers. How many other people in their small community were leading a double life? Did Dr Wentworth suspect someone? Someone she knew?

It was while she was lurking in the chemist's, hoping no one she knew would come in as she waited to collect her shady prescription, that it occurred to Harriet that Dr Wentworth's words could be interpreted, not as a warning, but a threat. 'I'd take care of yourself, Mrs Lee.' Had those words been said with menace in his voice? The more she thought about it, the more Harriet became convinced the doctor had been threatening her.

'Everything all right?' enquired Alix, opening the door.

'More or less,' muttered Harriet, following her into the spacious living room where Nicky and Imogen were sitting on the floor playing with Imogen's dolls' house.

From the outside, Alix's house was very like Harriet's in that it was red brick and Victorian and set back from the road. But once you stepped inside the resemblance ended for, instead of painting it herself, Alix had had designers in to recreate the exact colours and style of a Victorian interior. Like her daughter's clothes, everything about Alix's house was perfect. Harriet had only been in it once or twice. She had the impression Alix didn't much like having visitors. Perhaps she feared for the carpets.

'Before I forget, here's your key.'

'Thanks.' She took the key and sank down on to a sofa. 'Alix, I've been thinking. Maybe you're right, maybe Dr Wentworth is a suspect. After all, he's got an Apple Mac. I saw it sitting on his desk.'

'I've always thought he was a likely candidate,' agreed Alix. 'Hardly anyone in Apple Burton knows about my mother. Even you didn't. Well, it's not the sort of thing one talks about in general conversation, is it? "Hi, I'm Alix. My mother is paranoid. She's a bag lady living somewhere in London."'

'Is she?'

'Yes. She has my address. I've tried rescuing her, but it's hopeless. She always goes back. She's happier on the streets, I think. She knows where I am. She knows she only has to call and I'll fetch her home.' Alix glanced down. 'The thing is, Dr Wentworth's one of the few people who did know about her. He took over treating her from old Dr Cornforth –'

'I remember him,' interrupted Harriet.

'Yes, hopeless, wasn't he? Kept my mother more or less sedated for years. I had to do all the washing and cooking for Frances and myself while we were growing up.'

'Alix, I didn't know,' said Harriet guiltily. And she thought she had a hard life. But hers had only started when she was already grown-up.

'No, well, as I say, it's not the sort of thing people talk about, is it? My father hated people knowing. It was like some terrible dark secret. Of course, people's attitudes to mental illness were very different twenty years ago. And then when my father died, well, that put paid to my chances of going away to university. I had to stay and look after Mother. I wanted Frances to go, though. She did do a term at Newcastle, but then she became ill and had to come home.'

'Was that when her anorexia started?'

'Yes. They said it was psychological, brought on by living with Mother all those years. But she got better, got married, had children and it was just Mother and me again. Then suddenly, about seven years ago, Mother got up one day and buggered off down to London. As I say, I tried getting her back. In the end Dr Wentworth said leave her, she'll be all right. The Sally Ann keep an eye on her. So I tried to pick up the threads of what had been my life. I went to evening classes, met Tim, got pregnant and, well, that was it, we decided to get married.' She smiled wryly. 'I thought what I wanted was to go to university but I suppose I must have secretly been jealous of Frances and her children and wanted to have a child myself before it was too late.'

'So it all turned out right in the end.'

Alix flicked back her plait. 'Oh yes, it turned out all right in the end.'

But what a life she must have had, thought Harriet. It almost didn't bear thinking about. If it hadn't been for her mother, what might Alix have become? A diplomat? A high-flying civil servant? The managing director of a large multi-national?

'Anyway,' continued Alix, 'to get back to these anonymous letters, this does make Dr Wentworth rather a suspect, doesn't it?'

Harriet sighed. 'He's always seemed such a kind man. The perfect GP.'

'Yes. Almost too perfect, perhaps?'

'You think it's a mask? I suppose it could be. He was rather strange this morning. Told me to take care of myself in quite an odd tone of voice.'

'Did he?' Alix's eyebrows shot up.

'I couldn't make out whether he was warning me or threatening me.'

Alix pursed her lips. 'Perhaps we ought to lie low on the detecting for a bit then?'

'I can't help feeling we owe it to Peggy to keep on with it. After all, the police are never going to suspect Dr Wentworth, are they? He's much too well respected around town.'

Alix looked thoughtful. 'I wonder if he knew that Julian was gay?'

'How could a doctor tell that?'

'He might have caught something.' Harriet flushed. 'Or done himself some damage – from the newspaper account he went in for some pretty rough trade. Or he might have wanted to be tested for AIDS.'

'Yes, I see,' said Harriet, thinking how much more on the ball with all this Alix was. Presumably it came from her days in the Citizens' Advice Bureau, or perhaps she just read the newspapers very, very carefully. 'It does sound more and more plausible, I must say. It's a pity you're not ill.'

'Thanks.'

'No, I meant then you would have an excuse to go and check up on him.'

'Oh, that's easy,' said Alix. 'I'll ask him to renew some of my old prescriptions.'

'Good. Have a snoop around and see what you come up with. Meanwhile, I'll do the same with Humphrey Osborne. If I can arrange a baby-sitter.' Harriet felt that at last they were getting somewhere. She stood up. 'Come on, Nicky, we have to be getting back.'

'Why?' Nicky bent more closely over Imogen's dolls' house.

'Because we have things to do.'

'I haven't. I'm happy here.'

'Come *on*, Nicky.'

'Imogen's mummy's got a computer,' commented Nicky as he walked home rather sulkily.

'No, she hasn't.'

'Yes she has. I SAW it!'

'All right, Nicky. Don't scream. Oh, of course, you're right. Tim, Imogen's daddy, is very keen on computers.'

'You see, I was right.'

'Yes, you were right.'

'And you were wrong, Mummy.'

'I very often am,' replied Harriet.

When they arrived home, they found an enormous bunch of flowers on the doorstep. Irises and gypsophila. They'd been delivered by Interflora. There was a note with them. 'Sorry – Eddie.' She smiled. She'd taken one of Dr Wentworth's tablets and the soreness was beginning to wear off. She no longer felt so angry with him.

She carried the flowers into the kitchen. Nicky followed her.

'Are they for me?' he enquired.

'No, they're for me.'

'Who are they from?'

'A friend of Mummy's.'

Nicky scowled. 'Play with me, Mummy.'

'Just a minute, Nicky, while I put these in water.'

He kicked the leg of a chair. 'I don't want you to put them in water.'

'You don't want them to die, do you? How would you like it if you were thirsty and no one gave you a drink?'

'I *am* thirsty. Get me some juice.'

'Please.'

'I said please.'

She sighed and went into the scullery to fetch a vase. When she arrived back in the kitchen with the flowers and the juice, she found Nicky asleep on the floor. For a second, he reminded her of Eddie's cat. She moved him into a more comfortable position, took off his shoes and put a cushion under his head. He looked like being out for the count for some time. Harriet fetched her paints. She'd decided to paint Eddie's flowers. Though really, she thought, mixing colours, should anyone paint irises again, after Van Gogh?

Nicky stayed asleep for an hour and a half. By the time he awoke, she'd completed quite an acceptable water-colour and felt much more content with the world. She had forgiven Eddie.

Chapter Twenty

'I don't want you to leave me, Mummy.' Nicky stood on the landing, clutching his ragged pink towel.

'I'm not leaving you. I'm going out to dinner – supper, I mean – at Dominic's daddy's house. Caroline will be with you. You'll be asleep when I leave and asleep when I get back. You won't even notice I'm gone.'

'I will. I will.' He buried his face in his towel. 'What if I have a nightmare?' he mumbled.

'Caroline will be here. You said last time that you liked Caroline.' You said you liked Caroline better than Mummy, because Caroline let you stay up and watch television. And not children's television, either.

'I don't like her. I don't.' His face crumpled. 'Don't leave me, Mummy. I'm very little. I might get lost.'

Harriet sighed. In such moods, Nicky reminded her of Picasso's painting of *Child with Dove*. The little sad-eyed girl staring out of the frame, cuddling a dove as if it were the only thing in the world she had left to love. Harriet often thought that if it weren't for that painting she wouldn't give in to Nicky half so much. If Nicky turned out to be spoilt and capricious, it would be Picasso's fault. She went to phone Humphrey Osborne.

'I'm sorry, I'm afraid it's going to be difficult for me to come this evening. Nicky's in one of his clingy moods.'

'I see.'

The frigidity of his tone clearly implied he thought this was yet another excuse – and a bad one at that. It did sound weak, but that was because it was true. If she'd wanted to invent an excuse she'd have done better than this. Harriet thought for a moment. It was her last chance to get information out of Humphrey Osborne. After three refusals, he'd hardly feel like inviting her again. And what was she risking? He already knew where she lived. Wouldn't she be safer, after all, on home ground?

'Look, what if we change the arrangements? What if you came here for supper instead? Could Mrs Towers look after Dominic?'

'Only too happy to. She adores him. All right then. About eight?' He sounded mollified.

As well he might, having got out of the cooking. Harriet put down the phone. It would have to be pasta and salad again, she supposed. At this short notice, it was the best she could come up with. She was getting a bit fed up with it but she didn't dare risk anything new for Humphrey Osborne. She guessed he was demanding in the culinary line. Mrs Towers probably spoiled him.

The front door bell rang very promptly at eight. Involved with chopping things in the kitchen, Harriet was beaten to the door by Nicky.

'Mr Osborne? I'm Nicky Lee. You're very welcome.'

She arrived in time to notice Humphrey Osborne's eyebrows lifting. Perhaps he thought it was she who had trained Nicky to behave like a little Victorian. She flushed. 'Yes, come in,' she muttered.

He stepped into her hall. He was dressed in brown cords, checked shirt and the narrowest leather tie she had ever seen. He looked old-fashioned and formal. He was carrying a bottle of wine under one arm, chocolates under the other. As he divested himself of these, Harriet made a mental note to taste neither of them before he did. Or had she been reading too many Agatha Christie stories?

'The sitting room's upstairs.' She led the way.

He stopped at the threshold. 'Amazing colour!' He sauntered over to the window. 'Nice view of those chestnut trees.'

She held her breath for remarks about Paris and, when none came, awarded him a mark for originality.

'Make yourself at home.' Though not too much at home. 'Would you like a drink?'

He turned away from the window. 'I'd like a small whisky, if I may. If you have it.' He looked at her doubtfully.

'Of course,' she replied. It meant another raid on her father's 'cellar' but she had her pride to keep up. If Humphrey Osborne wanted whisky, that's what he would get.

As she brought it up to him, she heard Nicky demonstrating

his blue Power Ranger. She paused for a moment at the door. She loved to catch Nicky unawares, to glimpse new facets of his character.

'You see his legs and arms bend backwards so he can fight better.'

Humphrey Osborne bent down to inspect the toy. 'He certainly looks very frightening.'

Nicky raised his head. 'Don't worry. It's only pretend,' he said kindly. 'When Daniel was home last time he broke his Power Ranger.'

'Did he? Never mind, I expect it was an accident.'

'No, he did it deliberately.'

'What?'

'He did it deliberately.'

As Humphrey Osborne went on looking puzzled Nicky, rolling his eyes at the extent of grown-up ignorance, explained, 'That means on purpose.'

'Oh.'

Harriet smiled to herself. She knew just what it felt like to be wrong-footed by Nicky. She stepped hastily into the room.

'Here's your whisky.'

'Oops, silly me, I've bent his arm too far.' Nicky became absorbed in his toy.

'He's quite a – an extraordinary child.' Humphrey Osborne took a sip of his whisky. 'Amazing vocabulary for his age.'

'Yes. I sometimes think he knows more words than I do.' She plumped up a cushion Nicky had flattened earlier in the day by jumping on it. 'It's nothing I've done. He's just turned out like that.'

'We have less influence over our children than we like to think,' he agreed.

Nicky looked up. 'You're Dominic's daddy, aren't you?'

He nodded.

'He's a funny little fellow, isn't he?'

'Time for bed now, Nicky,' said his mother hastily. 'Say goodnight to Dominic's daddy.'

Nicky, ignoring her, remained squatting on the floor examining his Power Ranger.

Harriet smiled, falsely. 'I'll just get him off to bed – come *on*, Nicky – and then we can eat. Nothing elaborate, I'm afraid. It's pasta.'

'Fine by me. Do you know you have paint on your face?'

'Have I?' She went over to the mirror hanging above the fireplace. 'So I have. Sorry.'

'Why sorry?'

'It used to irritate Geoff – my ex-husband.'

'I can't think why. It shows you've been working. You must be doing very well,' he continued, with a glance round the room, 'to be able to afford all this.'

'I'm not. The house belongs to my father. He's sort of made it over to me. Well, he lets me live in it. Says he wouldn't get the right price for it if he sold at the moment. He thinks I've ruined the decorations.'

He smiled. 'What does he like? Off-white and magnolia, I suppose?'

'That kind of thing. No, my paintings barely bring in enough for me to live on. Sometimes I think I don't earn enough to cover the amount I spend on materials. I certainly couldn't afford a place like this.'

'That's a relief.'

'Why?'

'I'm always suspicious of creative people who earn vast amounts of money.'

'You live in a big house.'

He frowned. 'My wife was a wealthy woman,' he replied shortly.

There was an uncomfortable silence. Harriet thought she was beginning to get the hang of conversation with Humphrey Osborne. He was allowed to make personal remarks about you but you weren't allowed to make comments about him. Was this a technique he'd evolved for finding out about people's lives? Harriet pondered this as she put Nicky to bed. She also pondered the possibility that Humphrey Osborne might have married his wife for her money. And murdered her for her money?

She began to feel uneasy about having him in the house. Perhaps

Alix had been right. Harriet was half-tempted to phone her and ask her to come over. But then she thought how odd that would look and he might not be as expansive as she wanted him to be if there was a third person present.

Expansive, she thought, tossing the pasta in butter, he's about as expansive as a toadstool. The best solution would be to get him drunk. She opened the bottle of red he'd brought and sniffed it. It smelled all right (it was a Chianti) but she wasn't going to touch a drop of it till he'd tasted it himself.

Harriet doled the pasta out on to plates, put them and the bottle of wine and two bowls of salad on a tray and carried it all upstairs. She found Humphrey Osborne loitering by the mantelpiece looking furtive. She suspected him of checking his appearance in the mirror. Was he vain as well? As well as what, she wondered, and left the sentence unfinished in her head.

'I've been, er, looking at your pictures. I hope you don't mind?'

'No. Why would I? That's what they're there for.' She set down the tray, poured out a glass of wine and handed it to him. 'Cheers.'

'Aren't you drinking yourself?'

'Yes. Yes, of course.' She poured out half a glass. 'Cheers,' she repeated and waited till he'd taken a sip. Then she wet her lips cautiously. 'Very nice.' She handed him a plate of pasta and a fork and a spoon (better do things properly with Humphrey Osborne).

He sat down on the sofa, balancing his plate rather awkwardly on his knees. 'I particularly liked the sketches of your children.'

'Yes, I used to do a lot of those.' She sat down in an armchair. 'Now it's more difficult. Daniel's away and Nicky will hardly stay still for more than two minutes.'

He smiled. 'Like Dominic. How's Nicky getting on at St Cecilia's?'

'He loves it.' She twirled pasta around on her fork. 'What about Dominic?'

He hesitated. 'He's still settling in. He likes the work but he finds the play rather rough. Poor old Dominic, it's been a strange sort of life for him since his mother died. Audrey – Mrs Towers

162

– has been very good. I don't know how either of us would have managed without her.'

Harriet's forkful of pasta paused on its way to her mouth. Was it possible that Humphrey Osborne and Mrs Towers, that very respectable-looking widow, were having an affair? She scrutinised his face but it gave nothing away. She went over and refilled his glass.

'Thanks. Pasta's very nice, by the way.'

'Thank you,' she returned, all politeness, and sat down again.

They continued eating in silence. Life with Humphrey Osborne would probably contain lots of silences, she reflected. Silence while he wrote in his study, silence while he read the newspaper, silence while he meditated on things. He was that sort of man. His silence would be either soothing or unnerving. Harriet was inclined to find it the latter. She wished it was Eddie sitting opposite her on the sofa. She would have felt much more comfortable

'These letters,' he said suddenly, breaking the silence and catching her by surprise. 'Unsettling, aren't they?'

'Yes,' she agreed, on the alert but trying not to look it.

'So bad for our little community. And bad for the school. Just as Dominic was beginning to settle in,' he added, as if Dominic's frame of mind was all that mattered. 'There's a sort of tension in the classroom, I gather.'

'Do you?' It must have gone right over Nicky's head. 'Your son must be a very sensitive little boy to notice it.'

'He is,' he agreed rather smugly, making her feel that Nicky's sensitivities were being called into question.

'Perhaps Dominic's exaggerating?' she said stiffly. 'I'm sure Mrs Parker and Mrs Moss try their best not to let anything show in front of the children.'

'The trouble is,' he went on, as if she hadn't spoken, 'the police seem to be dragging their heels. They're not taking it seriously enough. I fear something awful may happen soon.'

'You mean apart from the breakup of at least two marriages, a ruined career and a child taken into care?' she said drily. And Peggy on the verge of a breakdown.

He looked abashed. 'Yes, well, that's bad enough,' he agreed.

'But I was thinking of −' He broke off abruptly. 'Are you still doing some detecting yourself?'

'Y-yes.'

Harriet shifted uneasily in her chair. Was he about to warn her off? What should she do if he started to threaten her? Make a run for it? No, she couldn't, there was Nicky. He had her trapped in her own house. Recklessly, trying not to think of gout, she poured herself another glass of red wine.

'I've been drawing up a list of suspects,' Humphrey Osborne went on. 'After all, I am a trained historian. I'm used to piecing together stories from clues dropped here and there.'

She looked at him over the top of her wine glass. 'And what have you come up with?'

He set his empty plate down on the tray, sat back on the sofa and folded his hands. It occurred to her that he was probably longing to have a smoke of his pipe. Let him long, she thought. He's not going to hide behind a cloud of tobacco smoke. I want to see his face.

'It must be a parent,' he began, 'and one currently connected with the school. I can't believe an outsider would know so much about us.'

'It could be someone who's left the school and has a grudge against it. Remember that fire bomb in that school in Northern Ireland? It was planted by a man who'd been expelled years ago.'

'That was a secondary school. *Is* anyone ever expelled from nursery? And would you still bear a grudge about it after so many years? Even supposing you remembered it, which you wouldn't unless you'd been told.'

She felt foolish.

'I'm excluding Mrs Parker and Mrs Moss,' he went on. 'They've always seemed to me to be two eminently well-balanced women and why should either of them want to do something that would put their jobs in jeopardy? Some of the parents have been talking about taking their children out of the nursery if this continues.'

'Have they?' It struck Harriet that he was remarkably well informed for someone as aloof and unknowable as he was. He must talk to someone at the school gate then.

'Our suspect must be someone with their finger pretty firmly on the button as far as details about people's private lives go –'

'A journalist?' she cut in eagerly, having just thought of this. 'Raking over people's filthy little secrets is exactly the sort of thing tabloid journalists go in for.' Why hadn't she thought of this before?

He gave her a withering glance. 'There aren't any tabloids in Apple Burton. Unless you count the *Herald*, which is mostly adverts anyway.'

'Mm.'

Deflated, Harriet piled the empty plates on the tray. Humphrey Osborne was turning out to be better than her at this game. Or was all this a very complicated trail of red herrings designed to mask the true identity of the letter writer, namely Humphrey Osborne himself?

'And,' he continued, 'our anonymous letter writer is obviously an expert in psychology. He seems to go unerringly for people's weak spots. I put Dr Wentworth high on my list of suspects. I took advantage of Dominic's having a slight cold to visit his surgery yesterday afternoon. He has an Apple Macintosh.'

'I know,' she said smugly. 'I was there too. But what does that prove? A lot of people possess Apple Macs,' she added pointedly.

He chose to ignore the point.

'But somehow I don't believe it's Wentworth,' he went on. 'He's such a skilled doctor. And he doesn't seem the type to harbour a grudge.'

'No, he doesn't,' she agreed, though Alix had counted Dr Wentworth as their chief suspect, apart from Humphrey Osborne himself, of course. 'Dr Wentworth's so open and friendly. I imagine the writer of those letters to be someone rather repressed and unsociable.' She glanced across at him. His expression didn't change. Perhaps he didn't think of himself as repressed and unsociable? 'What about the vicar?' she suggested. She wanted to keep him on this topic as long as possible. It was, after all, the main point of the evening. 'He must know plenty of secrets about people's lives.'

'Threlfall? Yes, I suppose he must. But I can't quite see it, can you? He's not – well – not clever enough. Very nice man and all that,' he added hastily. 'Anyway, he got a letter.'

'Oh, I think whoever is sending these letters and e-mails would be clever enough to send one to himself, don't you? To disarm suspicion.' Her eyes narrowed as she observed his reaction. But all he said was 'Perhaps', and, glancing down, brushed something – a crumb? a speck of dust? – from his corduroy trousers.

The conversation seemed to have ground to a halt. Remembering Eddie's comment, Harriet reflected to herself that it was not, this time, going to stretch to another bottle of wine. Smiling to herself, yet slightly disappointed that she had found out so little, she stood up and said, 'Coffee?'

'Please. We don't seem to have got very far, do we?' he added, echoing her thoughts. He looked up at her as she stood before him, holding the tray with the debris of their supper. 'Do you mind if I ask you something?'

'N-no,' she replied uncertainly, feeling she might mind very much indeed.

'Are you assuming our anonymous letter writer is a man?'

She rubbed one foot against the other. 'Yes, I was rather, weren't you? I mean it's the tone of them. The obsessive interest in sex.'

He smiled. 'Aren't women interested in sex?'

She adopted her coldest expression. 'Not in that way. That nasty little interest in raking over the most intimate details of other people's sexual lives.'

He stopped smiling. 'Yes, well, I rather agree with you. I think the writer must be a man. But if it *was* a woman, would you have any suspicions?'

'No,' she snapped, loyal to her sex. 'No, I wouldn't.'

Harriet marched downstairs to make the coffee. As she was measuring out the coffee into the filter, she thought over what Humphrey Osborne had said. She remembered Peggy's words, 'Do you still think it's a man?' Who were the women she might suspect? Brenda Barlow, who knew everyone's business better than they did? Mrs Parsons, who was almost as bad? But would she know how to work a computer? Women of that generation often didn't. And if it was a younger woman, who might it be? Fiona? She was certainly clever enough and she had a computer. What if the real story behind these letters was simply a wife seeking revenge on her husband? For what? For going with rent boys? No, that wouldn't work. Harriet poured boiling water into the filter. Julian's downfall must have dented Fiona's reputation too, at least in some people's eyes.

She would have to think about this and talk it over with Alix. Not with Humphrey Osborne – he wasn't entitled to know any of her thoughts. After all, what had he come up with? Nothing she hadn't already worked out for herself. And this idea of it being a woman might simply be another of his red herrings.

Upstairs in the sitting room she poured out the coffee and sat back to see where the conversation would go from here. Where it did go surprised her, for he said, looking up suddenly,

'You know, I haven't met many painters. It's a privilege for a writer like myself to meet an artist.'

'Is it?' she said, in a tone of disbelief.

'Yes.'

He stirred his coffee and appeared to ponder something. She waited. She'd had this sort of conversation with writers before, down in London. They never failed to put the boot into painting sooner or later.

'Of course writing's more difficult than painting,' said Humphrey Osborne, putting the boot in sooner than most.

She raised an eyebrow.

'The painter,' he went on, seemingly oblivious to her reaction, 'can withdraw from life into a silent world of shapes and lines and colours.'

Like Daniel, she thought.

'Whereas a writer has to remain involved in the world of human beings – their feelings, their ideas. Writers are forced to be exposed to life. Painters can retreat.'

She decided to go on the offensive. 'You see yourself as a creative writer then, do you? I thought you were an historian.' Silly me, as Nicky would have said.

He hesitated. 'Historians are edging closer and closer to the art of the novelist. From a few scraps and clues they build up a picture of a whole lost world, but it's not in any sense "the truth". It's just one person's picture. A construct. Someone else may come along and construct a more plausible account.'

Her head began to reel. If he was going to go on talking on this kind of level, he might as well go home.

'Anyway, I don't think what you said is right,' she said firmly, trying to wrench the conversation back on to her own territory. 'I would say I'm drawn more into the world because of my observation of it. Both nature and people. Think how much you can convey about a person's character simply in capturing the way they hold their head.'

He leaned forward, his hands closing round his coffee cup. He reminded her of Bogart in that study by Karsh. Bogart, lean and alert, looking like a French intellectual discussing the meaning or, more likely, the meaninglessness of life.

'All the same, writing can do everything paint can do and more,' he insisted. 'There's time, as well as space, in writing. Painting is static.'

'What? Look at the way the Impressionists used light. Look at Van Gogh's cornfields.'

'Mm. Maybe.' He shifted about in his seat like someone unwilling to let go of an argument. He reminded her of a terrier worrying away at a bone. He must be hell to live with. Seminars at the breakfast table, she expected.

'But you must agree that painting is easier than writing,' he went on. 'You paint an object or a landscape or a person. You have something there in front of you. Writers – at least writers of fiction – have nothing but a blank page. They have to spin it all out of their heads.'

Harriet sighed. 'I've never been able to theorise about my painting. I just do it.' She seized her half-drunk glass of wine. 'Come and see it.'

She led the way upstairs. On the threshold she hesitated. Seeing her studio for the first time through the eyes of a stranger made her realise what an incredible mess it must look. Easels stood about, the table in the middle of the room was covered with old newspapers, there were paintbrushes stuck in jam jars, half-used tubes of paint, odds and ends of filthy rags, dirty mugs. Canvases, framed and unframed, were stacked all along the walls. On a shelf stood her radio-cassette player. A heap of tapes lay scattered around beside it. The place reeked of oil and turpentine and stale cigarette smoke, and there was a layer of dust on the window ledges. This was the only room in the house that never got dusted. She felt more comfortable with it like that. She could only work in disorder.

'My God!' he exclaimed, practically pushing her out of the way. 'You work at it.'

'I do.'

He sniffed the air. 'Is this a room where I might be permitted to smoke?'

She smiled. 'It is. The only one in the house. For the children's sake the rest is a smokeless zone.'

'Very good.'

He took out his pipe and tobacco pouch. When he had successfully got it lit, he began wandering around looking at her canvases. They were grouped more or less according to subject. Some were finished. Some weren't. There were flower paintings. Flowers in a jar. Flowers in a jug in front of an open window. Flowers lying by a sink waiting to be arranged. There were still-lifes. Apples, oranges and an earthenware jug. A grey-blue background with two lemons, two yellow candles and some yellow flowers in a blue jar. There was a large painting of a room with polished wooden floorboards, a window open slightly, a breeze ruffling the blue and white checked curtain, a man's shirt (Geoffrey's) over a basket chair. It was the only painting she had left of their house in London. She hadn't wanted to part with it.

He stopped in front of an unfinished painting of Alix. 'That's your friend, isn't it? Imogen's mother.'

'Yes.'

'Interesting woman to look at.'

'She *is* interesting.'

'Strong face. Lots of untapped power.' He moved on to a small painting of a decorative cup and saucer on a patterned cloth. 'Bloomsbury.'

'A bit,' she admitted.

He straightened up. 'Not many landscapes.'

'I used to do them. I haven't the time now to go on painting expeditions. Anyway in this country the light always changes at the crucial moment.'

'Mm.' He paused in front of a picture of two avocados in a bowl. She'd been quite pleased with this one. She was sending it down to the Summer Exhibition.

'What do you see?' she asked, genuinely interested. She'd almost forgotten her suspicions about him. It was a question from one professional to another.

'Silence. Stillness,' he muttered, his pipe clenched between his teeth. 'A kind of privacy. No judgment. No moralising.'

'I can't moralise. I'm not interested in telling a story. It's the visual thing that's important to me – the shape, the colour, the outline.'

'Maybe I was wrong,' he said, after a moment. 'Maybe a painter is greater than a writer. You free us from the tyranny of language. Sometimes you can get awfully fed up with words.'

She thought of Daniel. 'We need words to live,' she said slowly. 'Else how do we know who we are?'

He took his pipe out of his mouth and looked at her. 'I like your paintings, Harriet. They're light and fleeting on the surface. A quick sketch, a small oil painting. But the longer you look at them, the more you become aware of the thread of steel running through them.'

'That's Daniel,' she replied, turning her head away and running her finger along the edge of a canvas. 'It wasn't there before.'

He coughed awkwardly. 'What's wrong with Daniel, exactly?'

She met his gaze. 'He's autistic. Good at some things – maths, diagrams, that sort of thing. Bad at language, feelings, life really.'

'Rough.'

'He's an improbable child.'

'We live in an improbable universe.'

Sympathy flashed in his eyes. She remembered the anonymous letter and hardened her heart. Was this all bluff? Did he want her to let down her guard so that he could find out more about her and send her another letter? Well it wasn't going to work. She was on her guard. She'd been on her guard all evening.

'And yet you manage to go on painting. You must work flat out to judge by all of this.' He waved a hand around.

'I have between nine-thirty and twelve-thirty, and if I didn't paint then I'd feel life wasn't worth living.' She looked at him. No harm in telling him this. There was nothing he could make a scandal out of. 'My brush is the only solid thing in my life. The only thing that never lets me down. When I've spent the morning painting I feel life isn't wasted. It helps me cope with Daniel.'

'He's away at a special school, is he?'

'Yes,' she replied shortly, thinking again of the letter. 'He needs the routine and the sort of specialised help I can't give him.'

'And then?'

'And then . . .' She sighed. 'Who knows?'

She knew what the future held for Daniel. She'd been to visit it. It was a long, low, one-storey building painted blue and surrounded by playing fields. Here, when he turned eighteen, Daniel would become a 'trainee'. He would learn to fill airline bags with a plastic spoon, a packet of sugar and a folded napkin (possibly he wouldn't be able to manage the napkin), sitting at a table, wearing a paper hat and paper gloves for purposes of hygiene. He'd have a break for juice and biscuits and then there'd be recreational activities such as throwing bean bags into a box, or football. This was if he was one of the lucky ones. If he slipped through the net (but he wouldn't, she'd see to that), he'd become one of those oddly dressed men endlessly playing the fruit machines in some greasy café until asked to leave. Or he'd be the man with the funny voice and the unnerving stare whom everyone avoids sitting next to on the train. This was Daniel's future and she couldn't bear to talk about it.

But Humphrey Osborne had already turned away from the subject. 'Your pictures have an extraordinary stillness about them,' he was saying. 'Almost a spirituality.'

'I'm not a Christian,' she said quickly. 'I don't go to church.'

He gave a smile that seemed malicious but was perhaps only alcoholic. 'You did last Sunday.'

'That was different. That was for Daniel.'

'And to spy on us? Eh?'

She shivered. Was this what the evening had been leading up to all along? A warning that he knew what she was up to and she'd better leave off?

He turned back to the paintings. 'This one of your friend, Imogen's mother, is different. There's a restlessness about it.'

Harriet put her head on one side and considered the picture. Alix was standing by an open window looking out, her face turned away from the observer. Her whole stance conveyed irritability and tension. She'd been a terrible model. Too impatient to remain still for long.

'Yes,' she said at length. 'I'm not very pleased with it. As you can see, it's unfinished. I couldn't seem to capture her very well. It's not Alix.'

'On the contrary, I think you've captured her very well indeed.' He puffed on his pipe and cast her a sidelong glance. 'How would you paint me?'

'A study in tone. Oils. Browns and blacks. I'd paint you in your dark study.'

'Gloomy. Is that how you see me?' He seemed faintly surprised. Unjustifiably, she thought. He must know he was hardly a subject who lent himself to bright colours. 'Perhaps I am gloomy. Now. I didn't used to be.' He paused. 'That letter, you know, accused me of killing my wife.'

Harriet's eyes widened.

'Indirectly. It said: *Your wife committed suicide because you neglected her.*' He chewed on his pipe. 'The thing is, it's quite possible to see it that way. I didn't do it on purpose, of course. I loved her.' At these words, Harriet felt a curious sense of relief. She sat down on a chair. 'But I was very distracted at the time. It was the year after Dominic was born. I had a big contract for a book. A deadline to meet. I was working all hours to get it finished. I knew Flora felt depressed after Dominic's birth, but I didn't realise how much.' He shook his head. 'The birth was a difficult one. Flora decided not to go back to work. She'd worked in stockbroking. Very high-powered. I suppose the loss of all that adrenalin, added to the normal hormonal disturbance after giving birth, left her feeling low. She took an overdose.' He turned away abruptly and went over to the window.

Harriet gazed at his back. It was a sad story. And it sounded plausible enough. But why was he telling her? It almost seemed as if he wanted to justify himself to her. Why? For the same reason she'd wanted to tell him about Daniel? *Did he suspect her of writing the letters?* She reflected on this as he stood staring out of the window. She was a woman living on her own. She supposed some people might think she was repressed. They might think she had a grudge against life because of Daniel. And then there were the drawings accompanying the letters. She wondered whether there'd been a drawing in Humphrey Osborne's letter. She hardly liked to ask.

He swung round suddenly to face her. 'Is this a good place to be for a painter? Don't you feel cut off?'

'From what?' she asked, bewildered by the abrupt change of subject, her mind still running on the possibility that Humphrey Osborne suspected her of being the letter writer.

He moved into the centre of the room. 'From galleries, exhibitions, all that sort of thing.'

'Oh, that. I lived in London for eighteen years.' Sharing a crummy, leaking flat in Kilburn with fellow students from art college (a week's dirty dishes in the sink, the electricity off because no one had remembered to pay the bill). No wonder she'd fled to Geoffrey in Fulham. 'I know the galleries pretty well. When I go to the Tate, I no longer go to look at what other people go to look at – the Turner rooms, Francis Bacon and so on. What I like to see nowadays are Vanessa Bell's flowers on a mantelpiece, or the funny things Winifred Nicholson does with her fingers in oils. As for exhibitions, I sometimes get asked to judge exhibitions around here. More than I would in London in fact.'

'Is it difficult?' He followed her back downstairs to the sitting room.

'A rough rule of thumb is the more expensive the frame the worse the artist. Amateurs set their work in the most elaborate and expensive frames, whereas professionals generally make do with the cheapest bit of plywood.'

He laughed. 'From what I've seen, you're a professional then.'

'Are you laughing at my frames?'

'Not at all. I'm not qualified to judge. Unlike you.' He looked at his watch and cast a half-regretful glance around her sitting room. 'Well, I suppose I'd better be off. Mrs Towers doesn't like to be kept up late.'

Harriet breathed a sigh of relief. Now they'd finished looking at her paintings, there didn't seem much else to talk about. They had little in common really. And there was this perpetual edginess between them. Whether it would have been there without the letters, she couldn't tell. As it was, they each seemed to be suspecting the other. He made her feel jumpy. Closing the front door behind him, she had a sense of being released from something. She thought with gratitude of Eddie, who was out of all this.

Later that night she lay awake in bed, feeling the pain stabbing her big toe. She must assert herself more in social situations. No one was going to think her odd or feel insulted if she refused their red wine. She thought how strange it was that her father and she, who weren't at all alike, should share the same disease. It linked them, his body to hers, proving a fact she'd often, when younger, been inclined to question, that she really was his daughter. There had to be something, she supposed. You couldn't expect to escape heredity scot-free. And, heaven knew, there was nothing else that connected them.

Chapter Twenty-one

Harriet was woken next morning by the sound of frantic knocking on her front door. She groaned, turned over and looked at the clock. Six-thirty. Who on earth could be calling at this hour? She lay in bed for a moment, still half-asleep, hoping whoever it was would give up and go away. But the knocking continued. Scrambling into her dressing gown, she hurried downstairs. Nicky appeared on the landing, clutching his pink towel. He peered through the banister at her.

'Who is it, Mummy? Is it the postman?'

'I don't know, sweetheart. Go back to bed. It's very early.'

Sleepily, he turned on his heel and padded back into his room trailing his towel behind him.

Halfway down the stairs, the thought struck her that it might be James. What if he'd decided to get violent? She began to wish she'd gone to the police after all. Cautiously, she unlocked the front door, prepared to slam it shut again if necessary. On the doorstep she found Alix, red-eyed and dishevelled in jeans and an old T-shirt, her hair uncombed and streaming wildly down her back. She was clutching a wide-eyed Imogen by the hand.

'Alix! What on earth's the matter? Come in.'

'I'm sorry, Harriet, I had to come. It's . . . it's Peggy. Harriet, it's awful!'

Alix burst into tears, let go of Imogen's hand and moved blindly towards Harriet for comfort. Harriet put an arm out to guide her into the house and held out her other hand to Imogen. Filled with a sense of dread, she led her friend down the hall to the kitchen. Imogen trailed along behind them.

'Sit down, Alix. I'll make a cup of tea. What on earth's happened?'

'Peggy took an overdose last night. Her mother rang me half an hour ago. I came straight over,' Alix blurted out, between sobs.

'An overdose!' Harriet abandoned the kettle and came to sit down at the table beside Alix. Out of the corner of her eye she noticed Imogen's face start to crumple. 'Why don't you take a look at Nicky's toy box, Imogen,' she said hastily. 'It's over there.' Obediently, the little girl trotted over to inspect the box. Harriet turned her attention back to Alix. 'Is she all right? Where have they taken her?'

'Hull Royal. But – oh, Harriet – it was too late.'

'What do you mean?' Harriet felt her head begin to spin. She grasped the edge of the table as if to keep a hold on reality.

'Peggy died at three o'clock this morning.'

'Oh God!' This couldn't be happening. It couldn't be true. Not Peggy. Not bright, cheerful Peggy whom she'd sat with and gossiped with and eaten Danish pastries with in the Apple Burton Arms. She felt the tears begin to roll down her cheeks.

'She can't have meant it, she can't! It must have been a cry for help that went wrong. Oh it's terrible! Terrible!' Alix put her head in her hands and wept.

Harriet sat beside her, holding her hand and weeping too. Pictures passed through her mind. Happy, smiling Peggy waiting at the school gate with Ben, beaming with delight when she caught sight of Simon coming out of infant school with the others, trailing his satchel along the ground, his tie and laces undone, his red hair, inherited from his mother, sticking out at odd angles. Peggy joking about diets and her inability to stick to them. And further back, Peggy at fifteen bemoaning her freckles and red hair, wondering whether she could dye it blonde.

Alix lifted her head. 'I never thought she'd do this, Harriet.' She fumbled in her pocket for a handkerchief. 'Honestly, I never thought she'd do anything like this.'

Harriet patted her arm. 'Of course you didn't. None of us did. We knew she was depressed but . . .'

Alix wiped her eyes. 'I knew she'd be miserable for a time but then I thought she'd get over it, make a new life for herself without Frank.' She looked at Harriet. 'I wonder how he's feeling this morning?'

'I can't imagine how he must feel.' She was silent for a moment. 'Poor Peggy,' she murmured. 'Now she'll never be a wicked old woman.' They smiled at each other through their tears. 'Those poor little boys,' Harriet added.

'I know.' Alix sniffed into her handkerchief. 'I should have tried harder. I should have got her away from her mother. That was my mistake.'

Harriet stared at her. 'It's not your fault, Alix. None of this is your fault. No more than anyone else's, anyway. We all could have tried harder. I wish I'd invited her here.'

She stood up to put on the kettle and glanced over at Imogen playing contentedly in the corner with Nicky's army tank, unaffected by the emotions of the adults in the room.

'Humphrey Osborne was right,' Harriet said, half to herself. 'He said something terrible would happen.' She shivered.

Alix looked up. 'Did he? I wonder why? Is he a prophet? Or did he know what effect these letters would have, sooner or later?'

'I don't know.' Harriet shivered again. She put two tea bags into the pot and poured in the boiling water. 'Peggy was the last person . . .'

'I know. She had so much to live for, if only she'd known it.'

Harriet poured out the tea. They sat side by side at the table drinking it. Harriet felt drained and exhausted, as if she'd been ill for a very long time.

'Did you get anything out of Osborne?' asked Alix at length.

'Not really. His letter accused him more or less of killing his wife.'

'He told you that?' For a moment Alix looked surprised. 'Did he try to defend himself?'

'In a way he did.' Harriet put her two hands round the warm mug for comfort. 'He admitted he might have neglected her.'

'Yes, well, that can be a type of killing.' Pain swept over Alix's face again and Harriet knew she was thinking of Peggy.

'He also floated the possibility that the letter writer might be a woman,' she added, in an effort to distract Alix's thoughts for a moment.

It worked. 'Typical!' Alix snorted through a mouthful of tea. 'Humphrey Osborne's always struck me as a bit of a chauvinist. I think you said the same yourself once.'

'Yes, but I'm not sure he is, now, after talking to him. Listen, Alix, we've always gone on the supposition that the writer is a man and we've got nowhere. What if it *is* a woman? Fiona, for instance? You suspected her at one point, didn't you?'

'Yes, but not now, not since those revelations about Julian. His career's ruined.'

'I know. But what if that's what Fiona intended all along? What if the other letters and e-mails were just a cover?'

'For revenge on her husband, you mean? Getting back at him for his gay lovers?'

Harriet nodded.

Alix pondered this for a moment. 'It's a possibility, I suppose. Fiona told us herself she has an Apple Mac at home, didn't she? She could easily have sent those e-mails.'

'Yes,' agreed Harriet. 'And if she was going to do a thing

like this, I imagine she'd go about it in a thoroughly professional way.'

'Oh yes, Fiona's no slouch.'

'You know, Alix, one of the last things Peggy said to me was that she was beginning to think the letter writer must be a woman.'

'Did she? Did she really? That's interesting. I wonder if she had anyone specific in mind.'

'She didn't say.'

A noise in the doorway made them both turn round. Nicky was standing there, forlornly clutching his pink towel.

'Oh darling.' Harriet went over to him and put an arm round his shoulders. 'Come in. It's all right.'

'I heard you crying, Mummy. Is it Daniel?'

'No, darling. It's something about Ben's mummy.'

'What about her?'

She hesitated. 'She's died, sweetheart. Gone to heaven. We must all be as nice as we can to Simon and Ben.'

'How did she die?'

'In her sleep,' she replied. It was almost the truth. She looked at him with concern. Was all this too much for a four-year-old to know?

'Why are Imogen and her mummy here?'

'They came to tell me.'

'Oh.' Nicky hesitated. He looked troubled. 'Mummy, can I whisper something in your ear?'

'Yes.' She bent down anxiously to him.

'Can I have some Coco Pops now, is it all right?'

She smiled in relief. 'Of course it's all right, Nicky.'

Alix rose. 'I'd better go before we all start crying again. Come along, Imogen, prise yourself away from that tank, darling. We must get home and get you properly dressed.' Imogen was wearing pyjamas under her coat. 'I'll give you a ring later this morning, Harriet.'

'Yes. Take care.'

Harriet gave her friend a kiss on the cheek. A first in their friendship. They'd never been given, either of them, to embraces. It had taken Peggy's death to bring them closer.

When Alix and Imogen had gone, Harriet poured Nicky some Coco Pops and sat down again at the table. She felt trembly and afraid. There was a shadow now hanging over the lives of everyone connected with St Cecilia's. Even if the letter writer was caught and stopped, things would never be the same again. There would never be the same happy, friendly atmosphere at the school gate. They all knew too much about each other now and because of the letters, one of them had taken her own life.

Peggy, Peggy, she thought, imagining her friend lying cold and alone in a drawer in the mortuary. She longed to speak to someone outside all this, someone who couldn't possibly be suspected. She went to dial Eddie's number. It was engaged. She left it five minutes and rang again. This time the answering machine was on. She didn't leave a message. Have a bit of pride, she told herself. She felt as if something hard and heavy was crushing her chest. She felt out of breath and her hands wouldn't stop shaking. She looked at Nicky.

'How do you fancy a morning off school?'

He nodded his head eagerly.

She rang Mrs Parker.

'That's quite all right, Mrs Lee. I don't expect many children today. A lot of parents have been ringing in. Poor Mrs Murray. I was thinking of closing the nursery school for a couple of days, at least until after the funeral. Only it looks like defeat, don't you think? As if the letter writer had won.'

'Yes, I suppose it might look like that. Only I'm beginning to think, Mrs Parker, that he, or she, has won already.'

Harriet and Nicky stayed in all morning and played endless games with trains and fire engines. Outside it was a sunny day but she didn't feel up to going out and facing the world. In her mind, as she staged crashes and fires and heroic rescues in the nick of time, memories of Peggy kept playing and replaying like an endless tape that couldn't be stopped. Peggy eating Danish pastries in the Apple Burton Arms. Peggy discussing clothes with Alix at the school gate. Peggy going sadly into her mother's house.

At eleven the phone rang. Harriet picked up the receiver.

'Alix, I've been thinking, we owe it to . . .'

The voice of a man cut across her. 'It isn't Alix. Whoever he or she may be. It's Geoffrey.'

Harriet was so taken aback she almost said, Geoffrey who? She caught herself in time and said 'Hello' instead.

'How are you? How are the boys?' Then, without waiting for a reply, he rushed on, sounding rather strangled, 'I thought I'd better ring you. I'm getting married again.'

'Are you?' It wasn't exactly a surprise. She'd been expecting something like this ever since the divorce had gone through. It wasn't a surprise and yet, for a moment, everything went wobbly again.

'Who is it? Anyone I know?' She'd be younger than herself, of course. In her twenties, probably. Young and bubbly, with short skirts and a perfectly flat stomach.

'You do know her, actually. It's Jane. Remember her? Jane Harrison.'

Harriet dimly remembered her. She was some kind of researcher in the House of Commons. Brown hair cut in a rather severe bob. Knee-length skirts. Must be in her early thirties, at least. Harriet felt her respect for Geoffrey rising. He'd avoided stereotypes. He'd gone for the sensible choice.

'I didn't want you to find out from the papers,' he went on, sounding slightly more relaxed. 'It's likely to be widely reported. I'm in the spotlight at the moment.'

'I know. I saw a piece about you.'

'Did you?' His voice became lower, almost tender.

'In the doctor's waiting room.' It was a cliché but she had to say it. She didn't want Geoffrey thinking she still followed his career with bated breath. 'Jane will be a good constituency wife, anyway,' she added briskly, to focus his mind on practical things. The last thing she wanted was Geoffrey becoming nostalgic on her.

'I think she will. She's interested in the children, too. Thinks I should see more of them.'

'Good idea.'

'She'll keep me right about their birthdays as well. I think I forgot Daniel's last time.'

'Yes, you did. He gave me hell over it.' Cards were the kind of thing Daniel remembered (he had forgotten his father but remembered the card).

'Sorry. I'll remember next time. Or rather, Jane will.'

'Good.' Harriet felt herself warming to the idea of Geoffrey's remarriage by the minute. Perhaps she and his new wife would even become allies? 'I hope you'll be very happy, Geoffrey. I was never the right wife for you.'

'It wasn't so much that.' He paused. 'We never had a chance, with Daniel always there.'

'Well he is our son.'

'I know but . . .'

'Have you told Jane he's autistic? You must, if she wants children, she must know there's a danger that –'

'She doesn't want children. At least, I don't want children. I couldn't face it happening again. Jane seems to understand.'

'Oh.' Harriet suddenly saw how much Jane must be sacrificing to marry Geoffrey. 'She must love you very much.' She felt ashamed of herself. Never again would she marry, or even live with, a man unless she felt absolutely head-over-heels in love with him.

'She's devoted,' he replied, a touch smugly.

'At least she'll understand if you have an all-night sitting.'

'Oh, I was never quite as busy as I made out. To tell you the truth, I couldn't bear to come home and see Daniel sitting in a corner grunting to himself. I was afraid of him and of the way you tore yourself to bits over him.'

'It's better now. I'm calmer with him. Most of the time.'

'And then there was your painting.'

'My painting?' she said in surprise. 'What did that have to do with anything?' She'd hardly had time for it during those early years, when Daniel had needed so much care and patience.

'I was jealous of it. Of your longing to get back to it. The quality of attention you gave to it. You never gave that sort of attention to me.'

'Didn't I?' Harriet felt a pang of conscience. She hesitated. 'Geoffrey, Nicky's here. I'm sure he'd like to speak to you.'

There was a pause at the other end. Harriet knew exactly what Geoffrey was doing. He was looking at his watch.

'Come on, Geoffrey! Five minutes won't kill you. He thinks you live in Arabia.'

'He what? Oh, all right then.'

She handed the phone to Nicky. 'Darling, it's Daddy.'

He looked up, his eyes shining. 'Daddy who lives in Arabia?'

She nodded.

Solemnly, he took the receiver from her.

Conversation with his father seemed to involve answering a lot of questions. Geoffrey must have got out of the habit of talking to small children; to tell the truth, he'd never been very much *in* the habit. 'Yes. Yes,' Nicky said at intervals. After about three minutes he nodded and hung up.

'Didn't Daddy want to speak to me again?'

'No.' He went back to his trains, a little subdued. 'Mummy, can we look up Arabia on the map? Is it a long way away?'

'It is. But Nicky, Daddy doesn't live in Arabia. He lives in London.'

'London town?' They had been reading Dick Whittington.

'Yes.'

'Is that a long way away too?'

'Yes.'

'As long as Arabia?'

'Not quite.'

'Will Daddy come and see us sometimes?'

'Perhaps.'

Nicky placed a brick in his truck and began wheeling it along the floor. 'He told me to look after you.'

'Did he?'

She suddenly felt weak and trembly again and had to sit down. What an exhausting morning it had been. She thought of what Geoffrey had said about Daniel. That he'd been afraid of him. She'd have to forgive him. When a person's afraid, you can't blame them for running away. How odd he'd been jealous of her painting. She'd never noticed. Alix said she never noticed things about people. Perhaps she wasn't fit to have a relationship with anyone? Would Eddie be jealous of her art? Very likely. He'd been jealous of the cat. And if she had to choose between Eddie and her painting . . . ?

The phone rang again. This time it *was* Alix.

'I've been talking to Peggy's mother again. The funeral's going to have to be delayed for a few days till the inquest's over.'

'Inquest!' exclaimed Harriet, appalled.

'There has to be an inquest. There always is when it's suicide.'

'This wasn't suicide, Alix. This was murder. If Humphrey Osborne can think he killed his wife by neglecting her, then Peggy was killed as surely as if someone put arsenic in her coffee.'

'I know. Frank's in an awful state. He rang me up this morning. Hardly coherent. Telling me he wished he'd never met Gemma if this was how it was going to turn out. I didn't know what to say. Serves him right, is what I thought.'

'I wasn't thinking of Frank,' said Harriet in surprise. 'He may have acted like a louse but it wasn't Frank who killed Peggy. It was whoever wrote those letters taunting her.'

'Letters can't kill anyone, Harriet. They simply pointed out Frank's behaviour, or misbehaviour. It was the thought that Frank had been unfaithful that made Peggy go out of her mind.'

'But perhaps if she'd heard about it in a different way, it wouldn't have had such a terrible impact on her?'

'Facts are facts, Harriet. However you find out about them.'

'Still, I can't help feeling sorry for Frank. He can hardly have expected this.' She thought of Geoffrey's phone call. 'You never know, he might have come back to her. If only she'd waited. Geoffrey, my ex, rang this morning. We had quite a rational conversation, for once.'

'Oh, Harriet! You're such a sucker for lousy men!' said Alix, exasperated. 'Frank was unfaithful. Peggy took her own life because of it. Why are you defending him?'

'I'm not defending him. I just can't help thinking . . . Oh, what's the use? Alix, why are we quarrelling like this? It's the last thing Peggy would have wanted.'

'You're right. Sorry.'

'I'm sorry too. These letters have got me into a state. What with those and now Peggy, and James stalking me –'

'Stalking you?'

'I think he is. I keep bumping into him in unexpected places.'

'Have you gone to the police?'

'They'd only say I was asking for it, joining a dating agency.'

'You need something to cheer you up. Have you heard from Eddie recently?'

'Not recently. Whenever I ring him up, his answering machine is on. I think he must have fled the country. Perhaps he felt he needed to get away from me.' Harriet gave a hollow laugh. 'Give me a ring tomorrow, Alix, or as soon as you hear about the arrangements for Peggy.'

'I will. Take care.'

Harriet put down the phone, then picked it up and dialled Eddie's number again. This time she did leave a message on his answering machine. Not being able to reach Eddie had given her an awful yearning for him that left her hollow and shaky inside, the way she used to feel in the early days when Daniel was having one of his awful tantrums and Geoffrey was working late – or, as it now transpired, pretending to work late – and she couldn't get hold of him. Eddie reminded her of Geoffrey. That undertow of desire she'd felt ever since she'd left him on Tuesday, it wasn't for Eddie. Or rather, it was, but it was also for Geoffrey. Eddie was handsome too, though in a less polished way than Geoffrey.

Five minutes later, her phone rang. She leapt to answer it.

'Hello? Oh, it's you.'

'I'm sorry. Were you expecting someone else?' said Humphrey Osborne drily. 'I rang to say I heard about your friend, Ben's mother. I took Dominic to school this morning and the nursery was in chaos. I had to bring him back again. I doubt they'll open it for a few days. Mrs Moss was in tears. Even Mrs Parker was upset. And several of the mothers who heard the news, as I did, at the school gate, broke down and cried. I just rang to say how sorry I am.'

'Thanks. So it turns out you were right after all. Something terrible *did* happen.'

'Believe me, I'd rather have been wrong.'

'It seems the letter writer is winning, doesn't it? If his aim was to ensure the breakup of our friendly little community he certainly seems to have succeeded, doesn't he? Or she,' she added.

'I think I've dropped that idea – about the writer being a woman, I mean.'

'Why?'

'This latest tragedy. Would a woman drive another woman to her death? Mrs Murray was quite popular amongst the mothers at St Cecilia's, wasn't she?'

'Yes, we all liked Peggy.'

'You and your other friend – Imogen's mother – were especially close to her, weren't you?'

'I don't know about close. We hadn't had time. You see, we were all at school together –'

'So you've known each other since you were young?' he interrupted her.

'Yes, but after we left Apple Burton High, we lost touch with each other till we met up outside the school gate at St Cecilia's. I'd been away eighteen years. I was gradually getting to know them again. Peggy occasionally comes – came – round for tea and a chat in the afternoon.' Her voice trembled. She fell silent.

'I'm sorry. I didn't mean to upset you.' Sounding embarrassed, Humphrey Osborne said a brief goodbye and rang off.

As Harriet wiped her eyes and blew her nose, it occurred to her that perhaps the reason why he had dropped his theory about the letter writer being a woman was because it had been herself he'd suspected, and Peggy's death had put paid to that suspicion. Oh, these horrible, horrible letters, she thought. They hang like a black cloud over all of us. It's impossible to have a normal relationship with anyone while we don't know who's writing them and why. Look how nearly she'd quarrelled with Alix this morning.

Everyone's nerves were bad. They would all soon become as deeply dysfunctional as those autistic adults she'd visited once at the day-care centre. The dark-haired man who'd rocked back and forth in his chair, with a perpetual grin on his face. The anguished woman who bit her knuckles whenever there was a loud noise. The pretty young girl who could work out the day people were born from their date of birth and who had come up to Harriet in a state of extreme anxiety saying, 'I think I've got your two names right. Now what about your address?' because that was the only way she could relate to people, through numbers and labels. The line separating the sane from the insane was a thin one. Was this what the letter writer wanted? To drive them all mad? Why?

Chapter Twenty-two

A week later, the sun shone down on the ancient church of St Cecilia as friends, relatives and parents from the nursery streamed in through the huge oak side doors to say their last goodbyes to Peggy. It was an afternoon to break your heart. The thick scent of the roses lining the narrow path up to the church made Harriet feel dizzy. She blinked as she entered the darkness of the church where, at the front, Peggy's coffin stood waiting. It looked so solitary there, so alone, that she almost burst into tears. She slipped quietly into a pew at the back.

The church was almost full. A few rows in front she caught sight of Alix's blonde plait. Across the aisle, Brenda Barlow had just taken her seat, her small, dark eyes busily scanning the congregation. Behind the high altar a brilliant stained-glass window depicting Christ of the Resurrection cast lozenges of deep blues and reds over Peggy's coffin and the mourners in the front pew. Suddenly one of those mourners turned round to speak to the person behind. For a second, Harriet's heart almost missed a beat. She looked so much like Peggy. It must be the sister she'd mentioned once or twice, the one who lived down in Surrey. She had Peggy's red hair and Peggy's round, freckled face. She had Peggy's way of holding her body, shoulders slightly hunched. Harriet drank her in with her eyes, concentrating on her every movement. It was like being given one last chance to see Peggy alive. Then the woman turned to face the front again and the service began.

They sang 'O what their joy and their glory must be'. Then the choir sang an antiphon, Micah 6, verse 8, to a setting Harriet dimly remembered having heard at school. Frank must have gone to a lot of trouble to get things right. Or had Peggy left instructions? No, she wasn't the sort. It must be Frank's doing. He sat through the service slumped in the front pew, an arm round each of his sons. Naturally, there was no sign of anyone who could be Gemma.

Martin Threlfall gave a short address about the tragedy of a life cut short and how they should all cherish their memories of Peggy. He also made a plea for the anonymous letter writer to give him- or herself up. Mercifully it wasn't Keith Graham, the curate, giving the sermon, thought Harriet. He'd probably have gone on about the wrath of God and this being a fitting punishment for our sins. On the other side of the church, almost hidden behind a pillar, she saw Humphrey Osborne sitting with his head in his hands. For a moment she was touched. Then she wondered whether he was overcome, not by grief, but by guilt.

She watched through a blur of tears as, prompted by his father, six-year-old Simon moved forward to place Peggy's wedding ring, a battered teddy bear and a photograph of her sons on the coffin. Then they were all invited to follow the coffin across the road to the cemetery. Peggy's mother, her head held high, took her remaining daughter's arm and walked briskly down the aisle, leading the procession of mourners. Suddenly Harriet knew who had done all the funeral arrangements. Not Frank, but Peggy's mother. That was why it had been so impeccably organised. She was going to give her daughter the perfect send-off.

As Harriet followed the mourners out of the church, someone came up to her and pressed her arm. It was Fiona Wilson-Smith.

'I'm sorry,' she whispered. 'I know how devastated you must be.'

She moved away and was swallowed up in the crowds. Harriet thought what a lot of courage it must have taken for Fiona to come here today, to show herself in such a public setting, after the scandal about Julian. Then she remembered having read somewhere that a murderer could seldom resist attending his victim's funeral. She looked at the line of mourners crossing the road. Mrs Parsons was among them, so was Dr Wentworth. Tony Richards and his Alsatian were standing on the other side of the road, watching. Sergeant Staples was directing traffic. Martin Threlfall was there and his wife, Joyce. Brenda Barlow. Mrs Parker. Mrs Moss. Humphrey Osborne. Everyone in fact whom she, or other people, had at one time or another suspected of being the anonymous writer.

Alix came up to her. Her face was tear-stained and blotchy but her appearance, in a short black skirt and jacket, was immaculate. 'I've got to go now and pick up Imogen. I'll give you a ring.'

Harriet nodded. She followed the rest of the mourners into the tiny cemetery. It too smelled of roses. She stood for a moment after they had lowered Peggy into the ground. Then she turned and walked slowly away. She didn't feel like going back to Peggy's mother's house, though she'd been invited. She wanted to be alone with her thoughts before it was time to collect Nicky from her father's.

Wandering in the hot sunshine in the park opposite, Harriet thought how thin the veil is that separates us, the so-called living, from the so-called dead. And yet how definitive. On any other day the sun, the roses, would have filled her with joy. Today the world felt suddenly empty because it was a world Peggy saw no longer. A guillotine had come down, cutting Peggy off from all those back in the graveyard who were left mourning her.

She walked slowly round the duck pond. She still couldn't quite believe in the reality of Peggy's death. Couldn't quite believe that when she next turned up at the school gate, Peggy wouldn't be there. She'd go on talking to Peggy in her mind, she knew she would. She was a wound inside her. It would join all the other wounds – her mother's death, Daniel, her broken marriage – which made her what she was. Oh but, Harriet thought, turning away and setting her face resolutely towards her father's house, how lonely I feel. Then she remembered Frank and how he must feel and thought that must be a million times worse. How strange of Alix not to see it.

'You've buried her, then?'

Her father had on his warning look. She knew it well. It meant don't let's have any emotional scenes. Not here. Thank you. When her grandmother had died – his own mother – he'd cut short her tears saying, 'She was old and frail. Surely you knew that.' Her brothers, five years older, had displayed manly self-control. Or if they had wept, they'd had the sense to do it in the privacy of their bedrooms. Looking at him now, a slim, smart, white-haired man, Harriet wondered whether he'd ever deeply felt the loss of anyone, even her mother. Pride had forbidden him to go to her funeral.

It wasn't entirely her father's fault, though. She watched him kneel, rather stiffly, on the floor playing with Nicky as he'd never played with his own children. He'd worked for years for a company which had paid its workers to put their careers before their families, which had encouraged them to be selfish since it was its managers' drive and ambition that gave the company its cutting edge. To this end, the hierarchies had been rigidly maintained. Wives were expected to give up their own careers and move around the country at the whim of their husbands' bosses. Husbands were given black marks if their wives refused to accompany them on social occasions or rebelled against entertaining foreign visitors in their homes. Bachelors were looked at askance and rarely got promoted beyond a certain point. There was no room for women or gays in the boardroom. The atmosphere in the company was definitely macho. The weakest went to the wall or the drying-out clinic. She supposed (she hoped) that this was all now being dismantled. Too late for her father. He'd been moulded by it. 'A toast to my son-in-law.' When she'd married Geoffrey, her father had ceased to see her as an individual. His daughter had joined the millions of nameless, featureless, insignificant women he lumped together under the general heading 'housewife'.

'Bit about the marriage in the *Telegraph*.' His voice broke in on her thoughts. 'Quite a do, by the sound of it. Register office, of course. Had to be.'

He sounded almost regretful, as if he blamed his daughter for the fact that his ex-son-in-law's second marriage couldn't take place in a church. She wondered where it would have been – St Margaret's, perhaps, or even Westminster Abbey.

Harriet wandered over to the table and picked up the newspaper. She read about the bride's elegant cream suit. She read about the Register office crammed with guests, among them the Princess of Wales . . . She read about the reception at the Savoy. She put down the paper.

'What do you think of it?' Her father glanced up, eager to

prolong the conversation about this social event of the month at which so many MPs, journalists and people generally in the swing of things had been present and to which he felt himself linked, however tenuously.

'He's done well for himself, hasn't he?' he added proudly, as if Geoffrey had been his son rather than his son-in-law. 'It looks like he's married the right kind of girl this time. He's going to need all the help he can get if he's going into the Cabinet. I'm no use to him now. I'm out of it all. Washed up,' he muttered.

'Geoffrey did seem to imply she was efficient.'

'Been talking to him, have you?' There was a note of envy in his voice. 'What else did he say? Did he tell you what the Government intends doing about the Crosswell deal?'

'What Crosswell deal?'

He let out a sigh of exasperation.

'We didn't say much,' she said, half-apologetically. 'He talked to Nicky.'

Her father shrugged his shoulders and went back to playing with his grandson, his one remaining hope. Who knew? Perhaps he'd be lucky. Perhaps Nicky would grow up to be the type of man who knew about Crosswell deals, who had his finger on the button. She hoped not, but there was no denying there was a lot of it in his genes, that determination to get on, to be at the centre of things. But what did it leave you with in the end?

She leant back against the table watching her father deal out cards for the memory game he and Nicky loved to play. As usual, her father hadn't asked if she wanted to play. So it will go on, she thought, till the end of his life. Him never really seeing me. Me waving frantically to get his attention. Hi, Dad, it's me. Me. Not Geoffrey's wife, not the mother of your grandsons, but me, Harriet. Not a housewife or a failed businesswoman, but an artist and, above all, a person. Not a woman. Women were always a bit of a joke to you, weren't they? Women and their irritable times of the month, women and their big hips, women unable to find their way from A to B without getting lost. Well, OK, if my womanhood gets in the way, try thinking of me without it. Try thinking of me as a person for a change. A human being. Can you imagine what it's like to grow up with someone who regards you with a faint sneer simply because of your sex? Can you? Was that why Mum left you in the end?

'Why don't you put on the kettle and make yourself a cup of tea while we finish this?'

His voice, cutting across her thoughts, had the effect of dissipating Harriet's anger. He wasn't as bad as she'd made him out to be in her mind. He was an old man, he'd been formed by his times. She went into the kitchen and switched on the kettle. If her father was irretrievably sexist, it had been branded into him by society. His father before him had been a racist. God knows what terrible prejudice Nicky would unearth in her when he grew up.

She made her tea and took it back into the living room. She remembered the five-pound note her father had given her after her O-levels were over, pressing it into her hand and saying 'Go out and enjoy yourself' (he'd always been generous with money). Taking it out of her pocket later in the disco she'd found doodled across it the words 'Good luck, Harriet' and knew he'd been thinking of her that day, though he'd never said a word. She'd held on to that note, had it still somewhere about the house. She put her hands round her mug and smiled to herself.

'That's the last one. Finished now, Nicky. Well done, my boy. You're getting good at this. You'll be beating me one of these days.' He glanced across at her suspiciously. 'Why are you smiling? He will beat me. He's got brains, has my grandson.'

'I know,' she said quickly. 'It wasn't that. I was remembering something. By the way,' she said, to change the subject, 'I think I've got gout.'

'Have you? It comes to all of us in the end. I have it. Your grandfather had it. It was to be expected. Let's hope Nicky takes after his father.'

'Yes, I know you hope that,' she said quietly, so quietly that beneath the clatter Nicky was making tidying away their game, her father didn't hear.

But, as they were getting ready to leave, it struck her suddenly how frail he was getting. He no longer walked with his shoulders back and his head held high. He'd developed an old man's shuffle.

As they went out of the door he said, almost forlornly, 'Come again soon.'

'We will.' She stopped on the steps outside. 'Dad, are you all right?'

'I miss your mother.' It was a great deal for him to admit. To Harriet's knowledge, this was the first time in twelve years her name had crossed his lips. But who knew what he'd been brooding about all these years? And then, as if to confirm her suspicions, he muttered, 'I was a damn fool.' He shook his head. 'It'll be my turn next.'

She came back up the steps and kissed him on the cheek. He looked mildly surprised (they rarely kissed) but made no protest.

'We will come again soon. I promise.'

She heard him double lock the door behind her. In his old age he'd become anxious about security. He never opened his door now after four in the afternoon. He's not the person he was, she thought, as she walked back home through the centre of Apple Burton, Nicky skipping along by her side. He's no longer the tyrant of my childhood memories. It's time to grow up. He needs taking care of.

At home, Nicky unexpectedly fell asleep on the sofa. Harriet wandered around the playroom, at a loose end. Absent-mindedly, she picked up a pencil and a piece of paper, sat down and began sketching automatically, her thoughts elsewhere. He did miss her mother then. That gave them something in common, something more than gout, at any rate. Her thoughts strayed over the three pictures of her mother that kept coming back to her again and again. Why those pictures? Why not others? She didn't know.

She must have been about five or six years old. She was in hospital with some childhood ailment. When her mother came to visit, Harriet screamed to be taken home. Her mother went in tears to plead with the staff nurse. Eventually she was given permission to stay in overnight with her daughter, a thing not normally allowed in those days.

The second picture was soon after her parents separated. Calling unexpectedly one day at her mother's new bungalow, on her way up to Scotland, Harriet had found her mother in the living room with Ralph, a family friend from way back who'd recently been widowed. There they both were (she could see them still), he in his slippers (did he keep them there or had he brought them with him?) reading a newspaper. Her mother was doing some sewing. A button on a shirt. Ralph's shirt? Something in the quality of the atmosphere in that room had stayed with Harriet (she'd tried, and failed, to recreate it with Geoffrey). It was more than companionable; the atmosphere breathed trust, affection and above all contentment. Yes, that was it. A deep contentment. She couldn't remember her mother ever having sat quietly like that with her father. For one thing, her father had never had time for sitting about. There'd always been meetings to be arranged, colleagues to phone. Besides, there'd been the bickering.

The third picture dated from shortly after Ralph's death. Her mother sitting up in bed in hospital (she'd had a stroke the day after Ralph's funeral) looked utterly bereft. 'I'm not going to leave you, Mum.' Harriet had picked up the brush lying on the hospital locker and begun brushing the short grey curls that were tangled and matted from lying in bed. 'You didn't leave me when I was in hospital.' And her mother, amidst all her bewilderment and confusion and speechlessness resulting from the stroke, had clung to Harriet like a child, as her daughter had clung to her all those years before.

Harriet had stayed with her mother for two weeks in hospital and during those two weeks she'd sensed that one circle in her life was being completed. She, the daughter, had grown up to mother her own mother. And when the end came, she'd realised that a certain kind of tenderness, that tenderness between women who have once been part of one another's bodies, was lost for ever.

'I'm losing all my mothers,' she said aloud. Then stopped, half-embarrassed at catching herself talking aloud when there was no one in the room but a sleeping child. She wondered what she'd meant. Peggy, she supposed. There was a kind of mothering that went on between women at the school gate.

She looked down at the scrap of paper in her hands and saw, with a shock, that what she'd sketched, almost unwittingly, was a profile of Humphrey Osborne. She crumpled up the paper and threw it in the bin. Then she went to dial Eddie's number again. His answering machine was still on. She left another message. 'What's going on, Eddie? Have you fled the country?'

Chapter Twenty-three

The next day they woke up to a blazing hot June morning. Harriet dressed Nicky in shorts, T-shirt and baseball cap and plastered his arms and legs with sunblock. They walked to school keeping under the shade of the overhanging chestnut trees. She wondered whether anyone else would be at the school gate or whether the letter writer had succeeded in his apparent aim of wrecking their small community.

When she arrived at St Cecilia's, she found that other parents had turned up, though in fewer numbers than usual. There was a scared look in everyone's eyes, scared and half-excited. What was going to happen next, they were wondering. People always believed their own secrets wouldn't be the ones to come out. They wouldn't be the ones caught slapping their children or fiddling expenses or groping a prostitute in a lay-by. She saw Humphrey Osborne in the distance. He gave her a short, embarrassed nod. Perhaps he did still suspect her. After all, she still suspected him.

Alix came up, leading Imogen by the hand. They were both wearing lemon-yellow sundresses, Imogen's a miniature version of her mother's.

'You're looking lovely, Alix.'

'Thanks. I had to do something to cheer myself up after Peggy's funeral. Imogen's not speaking to me though. She thinks her dress is frightful, don't you, darling?' Imogen frowned. Her mother rolled her eyes and flicked back her plait. 'Go and play in the playground with Nicky, darling. Off you go.' She sighed. 'What a fuss I had to get her into that dress, you wouldn't believe it.' Her tone altered. 'Wasn't it awful yesterday?'

'Yes.' Despite the heat, Harriet gave a shiver.

'Peggy's frightful mother, back like a ramrod, never shed a tear.

Whereas Frank hardly stopped. He looked terrible. As well he might,' she added.

Harriet opened her mouth and then shut it again. She didn't want to quarrel with Alix. Not now that Peggy was dead.

'Numbers are down a bit this morning, aren't they?' said Alix, looking around.

'I expect they'll creep back up again as the days pass, provided we don't have any more bombshells from our anonymous author.'

'I should have thought he'd pretty well exhausted all he had to say about us by now,' remarked Alix, stifling a yawn. 'After all, as a community, we aren't that interesting. Fiona's not here.'

'No, I noticed.'

'Perhaps one of us should seek her out,' suggested Alix. 'Say we were just passing by and wanted to show our sympathy and solidarity.'

'Yes, you're right.' The terrible news about Peggy had swept everything else from Harriet's mind. Fiona must have felt neglected. What if no one from St Cecilia's had been in touch? Would she think they all condemned her, were cold-shouldering her in a nasty puritanical way because of Julian? 'I'll go. I'll go this morning.'

'Keep your eyes peeled while you're there. You never know, you might come across something, some clue.'

Harriet winced. 'Do you realise that this is the first time we've targeted a woman suspect? Somehow it makes it all seem worse, snooping on another woman.'

'I'll go.'

'No, I'll go. It was me who persuaded you she was still a suspect. I don't want to go on thinking the worst about her. I want to find out the truth.'

'Be careful, Harriet. The truth is often the last thing most people really want to know. Have you got her address?'

'Yes, I've been there once before. Nicky was invited to Angelica's birthday party.'

As she walked – slowly, for the heat was intense – down the road of handsome Edwardian villas where Fiona lived, Harriet turned over in her mind all the reasons she had for suspecting her. First, she was head of a PR company. Presumably you didn't get that far without knowing what makes people tick. The anonymous letter writer might not have a degree in psychology, but he or she (Harriet supposed she must try to think of the writer as a she) certainly knew how to attack people's weak spots. Secondly, Fiona was probably bang up to date with the latest developments on the Internet and the Web (whatever that might be). Thirdly, unlike Peggy, she hadn't broken down over the disclosures about Julian. In fact, if her appearance at Peggy's funeral was anything to go by, she'd remained remarkably cool-headed. That made three reasons for suspecting Fiona to be the letter writer. The fourth reason, Harriet didn't quite like to spell out, even to herself. The fact was, she half-envied Fiona for being all the things she, Harriet, wasn't, all the things her father would have liked her to be – the well-dressed businesswoman, the highflying company executive.

She rang the bell of the three-storey double-fronted house. Fiona came to the door looking remarkably unlike her usual self. She was dressed in a pair of grubby jeans and a shirt that had a tear in it. Her hair was covered in a dusty red scarf.

'Oh hello, Harriet,' she said, brushing her dust-streaked cheek and making it worse.

Harriet hesitated. Perhaps she'd misjudged Fiona? Perhaps this was the real Fiona, grieving and quietly desperate? She was in PR. She knew how to put on an immaculate appearance in public. Harriet chided herself for having been so easily fooled by Fiona's cool, calm exterior.

'Er, Fiona, I came to say how sorry I am, we all are that . . .' That what? That your husband's turned out to be a louse who uses rent boys? Harriet's sentence wound down slowly into an embarrassed silence.

Fiona opened the door wider. 'Come in,' she said, clearly taking pity on her for her gaucherie. 'I was going to stop for a cup of tea anyway.'

Harriet stepped inside the square, spacious hall. There were packing cases everywhere.

'This is what I've been doing these past few days.' Fiona waved a hand around.

'Oh.'

Fiona hadn't been holed up at home then, too frightened to step out of doors and face people because of the scandal about her husband. She hadn't been crying her eyes out. She'd been packing.

'I've sent Angelica to stay with her grandparents while I get this finished. I wasn't going to send her back to that school again.'

She led the way down the hall to the kitchen. Skirting packing cases and stepping over piles of books, Harriet followed her. The kitchen was done out in pine and Italian tiles and must have been lovely, but now half the shelves were empty and the floor was littered with boxes.

'Take a seat. Move all that stuff.'

Harriet removed a pile of cookery books and sat down on a chair as Fiona put the kettle on.

'This is sudden, Fiona, isn't it? Leaving like this, I mean.' Harriet's eyes narrowed. Was Fiona the letter writer now taking flight, alarmed at what her letters had unleashed? 'You are moving, I suppose?'

'Oh yes, we're moving all right.'

Harriet assumed she meant Angelica and herself. Yes, of course, that was the logical next step. Move out of the house and leave Julian to face the music on his own. Perhaps they weren't going far, then. After all, Fiona still had her business to run.

'Where are you going?'

'The States.'

Fiona warmed the pot and put in real tea leaves. Harriet stared, fascinated. In the midst of all this chaos, both physical and emotional, when most other women would be climbing the walls, how on earth did Fiona stay so calm? Was it quite natural?

'Goodness! The States! What does Julian think about that? I mean he'll hardly see Angelica, will he?'

Fiona smiled. 'Oh, I think he will. You see, Julian's coming with us.'

'Is he?'

'There's no future for him here any more. And I can operate my company as well, if not better, in America. We're going to make a fresh start over there.'

'But Fiona . . .' Harriet fell silent. What was Fiona hoping? That Julian would somehow stop being gay?

Fiona set the cups on the table. 'I made my decision to stick with Julian years ago. I've always known he was bisexual. He's had affairs with men all through our marriage. It really doesn't bother me any more. As long as I'm the only woman in his life, I don't mind. Some of them have even become my friends.' She glanced at Harriet. 'It wasn't true about the rent boys. That was a set-up by the newspaper. If you notice, none of the photographs actually showed Julian with those boys.'

Trying to organise all this information in her mind, Harriet watched Fiona pour out the tea. It was Lapsang Souchong and tasted absolutely delicious.

'If what the newspaper wrote wasn't true,' she said at length, 'why don't you sue?'

Fiona shrugged. 'What's the point? Suing for libel usually makes things worse. The accusation sticks in people's minds more when there's a court case. And anyway, it is true that Julian's bisexual and that alone seems to count as a resigning issue round here.' She took a sip of her tea. 'We always knew it'd be risky settling here. In such a small community things easily get found out. And it's hardly in the forefront of liberal thinking up here. We thought it was worth taking the risk for Angelica's sake. Neither of us wanted her to be brought up in London.'

'So that's why you took it all so calmly,' said Harriet. 'I wondered.'

'I knew as soon as I got the first e-mail that the game was going to be up for Julian sooner or later. I've been planning this move for weeks. Julian's over in Boston now, scouting out places for us to rent.'

'Fiona,' Harriet decided to put her cards on the table, 'who do you think is writing these letters?'

Fiona shrugged and got up to pour them both another cup of tea. 'I haven't a clue. And now, quite frankly, it doesn't bother me a bit. I just want to get the hell out of here.'

'I know, but the rest of us have got to live here,' muttered Harriet.

Fiona's expression softened. She reached across the table and squeezed Harriet's hand. 'I'm terribly sorry about Peggy. She was an old school friend of yours, wasn't she?'

'Yes. We were at Apple Burton High together. We lost touch afterwards. Alix was there as well.'

'Was she? So you knew Alix when she was younger?'

'Yes. Not terribly well. She was several classes above us.' Someone else had asked her that question recently. Who? Harriet couldn't remember.

'I've been over and over in my mind who it could be,' continued Fiona. 'At first I thought it might be that bad-tempered-looking man – you know, the one who never speaks to anyone.'

'Humphrey Osborne?'

'That's right. But I deliberately took the opportunity of chatting to him once or twice at the school gate and I don't think he's the type. Then I thought it might be Dr Wentworth or the vicar. Then I wondered if it was a woman. And now I don't know.' She looked at Harriet. 'It must be someone who knows us all very well. Perhaps better than we know ourselves.'

Harriet felt a cold shiver run down her back. For some reason, Fiona's words struck a chord in her mind.

'And now,' concluded Fiona, 'I don't really care. It's Angelica and Julian I'm thinking about.'

Walking back home, Harriet thought how much she'd misjudged Fiona. Not a snob or a shark, she was simply a very successful businesswoman who knew when to put her success to one side and concentrate on her family when they needed her. Harriet felt almost ashamed. No wonder women didn't get on as well as they might when other women suspected them the minute they made a success of anything. Support, that's what women should give each other. Rapturous applause. Cheering from the sidelines.

As she entered the house the phone was ringing. She ran down the hall to answer it but as her hand reached the receiver, it stopped ringing. Damn, she thought. Ten seconds later, it rang again. She grabbed the receiver.

'Hello?'

'Hi, it's Eddie. I got your message. No, I haven't fled the country, darling. I'm still here. How are you?'

'I'm —' she hesitated — 'all right. How about you? You sound funny. Have you got a cold?'

'No,' he said nasally, 'I've had a face-lift.'

'You're joking.'

'No, it's true. That's why I haven't been in touch for a while. I've been flat on my back for ten days looking like Frankenstein.'

'Frankenstein's monster,' she said happily, dizzy with relief.

'What?'

'Never mind. What have they done to you?'

'I've had my nose reshaped.'

'What was wrong with it?'

'Too broad.'

'I didn't notice.'

'I felt it was. Anyway. I dunno, I've been feeling my age recently. Maybe it's living on my own. And the kind of women I've been meeting — apart from you, babe — have been duds. There's always been something off-putting about them. Halitosis or warts or something. So I thought if I smartened myself up a bit someone as beautiful as you might fancy me.'

'I do fancy you.' She'd thought that was obvious.

'I felt there was something missing. I've lost a lot of confidence lately. In the past, I've always had confidence with women.' He paused. 'I've had my cheeks lifted. It's a new technique from America. They use tiny cameras and put staples in. Then you have to lie in bed for ten days in case of neurological damage.'

'Does it hurt?'

'My entire face feels as if it's been stung by nettles.'

'It seems an awful lot to go through,' she remarked.

'It's worth it. I tell you, Harriet, when you see me next, I'll look ten years younger. I'll be booking my holiday on Club 21 to 30.'

She laughed. 'How much did it cost?'

'Seven thousand pounds.'

She whistled.

'I had it done in Harley Street. I wasn't taking any chances. There are a lot of cowboys about. Anyway, I thought I'd give you a ring to let you know what's going on in my life. You can't see me yet. Not for another couple of weeks. I'm going down to London tomorrow to have my capillaries loosened. They turn black, apparently. My face will look like a black and white patchwork quilt for a bit. I can't see anyone while I look like this. But let's keep in touch. How are things with you?'

'Not too good, to be honest. A friend of mine died recently.'

'Oh sweetheart, that's dreadful.' His manner changed. His voice sounded almost tender. 'How did she die? Cancer? A car accident?'

'No, she committed suicide actually. She'd found out her husband was having an affair.'

'My poor Harriet. Did you know her well?'

'We were at school together.' Her lip trembled.

'You need to look after yourself, girl. I remember what it felt like when my mother died. When you're in pain like you are, the only thing you can do is keep calm and quiet and nurse your pain. Give it time and space. One day you'll wake up and find that instead of it controlling you, you're the one in control again.'

Harriet smiled through her tears. This was why it was worth going on with Eddie. He talked a lot of rubbish but in between he threw out a few pearls which no one but he could have come up with. Insights about life, felt on the pulse. None of it out of books. He reminded her of her mother, sitting day after day, reading the newspapers, pondering over people's lives. Not in a malicious way, not with the spiteful glee that makes people scan the tabloids in order to gloat over the downfall of the latest public figure. Her mother had never taken sides but simply meditated on what made people behave the way they did. Sometimes she wept over a pensioner who'd been raped or a child who'd been battered to death.

Her mother hadn't *done* anything, at least not in the sense Harriet's friends had meant when they'd asked her 'What does your mother do all day?' But if you said her life had been wasted, you'd have also to say let's all turn our backs on compassion then, and on the everyday things of life. Or you'd have to ask yourself what was the point of spending hours studying a pair of home-made clogs like Van Gogh.

All this flashed through Harriet's mind as Eddie went on speaking about grief and healing. At the end, she said, 'You remind me of my mother.'

'Do I? What was she like?'

'Tender. Gentle. Wise.'

Only after she'd put down the phone did it occur to Harriet to wonder, if Eddie had been flat on his back in bed for ten days, who had been doing his shopping and cooking?

Chapter Twenty-four

Harriet got up late the next morning. With a headache. She'd lain in bed tossing and turning for much of the night. Think, think, she'd told herself, it ought to be easy enough to find a pattern behind the letters. To put two and two together and come up with the right answer. The heat in the room was unbearable. She got out of bed and threw open a window. The night air felt stuffy and over-used. They needed a good thunderstorm to clear the atmosphere.

She felt a yearning inside for Eddie. If only he were here now, to hold her in his arms and tell her everything was going to be all right. But he wasn't with her. Where was he? Was he going to turn out to be unreliable, like Geoffrey? Why couldn't she meet some calm, ordinary, dependable man? There must be one out there. Mustn't there?

She'd finally dropped off to sleep at around five. It was now eight. They were going to be late. Nicky was already up. He must have seen she was asleep and crept downstairs to switch on the television.

As Harriet came blearily down the stairs, she spotted a large brown envelope on the mat. She picked it up carefully. Her name and address were typewritten. Her heart sank. So the anonymous letter writer hadn't given up. What was she going to be accused of this time? Neglecting Daniel? Sleeping with Eddie? Gingerly she opened it.

A large black and white photograph fell out. Attached to it was a hand-written note saying 'Peggy wanted you to have this.' Harriet picked up the photograph and turned it the right way up. It was a picture of the girls at Apple Burton High School, taken years ago. There was Peggy, slightly left of centre, her red hair frizzed out and framing her plump cheeks. Harriet found herself at the end of a row, looking small and thin, with what appeared to be a streak of paint on her cheek. And there was Alix, standing at the back with the rest of the prefects, her blonde hair tied back in a ponytail, her tie perfectly straight, her shirt neatly tucked into her waist, not billowing out like most of the girls'.

Harriet gazed at the photo for a few minutes. Why had Peggy wanted her to have this? And who had sent it? Her mother? Frank? It was like a message from beyond the grave. You're not forgotten, it seemed to say. I'm with you still.

While Nicky stood eating Coco Pops in front of the television, Harriet sat on the sofa and looked again at the photograph as if it might provide some clue to Peggy's state of mind at the end of her life. How had Frank, or whoever it was, known Peggy wanted her to have this photograph? Had she left a note or had she made a will? In which case, was her suicide as spur of the moment as they'd all thought? The teachers sat in the front row. In the centre of them was Miss Barnesley. Harriet recalled only too well those brown lace-up shoes and long tweed skirts. But what had Peggy been trying to tell her by sending her this?

She glanced at the clock, put the photograph aside and began getting Nicky ready for school.

This morning there were slightly more parents and children at the school gate.

'They're creeping back,' said Alix. 'I thought they would.'

Harriet waved to Nicky as he disappeared round the corner with Mrs Moss and the rest of the children. 'Alix, did you get anything in the post this morning?'

'Only a couple of bills. Why? Oh!' She turned to Harriet in surprise. 'You don't mean you've had another anonymous letter?'

'No. I thought it was going to be, but it wasn't. Peggy sent me a photograph. At least, she didn't herself of course, it was sent by somebody else, perhaps her mother, or Frank. It was a school photograph from years back. You were on it.'

Alix flicked back her plait. 'Was I? How ghastly.'

'You looked very nice actually, much the loveliest of all of us. I was an absolute scruff. The thing is, Alix, I can't help thinking Peggy was trying to tell me something by sending me that photograph.'

Alix stared at her. 'Tell you something? About what?'

'That's what I'm trying to work out.'

'I shouldn't bother about it if I were you. It was probably just a sentimental gesture on her part. She wanted you to know how much you'd meant to her.'

'Maybe.'

'I'm sure I'm right.'

But as Harriet walked home, the thought of that photograph and what might lie behind it kept nagging away in her mind so that when she arrived home the first thing she did was phone Frank. He was back in his office.

'Oh, hello, Harriet.' His voice was polite, wary. After all, he hardly knew her, had met her once or twice at the school gate. 'What can I do for you?'

'Did you send an old school photograph to me?'

'Yes, I did. I found it yesterday when I was going through Peggy's things. It was in an envelope with your name on it, so I thought she'd intended you to have it.'

'Yes, I'm glad to have it. So you just found it, did you? I mean, er, there wasn't a pile of things Peggy left to different people?'

'No, nothing like that. She left no will or anything.'

He sounded rather frosty. Perhaps he thought she was some sort of fortune hunter.

'I'm sorry,' she said hastily, 'I didn't mean to pry. It's just I wondered why Peggy specially wanted me to have that particular photograph.'

'I don't suppose there was any special reason. Peggy had fond memories of school. It was an escape from home.' He sighed and let down his guard for a second. 'I suppose you all blame me for her death?'

'No one's to blame. Or if someone is, it's that letter writer. For meddling in other people's lives.'

He sighed again. 'I shall blame myself. Always.' He hesitated. 'Me and Gemma – our relationship's not going to survive this. She can't handle me feeling guilty all the time.'

Harriet didn't know what to say. On the one hand, she felt it only just that Gemma should have left him. On the other hand, Frank sounded so miserable.

'So Peggy got her way in the end,' he added bitterly. 'No Gemma.'

'I'm sure that's not why she –'

'No, I know. I didn't mean that. I don't know why I said it. That wasn't why Peggy killed herself. She killed herself because when you've been brought up to believe you're a failure it leaves you feeling hollow and desperate inside. I was always trying to get Peggy to believe in herself but she never could. And in the end I suppose I began to, well, get irritated by her not being able to stand on her own two feet, depending on me for everything, even to change the light bulbs.'

'I wish I'd done more for her too, helped bolster her confidence a bit. Stopped her going on those wretched diets.'

He gave a short, tired laugh. 'I know. I like plump women – Gemma's even plumper than Peggy – but she never would believe it. No, Harriet, there was nothing any of us could do. She'd been damaged in her childhood by that terrible woman telling her how useless she was and how she'd end up sweeping the streets if she wasn't careful. She never got over it. My – um – relationship with Gemma seemed to confirm Peggy's view about herself. Her mother had always told her she'd never keep a man looking the way she did.'

'It's a tragedy.'

'It is. My sons have been deprived of their mother. There's one thing though, I'm going to make damned sure Peggy's mother doesn't get her hands on them. When Gemma was still around, she was making noises about suing for custody on the grounds of my being an unfit parent. She can't do that now. And I'll be keeping my nose clean in future so that the boys stay with me.'

'No, you couldn't let her have them, not after what she did to Peggy.'

Harriet rang off. Frank had convinced her that there was nothing behind Peggy's photograph other than a nostalgic glance back at their shared schooldays. It's these letters, she thought. They make everything seem so complicated. I'm losing my sense of life's simplicity. I'm not going to think about the letters for a bit. She spent the morning studying an apple and a pear in great detail, preparing to compose a still-life. It would be fatal to her as a painter if she were to lose her sense of simplicity.

The next morning, she had arrived home after delivering Nicky to St Cecilia's and was about to go up to her studio when the phone rang.

'About this letter business,' began Humphrey Osborne, in his usual abrupt fashion. 'I've arranged a meeting for ten-thirty this morning. Can you come? I didn't want to mention it outside St Cecilia's. You never know who might be listening.'

'Yes, but –' This was so annoying, just as she'd resolved to forget all about the letters for a while and was getting on so well with that still-life. 'I suppose I could come,' she said grudgingly. 'Who else will be there?'

'Sergeant Staples, Martin Threlfall and Dr Wentworth.'

'Is that all?'

'They're the only people I trust.'

She was about to ask whether she might bring Alix along for moral support when he went on, 'This isn't a public meeting, it's going to be held in my house.'

'Oh.' If that was the case, she didn't feel she could suggest bringing Alix.

'We'll see you at ten-thirty, then. I want to get to the bottom of this.' He rang off.

Harriet had never heard Humphrey Osborne sound so determined. He had the bit between his teeth now over this letter business. It looked like he was set to ferret out the facts with as much tenacity as she supposed he set about deciphering old manuscripts. Their anonymous letter writer had better look out.

But at ten-fifteen, reluctantly abandoning her still-life to walk under the shade of the chestnut trees to Humphrey Osborne's house, Harriet wondered whether what she was about to participate in was not in fact a brilliant piece of double bluff, performed under the very eyes of the police, in the shape of Sergeant Staples. Call a meeting, seem to be anxious to track down the letter writer, pretend to trust only a select few – what better cover could there be if in fact you yourself were the writer of those letters?

She began to wish she'd phoned Alix to tell her about the meeting and discuss with her how to handle it. She was sure Alix would have had some good ideas. At any rate, she must be on her guard. She owed it to Peggy's memory. And Humphrey Osborne was certainly clever enough for anything.

Chapter Twenty-five

Everyone else was already present, seated in a circle in Humphrey Osborne's dark study, when Harriet was shown in by Mrs Towers.

There was Dr Wentworth, slim and dapper in his three-piece suit. He was leaning back in his chair, frowning. Harriet writhed inwardly with embarrassment as she remembered where he'd last seen her – lying on his couch with her legs wide apart. Martin Threlfall was leaning forward, his face, with its long thin nose and cadaverous cheeks, focused on Sergeant Staples.

'. . . clearly unbalanced,' the latter was saying. He broke off when he noticed Harriet.

'Welcome,' said Humphrey Osborne. 'Have a seat.'

Harriet sat down, feeling as perhaps some of Picasso's models must have felt, wondering what they were going to be turned into and how many chins they would end up with. She found herself directly opposite Humphrey Osborne. Good, she thought. This would give her plenty of opportunity to observe his reactions during the meeting.

Sergeant Staples continued, 'I was just explaining, Mrs Lee, that cases like this one are always slow. I worked on one twelve years ago up in Northumberland. It's a matter of checking and rechecking the facts, the steady elimination of suspects.'

She glanced around. 'So we've all been eliminated, have we?' Was that wise?

Sergeant Staples nodded. 'You, for instance, Mrs Lee, have no computer.'

'No, that's true. And I wouldn't know how to operate one if I did. But,' she added as she wondered on what grounds the other people in the room had been eliminated, 'is it necessary for the writer to possess his own computer? Aren't there places where you can go if you want to send e-mails?'

'Cybercafés?' Sergeant Staples grinned. 'I'm afraid they haven't hit Apple Burton yet, Mrs Lee. The nearest one is Birmingham. Too far to keep popping back and forth on a regular basis.' He gave her a tolerant look; he was used to dealing with dim members of the public. Harriet suddenly felt foolish and isolated amongst this company of professional men.

'Besides,' added Humphrey Osborne, 'the anonymous writer can't be an occasional computer user. It's quite tricky to send e-mail anonymously. I know. I tried it as an experiment last week. Wasted a whole day on it and got nowhere.'

Harriet observed him closely. Her eyes narrowed. Was this a double, or even triple, bluff? Just how clever was he?

'No, it's someone who knows what she's doing all right.'

Harriet's eyebrows shot up. 'She?'

'We're now working on the supposition that the anonymous writer is a woman,' explained Sergeant Staples.

'Why?'

'Our psychologist at Scotland Yard has made a careful study of all the letters and e-mails that have been handed in to us. He believes the writer is a woman cleverly imitating male language about sex in order to throw us off the scent.'

'Oh.' She glanced across at Humphrey Osborne. Or was it perhaps a male writer pretending to be a woman imitating a man? As with Shakespeare's comedies, the permutations on gender in this case seemed endless. 'Are you sure about this, Sergeant Staples?'

'Well, obviously, we can't entirely eliminate all male suspects,

Mrs Lee, but the psychologist was quite convinced.' He looked round the circle at them all. 'What we have to look for in a case like this is someone who's deeply unhappy. Whose life feels so empty and drab they enjoy the power they get from uncovering other people's secrets and publishing them. You see,' he pressed his large hands firmly down on his knees, looking like nothing so much as a Yorkshire farmer, 'this case is rather different from the usual run of poison-pen cases. Generally what happens – what happened in the case up in Northumberland – is that the writer – and it turned out to be a woman in that case – simply hits out wildly in her letters, spreading scurrilous insults, generally of a sexual nature, blind accusations without any foundation in truth. Occasionally, by chance, one of these accusations strikes a chord in the recipient and then tragedy occurs. That's how we solved the case in Northumberland – a woman took her own life in circumstances very similar to those of the unfortunate Mrs Murray.' He paused. 'Our writer is much cleverer. For a start, she uses e-mail, which I've never come across before in a poison-pen case, and then every single one of the accusations, without exception, has turned out to be true. So we can't even get her for libel.'

'What could we get her for?' asked Humphrey Osborne.

Sergeant Staples shrugged. 'Disturbance? Some minor charge, anyway. With luck, we might be able to persuade her to go into hospital for a time. She obviously needs help.'

'Section her, you mean?'

'Yes.'

Humphrey Osborne glanced across at Harriet who gave an involuntary shiver. She'd read the literature. *Jane Eyre*, *The Yellow Wallpaper*, *Wide Sargasso Sea*. She knew about men who shut up troublesome women in lunatic asylums. Was this a trap? Had Humphrey Osborne invited her here today to try to get her to implicate herself in some way? Was he manoeuvring her into the position of chief suspect in order to throw suspicion off himself? She clenched her hands tightly in her lap. Artists, in the public mind, were notoriously unbalanced people. So, traditionally, were women. It was easy, once a woman was established as a witch in the public eye, for her to remain a witch, whatever she did. Look at

Myra Hindley. Harriet wondered how on earth she could fight these powerful professional men, if it came to a fight, on her own.

Martin Threlfall leaned forward, resting his bony chin on his hands. 'Whoever wrote these horrible things must be feeling quite desperate and alone. Are they a cry for help more than anything, do you think, Sergeant Staples?'

'It's possible. But I think there's more to it than that,' the Sergeant replied. 'Think how carefully the whole thing has been planned. To uncover what the writer has about other people's lives, she must have been storing up her information for months, if not years.'

Martin Threlfall gave a shiver. 'I should have realised. If there's someone in my parish as unhappy as that, I should have been able to discover it by now if I'd been doing my job properly. I should have been able to prevent all this.'

He sank his head in his hands, overcome by what looked like genuine remorse. Harriet decided it was genuine and struck Martin Threlfall off her list of suspects once and for all.

Dr Wentworth leaned across and touched the vicar's arm. 'I'm as much to blame as you, Threlfall. If you're in charge of these people's souls, I'm in charge of their minds and bodies. I should have noticed something too.'

'A neurotic, unbalanced personality, possibly severely deprived,' mused Humphrey Osborne. He broke off and nodded as Mrs Towers brought in a tray of coffee, set it down discreetly and went out again, closing the door firmly behind her, leaving Harriet once more alone with the men. 'Is there no one in our little community who fits the bill, Wentworth?' He began pouring out the coffee and handing round the cups.

'I can't divulge patients' secrets, Osborne,' replied the doctor, taking a cup.

His gaze met Harriet's and he frowned. She flushed, remembering that session on his couch. Then she thought, he clearly suspects someone. Is it me? Does he think I'm neurotic and unbalanced because I sleep around enough to get STDs? After all, he knows I have a mentally handicapped son. They all know. Somebody must have handed that gene on to Daniel – was that what they were thinking? She shivered and set her cup down on her saucer with a clatter. Once again she felt like an outsider in this room full of professional men who addressed each other by their surnames and whose professions had once been and still were, in part, profoundly misogynist.

Dr Wentworth was still speaking. 'Whoever the letter writer is, she's enjoying her power over us all. She's got us on tenterhooks, wondering what dark secret she's going to reveal next. The number of people I've had in my surgery during these past few weeks complaining of insomnia or problems with their digestion or trouble with their backs. All symptoms of stress. We're not a healthy community at the moment.'

He fixed his gaze on Harriet as he spoke, very slowly and deliberately. It was almost as if he was trying to tell her something, to warn her. To warn her off? She bit her lip.

'Perhaps the letters will stop, now that she's shown us how clever she is, do you think?' she suggested, turning to Sergeant Staples.

He shook his head. 'The letters haven't stopped, Mrs Lee. I know that for a fact.' He drew a piece of paper from his pocket. 'There was a bit of a lull till Mrs Murray's funeral was out of the way. I expected that. She didn't want anything distracting attention from her letters. She likes the limelight, does this one. No, Mrs Lee, the letters haven't stopped. Whoever it is has a craving to write them. It's like an obsession with her. She won't stop till she is stopped. This arrived yesterday. It's an e-mail sent through the post to Brenda Barlow at her place of work. I'm showing it to you because I want to see if any of you can help me with it, but I expect absolute discretion about its contents.'

They all nodded. For two of them anyway, Martin Threlfall and Dr Wentworth, keeping secrets was part of their job.

'As you can see, there's an e-mail address on it this time. Not that that helps us much, since it isn't a real address. But it does contain a name. A code-name, most likely. There's no one of that surname living in the area, I've checked. I want to know if any of you recognise it. Take your time.'

He handed the print-out to Humphrey Osborne who read it, shook his head and passed it on to Dr Wentworth.

'Doesn't ring any bells with me, I'm afraid. She's getting a bit careless, isn't she?' he added. 'Leaving that on.'

'Well if it's a slip-up, it's the first one she's made. Which is a remarkable record. Normally we'd have expected many more by now. Bill down at the station thinks that what happened is that she tried to get through to Finland in order to send the e-mail anonymously, failed to get through, so printed out the e-mail and sent it by post, forgetting to erase the e-mail address.'

Dr Wentworth shook his head and passed the print-out to the vicar. Martin Threlfall hesitated. 'I think I have seen that name before. No one I know, but written down. Where, I can't remember.'

'Think, Threlfall,' urged the Sergeant. 'Could it be on your parish register?'

'Well not the current one. I know everyone on that. Perhaps on some past one? I'd have to go back and check.'

Sergeant Staples nodded. 'Do, please. I'll send an officer to help you.'

The vicar passed the e-mail to Harriet. It said *Done any shoplifting recently Brenda?*

'It's true, incidentally,' said the Sergeant. 'Mrs Barlow was caught shoplifting about four years ago. She was prosecuted and fined. As far as we know she's done nothing similar since.'

So that's the reason Brenda Barlow has always been so keen to ferret out other people's secrets, thought Harriet. A guilty conscience. Wanting to prove to herself that other people aren't saints either.

Humphrey Osborne shifted in his chair. 'You know what I think? I think that e-mail shows our letter writer's running out of inspiration. She hasn't found any new misdemeanours so she's had to resort to digging up old ones.'

Sergeant Staples nodded. 'Possibly.'

'It comes to the same thing though, doesn't it, Osborne?' said Dr Wentworth. 'People are still going to be unnerved by receiving these things, especially if, like many of us –' he coughed – 'they'd hoped to put their pasts behind them.'

'Do you recognise the name of the sender, Mrs Lee?' enquired Sergeant Staples.

Harriet looked again at the e-mail. The code-name of the sender began with Barnesley. She felt the blood rush to her cheeks. Her hands began to tremble. For a moment she thought she was going to faint.

'Well, Mrs Lee?'

'Are you all right?' Humphrey Osborne's voice cut across the Sergeant's.

Slowly she lifted her head and willed herself to meet his gaze. 'I'm all right. Yes, I recognise the name. It's the name of my old headmistress at Apple Burton High.' The witch with the warty hands who could silence three hundred girls at a glance.

'Of course!' exclaimed Martin Threlfall. 'That's where I've seen the name. I go into Apple Burton High quite often. I sometimes take assembly there. I was shown some old photographs of the school the other day and that's where I saw the name.'

School photos, thought Harriet. Was there a link between the photograph Peggy had sent her and this e-mail? Surely the name couldn't be a coincidence. The sender must have had some connection with Apple Burton High. It couldn't be Miss Barnesley herself – she'd retired the year after Harriet had left. She must be well into her eighties by now, if indeed she was still alive.

Looking up from the e-mail, Harriet caught Humphrey Osborne exchanging a glance full of significance with Sergeant Staples. They know something, she thought, that the rest of us don't. Just those two. Why? Was it true that the people in this room were the only people Humphrey Osborne trusted in this affair? Or was it the case that three of the people – Dr Wentworth, Martin Threlfall and herself – had been got here on false pretences, namely because they *were* the suspects? If so, she must just have given herself away in their eyes as the chief suspect.

Humphrey Osborne rubbed his hands. 'We're getting closer,' he said. 'We're on her tracks.'

He sounded, to Harriet's ears, just a little too gleeful. He seemed to be treating this as some sort of intellectual game. Had he forgotten the damage the letters had wrought on their community? Had he forgotten Peggy and Julian and Beverley and Denise and many others whose lives had been wrecked or irretrievably altered?

Sergeant Staples nodded. 'Yes, we're getting closer. Now I want you all to be vigilant. Report to me anything you find odd in the behaviour of people you come into contact with, no matter how trivial it may seem to you to be. Detective work's all in the detail. And be on your guard. The letter writer may strike again at any moment.'

Harriet wondered whether it was her imagination or whether Sergeant Staples was really concentrating his gaze on her as he spoke. Again she thought how odd it was that she'd been invited to this meeting. Dr Wentworth and the vicar had plenty of opportunity to meet a wide range of people during the course of their day. She met almost no one.

The meeting broke up. In the hall, as they were being shown out, she was conscious of a pressure on her arm and Humphrey Osborne's voice in her ear saying, 'Take care.' That phrase again. Was it a warning, or a threat? She shook her arm free, said goodbye to the others and began walking very quickly down his drive. Let them think her a suspect. They'd have to find proof before they could arrest her.

When she reached the main road she slowed down and took a couple of deep breaths. Her head was beginning to clear after the smoky atmosphere of Humphrey Osborne's study. Were they right in believing the writer was a woman? This person had wrecked their community, struck at the heart of their nursery school. Would a woman do such a thing? Women were builders and healers, not destroyers. Sergeant Staples was too fixated on that case up in Northumberland. He wasn't seeing clearly. What had Peggy been trying to tell her through that photograph?

As Harriet walked home in the heat, her thoughts went round and round in her brain, like rats in a cage. This was no good. She must sit down and discuss all this calmly and coolly with Alix. She needed to borrow some of her friend's capacity for logical thinking. But when she arrived home and dialled Alix's number it was engaged. She rang again five minutes later. It was still engaged. She left it ten minutes. It was still engaged. Who on earth was Alix on the phone to?

Feeling alone and sad and slightly afraid, on impulse she rang up Eddie.

'Harriet! Hi, darling. Just a minute.'

In the background she heard the sound of women's voices. There were at least two of them. She heard the clink of ice in glasses and Eddie saying, 'I'll be back in a second. Enjoy your drinks.' He added something else which she didn't catch. The women laughed. What had he said? Were they laughing at her? Had he said something like, 'These dating agencies – Christ! I had a couple of dates with this woman and now she won't stop ringing me up.' Was she becoming like James?

'Sorry about that. I've brought the phone into the bedroom. I've got visitors.'

'So I heard,' she said frostily. 'I thought you were incommunicado.'

'What? Oh, these are just old friends. I don't mind them seeing me like this.'

She was silent.

'What's the matter, babe? Aren't I allowed to have friends?'

'Of course. Only, you know, I wouldn't have minded about your face.'

'I would. I want to look my best for you. Hang on in there, girl. Just another couple of weeks and I'll look less like I've been through a mangle.'

Was he telling the truth? Or was this whole story about a facelift simply a ruse to get her off his back? The awful thing was, with the past he seemed to have had, she'd no way of telling what the truth was. Perhaps a dating agency was the wrong place to meet people after all. You never got enough information about them. Or the right information.

'Come on, you know the chemistry is good between us. It is, isn't it?'

She pictured his body. 'I suppose so,' she agreed reluctantly, knowing that if Eddie had been there with her now, if he'd been available, she'd have liked nothing better than to go to bed with him and spend all afternoon there.

'There you are. Why throw it away? You just need to loosen up a bit, that's all.'

'Oh?'

He chuckled. 'I divide women into swallowers and non-swallowers,' he said confidentially. 'With a bit of tuition, you'll soon make the grade.'

From the other room came the sound of women's laughter. Without replying, Harriet slammed down the receiver and pressed the tips of her fingers against her forehead. She was shaking. She'd phoned Eddie for a bit of comfort and the phone call had made everything worse. Was everyone against her this morning? Or did she only think they were? Was she becoming paranoid? Was this what the letter writer wanted – to reduce them all to nervous wrecks?

Harriet went slowly up the stairs to her studio and lit a cigarette. After a few moments, she felt calmer. She'd have had a shot of her father's whisky, only she had to collect Nicky from school and to turn up at St Cecilia's smelling of alcohol would surely not go unnoticed in the current climate of suspicion and innuendo. She gathered up all the letters she'd received from Sweethearts Inc. and set a match to them. She held them over an empty paint tin and watched the ash drop into it bit by bit, blackened fragments of her past.

You couldn't take short cuts with life. All you could do was go on with your daily routine, trying faithfully to make the best of it, instead of crying for the moon. What a bad idea that dating agency had been. Alix's idea. Why had she been so keen on it?

Chapter Twenty-six

Alix was there, waiting at St Cecilia's gate, her dress a splash of yellow amongst the drabber colours of the other parents.

'Alix, I need to talk to you.' Harriet pulled her over to one side and spoke in a low voice, glancing over her shoulder.

'What's the matter? Has something happened?'

She thought of Eddie. 'Lots of things have happened but what I really want to talk to you about is these letters. I tried to ring you this morning. Your phone was engaged.'

'Yes, I, er . . . Tim phoned from Singapore.'

'You see, we had a meeting this morning over at Humphrey Osborne's house and –'

Alix's eyes widened. 'Did you? Who was there?'

'Sergeant Staples, Dr Wentworth, Martin Threlfall, Humphrey Osborne and myself,' said Harriet impatiently. 'That's not important. What is important is that Brenda Barlow received an e-mail yesterday.'

'Did she?' Alix looked interested. 'What did it say?'

Too late, Harriet recalled that Sergeant Staples had asked for secrecy over this e-mail. She flushed. 'Er, you know, the usual allegations. The thing is, Alix, this time the writer left a clue. She'd forgotten to erase the e-mail address. She's using the code-name Barnesley. Alix, the letter writer must be someone we were at school with. Miss Barnesley was head all the time we were there and then she left the year after me, remember?'

'Yes, I remember,' said Alix slowly.

'Alix, we need to talk, rake over our memories and see if we can come up with the name of anyone. Perhaps look again at that photograph Peggy sent me. I still think she was trying to tell me something.'

'Mm. Yes, I see.' Alix thought for a moment. 'Look, I can't make it this afternoon. I've got to take Imogen into town to get her eyes tested. What if I come home with you tomorrow morning after we've dropped off the children and we can have a good mull over everything then?'

'All right,' replied Harriet, disappointed. She'd been looking forward to spending the afternoon talking things over with her friend.

'Did they mention any names?'

'What? Oh no . . . though I had a feeling Dr Wentworth knows something.'

'What kind of thing?'

'Something about a patient of his, I should think. He hid behind patient confidentiality. Personally I'd have thought this was as good a case as any for breaking it.'

'Perhaps he just wanted you to think he knew something.'

'Why would he do that?'

'To make himself look important? To throw you off the scent?'

Harriet looked at her. 'Do you still think the letter writer could be a man, Alix? I would so prefer it if it were. It's just that the Scotland Yard psychologist is sure it's a woman.'

Alix snorted. 'I wouldn't believe anything any psychologist said. It's a charlatan's science. I should know. I spent years dragging my mother from one to another.'

Harriet felt a sense of relief. She'd begun to suspect – she didn't know what – that the writer was someone she'd known, had been at school with. But perhaps the name Barnesley was just a coincidence. The writer could have picked it up from anywhere.

The children came out. As Harriet moved forward to hug Nicky, she noticed Humphrey Osborne standing across the other side of the road watching her. She felt a shiver of fear run down her back. How long had he been there?

That afternoon, in between playing with Nicky and reading to him, Harriet prowled restlessly around the house. She found it hard to concentrate on anything for long. The events of the morning had thoroughly unnerved her. There was no one she could trust and no one she could turn to any more. Eddie had proved himself unreliable. Humphrey Osborne was too heavily implicated in all this himself. Her father – but how could she begin to explain this to her father – and wouldn't he think it just the perfect excuse for taking Nicky away from St Cecilia's and sending him to a private school? No, there was only Alix. She must wait till tomorrow morning when the two of them would put their heads together and maybe come up with an answer once and for all.

After she'd put Nicky to bed, Harriet went up to her studio to work on her still-life, but after half an hour she put down her brush and came back downstairs again. She couldn't concentrate this evening. She was in danger of ruining her picture. Idly she wandered into the playroom and switched on the television. She watched a laddish comedy made in Britain, a slightly slicker version, with babes instead of lads, made in America. Then *News at Ten* came on. Another body had been dug up in Gloucester. The heat wave showed no sign of breaking. Yorkshire Water was applying for a drought order. There was a picture of a tearful Princess of Wales emerging toned, tuned and sleek from her gym in shorts and T-shirt. Harriet wondered if Alix dressed like that to go to her gym. Perhaps she should give it a try. She couldn't remember the last time she'd felt good about herself in shorts . . .

All of a sudden, Harriet's attention was distracted by what she could have sworn was a noise in the kitchen. She turned down the television and listened. Then she got up and went through into the kitchen to check. Naturally, there was nobody there. Nobody outside the door (she peered out of the window to make sure), nobody standing outside the window with a hammer, preparing to break in.

She double locked the back door and poured herself a glass of white wine. It wasn't going to be one of those nights, was it? When each creak of the floorboards or rattle of the windows or gurgle of the hot water pipes made her jump? Harriet had these nights less frequently now; she'd more or less got used to sleeping on her own in the house, or at least without another adult. But strange noises at night still made her tense up (she was tense now) and then she'd find it difficult to sleep, would lie in bed for ages, her legs as stiff as boards, fearing a dark shape was about to loom out of the darkness and strangle her.

She went back into the playroom. The news was still on. She forced herself to concentrate. Beneath the rattle of gunshot in Bosnia, she heard the small but unmistakable sound of a key being turned in the lock, the front door opening and then closing again behind someone. Her thoughts flew to James. He was coming to get her. He was coming to exact his revenge. To rape her, to murder her in her own home. Harriet sat on the sofa, rigid with fear. She heard footsteps coming down the hall. As she watched, unable to move, the door of the playroom opened. Alix stood in the doorway.

Her shoulders went down. 'Alix, you gave me a fright. I thought it was James. What are you doing here? How did you get in?'

Alix held up a key ring. 'I've got a key.'

'How? I don't understand.' She didn't remember having given

Alix a key. No one had keys to the house except herself and her father.

Alix came further into the room. She was wearing jeans, a dark jacket and, for some odd reason, gloves. 'I got it copied that afternoon I looked after Nicky. Remember? You gave me your key,' Alix replied, with a faint air of boredom.

'Did I? Oh yes, so I did.' Harriet gave a short laugh which, even to her own ears, sounded faintly hysterical. Her nerves still felt strung up after expecting James. 'Fancy copying it.' It wasn't a crime, she supposed, but what an odd thing for Alix to have done. Embarrassing, really, to have caught your friend out in such a social solecism. But Alix didn't seem in the least embarrassed as she stood staring down at Harriet. There was something strange about her expression.

'Where's Imogen?'

'Caroline,' replied Alix briefly, not taking her eyes off Harriet.

Under the intensity of her friend's gaze, Harriet stood up. 'Well, er, would you like a glass of wine? I suppose you've come to talk about the letters?'

'I have,' replied Alix in a tone so abrupt as to make Harriet feel uneasy.

She switched off the television. 'Come into the kitchen,' she said.

She led the way down the hall. What was the matter with Alix this evening? She was quite unlike her usual self. It was almost as if she'd found out that Harriet had done something terrible and had come here to punish her.

'Alix,' she said, pouring out a glass of wine and handing it to her friend, 'is something the matter? You don't suspect me of being the poison-pen letter writer, do you?'

Alix gave a sharp bark of laughter, tossed off the glass of wine in one go, set it down on the table and turned to face Harriet.

'You haven't twigged yet, then? I thought you had. Never mind. It's done now.' She flung the key to Harriet's front door on the table, pulled out a chair and sat down.

'Twigged what?' asked Harriet, puzzled. 'What's done?'

'I've given the game away. As good as. Because I thought you'd already guessed.'

'Guessed what?' asked Harriet, utterly bewildered.

Alix looked smug. She stretched out her long legs and gazed at her feet. 'I'm an artist too, you know. In my way. I've certainly put the wind up among them all, haven't I?' She sighed. 'But I'm bored with it now. Utterly bored.' She flicked her plait over her shoulder. 'It's been too easy.'

Harriet stared at her friend. It couldn't be true. What Alix was hinting to her, telling her, couldn't be true because then if so . . . Harriet felt her thoughts turn several somersaults. Her legs gave way beneath her. She sat down on a chair.

'No!' she gasped. 'No, you can't have . . . !'

Alix looked across at her and smiled. Even now, Harriet thought how beautiful she was, with her high cheek-bones and finely chiselled nose.

'You really didn't guess then? I thought you had. It was my fault, leaving that e-mail address on. You were the only one who knew about Barnesley, how she stood in my mind for a witch, a witch demonising a community of little girls.'

Harriet shivered at the glee in Alix's voice. 'But you don't know anything about computers,' she said.

'Did I say that? I went to evening classes to learn. That's where I met Tim. Computers are easier to use than people think. With what Tim taught me and what I've picked up myself, the whole thing was a piece of cake,' she replied, with an air of satisfaction.

Harriet remembered then what Nicky had said, that afternoon Alix had looked after him. 'Imogen's mummy has a computer.' If only she'd listened to him, really listened, Peggy might still be alive today. She groaned. 'Alix, you killed Peggy!'

Alix flicked a bit of fluff off her jacket. 'I didn't kill Peggy. That was Frank's doing. Of course I didn't intend that to happen. I was very upset about it, if you remember. I hadn't intended for Peggy to kill herself. I was trying to get her to stand on her own two feet for a change. I thought it would be good for her. I was disappointed in her, to tell you the truth.'

Harriet's blood ran cold. This couldn't be happening. It was a nightmare. Only a nightmare. She'd wake up tomorrow morning and laugh about it with Alix. The real Alix. Then she looked up and saw the strange glitter in Alix's eyes and knew that this was also the real Alix.

'You can't go about playing with people's lives like that,' she said slowly. 'Tragedy was bound to happen. *Alix, why did you do it?*'

Alix shrugged. 'I was bored.' She tapped her fingers on the table. 'There's nothing for me here. All these smug little people with their smug little lives. Not you, Harriet, you're not smug, you've got Daniel. But the rest of them, all enjoying life while I . . . can never . . .' For a moment she faltered. She broke off, but when she spoke again, her voice was clear and calm. 'I told you about my mother. I thought you might guess then. But you didn't.'

'I trusted you,' muttered Harriet.

'Yes, well, you trust too many people, don't you, little Harriet? Head in the clouds as usual.'

'So you always say.' Then she remembered Alix had said once, 'I sometimes think I know you better than you know yourself, Harriet'; and Fiona saying, 'The letter writer knows us better than we know ourselves.' How stupid I've been, she thought. Alix always said I didn't know much about people. I was the perfect stooge, her stooge. 'You've been very clever.'

'Haven't I?'

Harriet covered her face with a hands for a moment, unable to bear the look of triumph in Alix's eyes. Then she looked up and asked again, 'Why?'

'Have you any idea what it's like to come home from school every day to listen, scared rigid, to your mother raving? No, of course you haven't. None of you have.' Alix got up and began pacing up and down the kitchen. 'Or come home to find her sitting, catatonic, in exactly the same chair you left her in at breakfast? And grow up afraid you'll go the same way yourself? Look at Frances. Our mother's illness cost me my childhood, my adolescence and any hopes of a career; it's scarred Frances for life.'

Alix paced up and down, her fists clenched. Harriet had the sense of watching someone very close to the edge.

'I thought you were so strong,' she murmured.

Alix came to a halt in front of her. 'No one can be that strong,

Harriet, it's impossible. I had to take care of my mother from the day I left school until I was well into my thirties. What life have I had? Never being able to get away from here, never being able to use my skills?' She resumed her pacing. 'Dr Wentworth suspects. He suspects. But what can he prove? He's been giving me tablets for my nerves for years. To turn round and point the finger at me would seem like discriminating against the sick.'

Alix laughed. A hard, unnatural laugh. It sent shivers down Harriet's back. She looked at her. '*Are* you sick, Alix?'

Again the laugh. Harsher this time. 'Not me.'

'I still don't understand, Alix. Why this? Why all those letters?'

'No, you don't understand, do you, Harriet? That's because you're not me. You haven't lived through what I've lived through.' Alix put her hands in the pockets of her jacket and sat down on her chair again. 'It was a game. I enjoyed it. I enjoyed seeing people becoming less and less pleased with themselves. That was fun. Sending the letters out and watching people's reactions. When people are as stupid as the people round here, it's amusing to play games with them.'

'Why did you encourage me to go detecting? Weren't you afraid I'd find out something?'

Alix gave a condescending smile. 'Not really, Harriet. You know nothing about computers and I'd covered my tracks well. You were useful for letting me know how people had reacted to their letters. You allowed me not to have to look too interested in the letters myself.'

'I was your pawn,' Harriet said bitterly.

'Not quite. I told you, I felt differently about you. You weren't smug. You weren't trying to hide things. Besides, as I said, it was a game. Encouraging you to do some detecting was part of the fun, like getting you to join that dating agency.'

'Rather a horrible game, Alix,' replied Harriet, not registering that Alix had spoken of her in the past tense.

'I protected you by sending you that letter when everyone suspected you. I could have gone on letting them suspect you, couldn't I? And I only told the truth about people. I never made things up.'

'How did you find out all those things about everybody?'

'I've got a good memory. I keep my eyes and ears open. I read the newspapers from cover to cover. What did you think I did all day?'

'I don't know, I . . . Alix, you made public things about people's private lives. What right had we to know about them? You've destroyed a community.'

'It deserved to be destroyed!' exclaimed Alix. Suddenly her features, which had been so lovely, became ugly and harsh. There was a dangerous glint in her eye. She took one gloved hand out of the pocket of her jacket and banged it down on the table. 'All those people living lies. Keeping up appearances. I never had any appearances to keep up. Everyone knew about my mother. Have you any idea what it's like growing up in a small town with a mother who's crazy? Everyone laughing at you or, worse, pitying you.'

'Alix, no one laughed. No one knew. No one at school, anyway. We didn't know.'

'No, but plenty of people outside did. As a teenager I'd walk into a shop and there'd be a sudden silence. Looks. Sneers. False, pitying smiles. Ugh!'

Harriet, watching her friend – former friend – wondered how much of this was true, how much imagined. She had no way of telling. Her uncertainty made her head spin. It was as if she'd entered another dimension. Or stepped behind a mirror and seen everything reversed.

'Everyone knew about my mother,' Alix continued. 'So I thought, why shouldn't other people's filthy little secrets be made public? I knew enough of them. God knows, I'd lived here long enough. Apple Burton sets itself up to be such a respectable community. What a sham!'

Harriet gazed at her. 'Alix, I think I'm beginning to understand why you did all this,' she said slowly and carefully. 'But now you've proved how clever you are, won't you stop it?'

'There's one small snag in that, Harriet. If I say yes and go meekly away, the minute my back is turned you'll be on the phone to the police, law-abiding citizen that you are.'

Harriet thought quickly. 'No, I won't turn you in to the police,

Alix, if only you'll stop. I'll never forgive you for what you did to Peggy. Never. But even if I did tell the police, there's practically nothing they could charge you with. Sergeant Staples said as much this morning. As you pointed out, none of the letters were libellous.'

'It would get out, Harriet.' Alix put her hand back in her jacket pocket. 'You know the identity of the letter writer now. Sooner or later you'd tell someone else, perhaps Humphrey Osborne.'

'Why –?'

'Let me continue. And he would tell someone else and so rumours would spread.'

'You could move away. Make a fresh start somewhere else. Tim could get a job at another university. He'd help you, I'm sure.' At least after I've talked to him he will, she thought.

'Tim mustn't know anything about this. I can't risk that. I need his money for Imogen. At my age I'm too old to start learning how to earn a decent wage.'

'But –'

'You don't understand, Harriet, do you? I want to be free to go on with this, or to try something else. If I'm known as the letter writer it would make it too difficult for me ever to do something like this again.'

'Why would you want to?'

'I've got a taste for it. And I'm good at it. It's my career, if you like, the career I never had. I like having so much power over people's lives.'

'Poor Alix.'

'Don't you dare pity me.'

'I –'

Harriet stopped. She drew in her breath. The madness had gone out of Alix's eyes. She was staring at her coldly, icily, as Harriet had never seen anyone stare in her life.

'I don't want your pity, Harriet. I don't want your forgiveness. After tonight, you'll no longer matter.'

'Why? Have you decided to leave town after all?'

Alix smiled. 'No, but you are, my dear. You're leaving. You don't think I can keep you alive after what I've just told you, do you? You know too much about me, Harriet. I've never liked people knowing too much about me.'

Harriet's blood ran cold. She tried to get up from her chair and found she couldn't. Her legs just wouldn't work. What was Alix's plan? 'Why have you come here?' she asked.

'I told you. After our conversation at the school gate at lunchtime, I thought you'd rumbled me. I made a mistake. But it makes no difference. You'll still have to go.' She took a small brown packet from the pocket of her jacket. 'Cyanide. Surprising how easy *that* is to get hold of. You've only got to mention wasps' nests and they hand it over to you. I've already composed the note. No one will think it odd. You've been unsettled by the letters and by Peggy's death. Your ex-husband's remarried – yes, I saw that in the paper. You've got a handicapped son. Things got on top of you. Suicide's catching. You followed Peggy's example.'

Harriet glanced contemptuously at the packet lying on the table. 'You can't force me to take that.'

'I can't force you. But I think you will.' Alix drew her other hand out of her jacket pocket. It held a gun. 'Nicky's sleeping upstairs, I suppose?'

Shock propelled Harriet out of her chair. 'Don't touch Nicky! Don't you dare touch Nicky!' She stared at the gun in horror. Where on earth had Alix got hold of that?

'Careful, Harriet.' There was a click as Alix slid back the safety catch on her gun. 'Don't let's get hysterical, shall we?'

'Don't touch Nicky! Think of Imogen.'

For a second Alix looked as if she didn't know who Harriet was talking about. Caught up in the drama she'd staged, she'd forgotten her own daughter. As she must have forgotten her many times, thought Harriet, to go on doing what she did. She must have known Imogen would suffer in some way in the end. But perhaps not if her mother got off scot-free.

'All right, Harriet, I'll leave Nicky alone. If you take the cyanide.'

Harriet stared at Alix, at her gun and at the small packet lying on the table. She didn't dare make a grab for the gun. Alix was fitter and stronger and taller than Harriet. And mad enough to shoot straight off. Play for time, she thought. 'How am I to take it, that stuff?'

'Put on the kettle. Make yourself a nice cup of coffee. It helps mask the bitter taste. So I've read.' Alix laughed. It sounded like a snarl.

Harriet filled the kettle right to the top and switched it on, praying it would take an exceedingly long time to boil. Then she sat down again before her legs gave way beneath her. There must be some way out of this, she thought.

'I won't give you away, Alix, I promise. You know I can keep a secret. If you go away now, the police will have nothing to charge you with.'

'I don't like you knowing. As I said I want to be free to do this again. You don't know how wonderful it is to be using my brain after all these years. At school they always said how clever I was, but what could I do about it? I had to look after mother. With you out of the way, I'll be free.'

'What about Tim? Won't he suspect?'

'There'll be nothing for him to find. When he comes back from Singapore, I'll have erased all the discs.'

'And then?'

'Then I start again, perhaps spreading it round the whole of Apple Burton this time, what do you think?'

You're mad, thought Harriet, but she didn't dare say it out loud. With one eye on the kettle which was starting to bubble ominously, she said, 'So I take the cyanide. Then what?'

'I leave you. It works pretty quickly, I've been told. You'll notice how careful I've been not to leave fingerprints anywhere.' She held up one gloved hand.

'Alix, what will happen in the morning? Have you thought of that? When Nicky wakes up and . . .' The picture filled Harriet with terror. A child's voice calling and calling in the empty house, then coming down and finding . . . ? She let out a strangled sob. 'You can't do this to him, Alix. It'll mark him for life. Have a little pity. Find some way out of it for him.'

'OK, I've no quarrel with Nicky. Phone your father.' Alix nodded towards the phone.

'What? Now?' A tiny sliver of hope sprang up in Harriet's mind.

'Yes. Tell him to call round here early tomorrow morning. But mind, no funny business.'

With trembling hands, Harriet dialled her father's number.

'Hello? Dad? Yes. I know it's late. I wanted to ask you, would you mind coming round here tomorrow morning? Yes. As early as possible. Before Nicky wakes up.' Behind her she heard the click of the kettle as it finished boiling. 'In fact, could you get him up? I have to . . . go out. Yes, I know it sounds odd, but there is a reason. You'll find out tomorrow.' Dare she say more?

Harriet glanced across at Alix. Alix tightened her grip on the gun and raised her eyes up to the ceiling on the other side of which Nicky was sound asleep. No, she daren't say more. Nicky's safety must come first. She rang off.

Alix looked pleased. 'Good. A nice little touch that, phoning your father. They'll think you planned it all out in advance, like Sylvia Plath leaving milk and biscuits beside her children's cots before she gassed herself.' She glanced across. 'Kettle's boiled. How about that coffee?'

As slowly as she dared, Harriet took out a cup, spooned in the coffee and poured in the water. All the while, thoughts were going round and round in her head. What would happen to Nicky? And to Daniel? Would her father look after them? He was an old man, too old. Geoffrey? No, despite his new wife, he wouldn't want to know. Never had Harriet felt quite so starkly how much she was needed. Was it worth making a run for it? She might be shot anyway. And that might make Alix furious and go on the rampage upstairs. She shuddered, then felt a jab in her back. She'd never understood till then how deeply unpleasant it is to have the barrel of a loaded gun stuck in the small of one's back.

'Get a move on,' snarled Alix. 'Hand me that cup of coffee.'

Harriet handed it over and watched, almost mesmerised, as Alix unfastened the packet with one hand and shook white powder into the cup. It dissolved with a faint hiss. Death's as easy as that, thought Harriet. Why did I never realise it?

228

'There we are then,' said Alix, in a tone of satisfaction. 'All ready. Any last thoughts?'

'Can I say goodbye to Nicky?'

'I don't think so. That might create complications. The essence of successful crime is to keep it simple and my plan is beautifully simple. Now drink up, there's a good girl.'

Harriet listened. There was not a sound in the house. A picture of Nicky sleeping soundly in his bed upstairs, his cheek resting against his pink towel, came into her mind as she lifted the cup to her lips.

Then the phone rang.

'What the . . . ?'

Alix glanced aside for a fraction of a second, just long enough for Harriet to dash the contents of the cup in her face and knock the gun out of her hand. It fell to the floor with a clatter.

Alix sprang, literally sprang, on Harriet like some wild, demented animal, her face contorted with fury. The two women grappled on the floor for the gun. Alix was the stronger, but Harriet was more desperate. The phone kept on ringing. Somewhere in the distance, Harriet heard the faint sound of breaking glass. She punched out wildly and felt her arm being grabbed and pinioned to the floor. Alix was on top of her. In her hand, Harriet saw the glint of cold steel. She opened her mouth to scream. Then she heard footsteps pounding down the hall.

'In here!' shouted a voice she recognised.

Alix turned and fired. Lying underneath Alix, half-fainting with fear, Harriet was conscious of a figure slumping in the doorway and another figure coming up behind, pushing his way through, lunging straight for Alix and dashing the gun from her hand. Sergeant Staples hauled Alix off Harriet. She kicked and fought, but Sergeant Staples held on to her firmly. Shaking, Harriet pulled herself up into a sitting position. At the same time, the figure in the doorway uncurled himself.

Harriet crawled over. Humphrey Osborne was inspecting his bleeding shoulder.

'Hello there.' He gave her a smile, the first real smile she'd ever had from him. Then he fainted.

'Leave him!' shouted Sergeant Staples, as Harriet began scrambling to her feet. 'Dial 999 for God's sake! I can't hold on to this bitch much longer!'

Harriet staggered over to the phone. It was still ringing. She picked up the receiver. Her father was on the other end.

'Harriet? Are you all right? What's going on? I was worried about you. You sounded so odd. And then when you didn't answer the phone, I was about to put on my coat and come round.'

'Oh Dad,' she said weakly, 'I think you saved my life. But please, get off the line, I've got to phone the police.'

'What's happened? Where's Nicky?'

'I can't talk now, Dad. Nicky's all right. I'm all right. I'll speak to you in the morning.'

She put down the phone, lifted it again, dialled 999 and requested police and an ambulance. Then, filled with an immense and irrational fear, she left Sergeant Staples grappling with Alix, stepped over Humphrey Osborne still prone in the doorway, and raced up the stairs two at a time to check on Nicky. She found him sleeping soundly in his bed, his pink towel wrapped round his face. Harriet gazed down at him for a moment with her heart full of the immeasurable blessings of life. Then she ran downstairs again.

Sergeant Staples had succeeded in forcing Alix on to a chair. He glanced up as Harriet came into the room, stepping once more over Humphrey Osborne.

'Rope?' he said briefly. 'Washing line? Anything like that?'

'The children's skipping ropes.'

She went to fetch them. Sergeant Staples ripped off the handles and bound Alix securely to Harriet's kitchen chair. For his pains, he got his hand bitten.

'Ouch! Bitch!'

Alix looked sulky and defiant. Her shirt had got ripped. Her hair had come loose from its plait. She looked stunning. What a waste, thought Harriet, all those brains and those looks. She bent over Humphrey Osborne. His eyelids fluttered.

'Oh God!' he groaned. 'My shoulder!'

She examined it. There was a large and spreading patch of dark red blood on his shirt. She ripped the shirt open, got a towel, wet it and held it to the wound.

'Let's have a look.' Sergeant Staples came over. He inspected the shoulder. 'You'll live. Next time, Osborne, try to move *out* of the line of fire.'

Humphrey Osborne grimaced. 'Are all police officers as callous as you?'

'I'm one of the decent ones.' Sergeant Staples moved back to Alix who was rocking back and forth on her chair. 'No chance, my girl.' He laid a hand on her shoulder. 'You're never going to get those knots undone. Better stay quiet.'

Alix's face lit up in anger. 'Fuck you! You fucking interfering bastards!'

'Watch your language, Mrs Greenwood. Or it'll be the gag for you. I never like to hear a lady swear.'

'Piss off!' growled Alix. She lapsed into sulky silence.

Sergeant Staples sniffed the air. 'That smell. I recognise it. What is it?'

'Cyanide,' said Harriet, still bending over Humphrey Osborne.

'Wasn't the gun enough then, Mrs Greenwood?'

Alix simply glowered.

'What I don't understand,' said Harriet, dabbing at Humphrey Osborne's shoulder, 'is how come you're here?'

'I've suspected your friend for some time,' said Humphrey Osborne, slowly and a little thickly. 'So has Wentworth – he came to me privately a little while ago. He was worried about you. He thought you might be in danger. But then your other friend, Mrs Murray, died and we thought we must be mistaken. We didn't think a woman would be so ruthless. We underestimated Mrs Greenwood,' he said grimly. 'Then when you told us Barnesley was the name of one of your teachers, I went over it all with Sergeant Staples and we decided Mrs Greenwood couldn't be ruled out. I've been keeping a sort of unofficial watch on her movements. This evening was pure chance, though. I'd been working late and had gone out for a walk to clear my head before bed when I saw Mrs Greenwood walking down the street. It was a purposeful sort of walk, so I decided to follow her to see what she was up to. When she let herself in here, I felt uneasy. I hung around for a bit but there's no easy way to get into your house. So I called up Sergeant Staples. I'm afraid we broke a window.'

'Never mind about that. Why didn't you warn me of your suspicions?'

'I think Wentworth did try to, from what he said. Sergeant Staples and I were afraid you'd give the game away. Start behaving differently with her and then we'd never catch her.'

'You took a bit of a risk,' she said frostily. 'I was nearly killed.'

He looked up at her. 'I knew you'd be able to handle things. Ouch!'

'You deserved that.'

There was a blare of sirens in the street outside. Sergeant Staples went to open the door. Harriet's house seemed suddenly crowded with policemen and women. Alix was untied and led away, sullen and silent, between two officers.

Watching her disappear out of the door, Harriet felt something go with her. A friendship. She sat down on a chair and burst into tears.

'Now, now, it's the shock.' Sergeant Staples patted her clumsily on the shoulder. 'Constable, make Mrs Lee a cup of tea.'

Harriet wiped her eyes. She felt such a fool, crying in front of Humphrey Osborne. But perhaps he hadn't noticed. There was a lot of groaning coming from his side of the room. Two ambulance men were trying to lift him on to a stretcher. Whatever else Humphrey Osborne might be, he was certainly no martyr. She took a sip from the cup of tea a policewoman thrust into her hands and glanced up at the officer beside her.

'Is Alix mad, Sergeant Staples?'

'Not clinically, perhaps. But criminally, yes. She possesses one of those cool, ruthless minds that stop at nothing. A brilliant mind, I'd say. Who knows what she'd have tried next? Thank Christ she was stopped in time. I'll get the full details later from you, Mrs Lee, but it looks to me as if you've been very brave tonight.'

Harriet looked down at the floor where recently she'd wrestled for her life with a woman she'd thought of as her friend.

'I feel such a fool. Talking with her every day about those letters and never suspecting a thing. Alix always said I knew nothing about people. I was on the wrong track all the time.'

'Whom did you suspect?' enquired Humphrey Osborne, from his stretcher.

She looked at him.

He raised his eyebrows. 'Oh. Like that, was it?'

'Sorry.'

'I did wonder why you were so terrifically icy on occasions,' he muttered, as he was carried out past her.

'We'll fix up that window before we go,' said Sergeant Staples. 'Make sure it's secure for you. You've had a nasty shock, Mrs Lee. Would you like Constable Lawrence here to stay the night with you?'

Harriet looked at the policewoman who was moving round setting the kitchen to rights and shook her head. 'No. Thanks. I want everything to be back to normal when Nicky wakes up in the morning. We're safe now, aren't we?'

Sergeant Staples nodded. 'Yes, Mrs Lee, you're safe. You go off to bed,' he added, as she gave a huge yawn. 'We'll lock everything up for you.'

'Thanks, Sergeant. I suddenly feel terribly, terribly sleepy.'

Harriet went upstairs, lay down beside Nicky and fell fast asleep.

Chapter Twenty-seven

'Why are you in my bed, Mummy?'

'I had a bad dream.'

'Don't worry, I'll protect you.' Nicky crumpled up his towel and stuffed it into his mouth. 'Wa, wa, wa.'

'What? Nicky, I can't hear you.' Harriet disentangled her arms from his and sat up.

He took the towel out of his mouth. 'I said, I dreamed of police cars.'

'Did you?'

'I heard sirens. EE AW, EE AW, EE AW.'

'Did you? Well, never mind now. It's morning. We're safe. Everything's all right.' She swung round out of bed. Except that I've lost a friend, she thought. 'Come on, Nicky, time to get up.'

'Am I going to school today?'

'No, not today. Monday, maybe.'

He followed her downstairs, trailing his pink towel. 'Why not today?'

'Because Mummy wants you all to herself today. I know, shall we take the train to the seaside? Let's go to Scarborough, shall we?'

'Goody!' He jumped around, clapping his hands, then peered into his toy box. 'What happened to my skipping rope? It's gone.'

'It's a long story, Nicky.' She switched on the kettle for a cup of tea. Not coffee. She wondered whether she'd ever be able to drink coffee again. 'I'll tell you some day. When you're older.'

He pouted and stamped his foot. 'I want my skipping rope back!'

'We'll get you another one, Nicky, don't cry. Please don't cry.'

'Mummy, why are you crying?'

'I'm not really.' She sniffed. 'I've lost something too, Nicky. I've lost a friend.'

'Why have you lost a friend?'

'She did something bad and the policeman came and took her away.'

Nicky stared at her solemnly, skipping ropes forgotten. 'You mean he rescued her?'

She smiled. 'Arrested her, yes.'

'What did she do?'

'She wrote some naughty letters.'

'Why were they naughty?' He drew in his breath. 'Did she say bugger? Was that what she did?'

'Something like that. Where did you learn that word?'

'You said it when you dropped the saucepan.'

'Did I? That was naughty of me.'

'And when you hurt your finger in the door and when you . . .'

'Yes, all right, Nicky.'

That afternoon the weather broke. Harriet and Nicky were sitting on the beach at Scarborough when they felt the first drops of rain. By the time they arrived home, a thunderstorm was brewing. Later that night, after Nicky was in bed, Harriet sat in her studio smoking a cigarette and listening to the rain lash against the windows. Studying again that photo of Alix as a schoolgirl, she saw a different Alix now, one driven by rage and the desire for perfection. Thoughts went round and round in her head as she strained to understand. All those sessions of Alix's down at the gym – what had they been for? To get fit, or were they a compulsion? A compulsion, as deep as her sister Frances' need to dominate her hated female body by starving it? Had Peggy suspected Alix at the end? Had Peggy recognised in her friend that same obsessive drive for perfection that she'd lived with in her own mother? I shall never know, thought Harriet. And I shall never really understand what made Alix behave the way she did. Years and years of living with a crazy mother must have warped her mind.

The next day she went with Nicky to see her father. She gave him an edited version of events.

'Thanks, Dad,' she said awkwardly.

'What for?'

'For saving my life.'

'You're my daughter,' he said unexpectedly. 'What else would you expect me to do?' She must have looked surprised, for he sighed and went on, 'I know I've never been very good at expressing my feelings – I belong to that generation of males which was brought up to repress emotion and it's too late to change now – but I do care for you, you know, you and Nicky.'

She hesitated. 'And Daniel?'

The pause was infinitesimal before he said, 'And Daniel.'

'Dad, why is it so hard for you to accept Daniel?'

Her father ran his fingers through his white hair and glanced down at the floor where his other grandson was doing a jigsaw. 'Daniel reminds me of myself. Oh, I know on the surface there doesn't seem to be any similarity but, as I get older, I can't help feeling that we're all in some way or other autistic. Look at you with your painting. It's not entirely a normal life you lead, is it? I was never much good at getting on with other people either. At work it was different. You had a job to do and you got on with it. But at home . . . well, I never really got the hang of family life, did I? That's why I feel awkward with Daniel. He reminds me of my failings.' He glanced across at her. 'We're all handicapped in some way or other, aren't we? And we all try to compensate for it. My solution to my inability to deal with emotion was to throw all my energies into my work. At least you don't do that. At least you spend time with your children.'

'I always thought you disliked me rather,' she said slowly.

'No, Harriet, I loved you. I loved you more than the boys, if it comes to that. But because I loved you so much, I feared for you. I feared about how you'd survive. I thought you were taking a wrong turning with your painting. I was mistaken.'

She wiped a hand over her eyes. 'I'm afraid, Dad,' she murmured. 'I'm afraid for Daniel. How's he going to manage in the real world?'

Her father shrugged. 'What's real? Scientists tell us we ourselves choose the reality we see. They say we're discovering, not what nature is, but what we can say about it. Our knowledge of the world is limited by our language. In that sense, we're all deeply autistic.' He bent down and fitted in a piece of Nicky's jigsaw. 'You know, Harriet, our world is an asymmetrical remnant of a once perfect world. I see Daniel as part of the risk of living in an imperfect world. Perfection leads nowhere – to sterility. In a perfectly ordered world, though there'd be no flaws, there'd be no life, either. No freedom. No creativity. Out of imperfection came life. Without the possibility of error, our freedom is meaningless. A child like Daniel is the price of our freedom.'

'But what a price to pay,' she said, her hands shaking in her lap. 'What a price to pay.'

He paused for a moment and swallowed. 'I know I always pushed you children hard. Too hard perhaps. Since I've retired I've come to see that it's all only playing, isn't it? Playing at careers, accumulating possessions in order to pass the time and help us forget we all of us, successful and unsuccessful, come to the same in the end. "Remember that you are dust, and to dust you shall return." They didn't entirely get it wrong, the old writers. We *are* all made up of the ashes of dead stars.' He glanced over at her. 'Don't worry about Daniel's future. I'm putting money aside for it.'

'Oh Dad,' she said, and burst into tears.

Chapter Twenty-eight

It was three days before Harriet plucked up courage to take Nicky back to school. It was strange walking there, knowing there'd be no Alix to talk to at the school gate. Sergeant Staples had confirmed that Caroline had been with Imogen the night Alix was arrested, so she had thought of her daughter to that extent. Tim had flown back from Singapore immediately on hearing the news. Presumably he was at home with Imogen now. Harriet wondered if Imogen would ever return to St Cecilia's. She must give Tim a ring in a day or two, invite Imogen round to play. The little girl mustn't be ostracised because of her mother. There must be no more burdens on daughters in that family.

Harriet walked along, Nicky hopping and skipping beside her. The air was fresher and cooler now, after the storm. It was as if the time of madness had been brought on by the heat and had disappeared with it. She wondered what the atmosphere was going to be like at the school gate. Would she find everyone silent and distrustful? After all, she'd been seen as Alix's friend. Perhaps the other parents would turn their backs on her?

She arrived at the school gate. There was quite a crowd of parents. Presumably, the news of Alix's arrest having got round, they felt it was safe to turn up, knowing there'd be no more letters. Harriet stood with Nicky slightly apart from the other parents under a chestnut tree. She suddenly felt terribly lonely. Alix had gone, Peggy had gone, Fiona had gone. There was no sign of Imogen, or of her aunt, Frances. Harriet wondered how Frances would survive without Alix to look out for her.

She felt someone touch her arm. She turned round. It was Dr Wentworth.

'Well done,' he said, as if she personally was responsible for tracking down Alix.

'Smart work,' added Tony Richards, passing by with his little girl and his Alsatian.

One by one, parents came up to congratulate Harriet. They were treating her as some kind of heroine. She felt overwhelmed and also a bit of a fraud. She didn't deserve this. If anyone had tracked down Alix, it was Humphrey Osborne. There was no sign of him at the gate. She supposed he was still in hospital. Sergeant Staples, dropping his daughters off, came over with a parcel for Nicky.

'Here you are, young man. This is to replace something of yours that I used.'

'What did he say?' whispered Nicky, unwrapping the parcel. Inside was a brand new skipping rope with red handles. 'Oh thank you, thank you.' He rushed into the playground to show his present off to the other children.

'Thank you,' began Harriet. 'I −' She bit her lip.

'All right?' Sergeant Staples placed a hand on her shoulder.

She nodded. 'Sort of.' Tears pricked the back of her eyelids. With difficulty she restrained them. She'd cried such a lot over the past few days.

'I know she was your friend, Mrs Lee, but don't waste too much time pitying her. She's a hard nut, that one. Hasn't spoken a word since we brought her in.'

'I know but . . . I can't help thinking . . . she's had a difficult life. Her mother was unbalanced. It was Alix who had to sacrifice her life to look after her.'

'Plenty of people have hard lives, Mrs Lee. It doesn't turn them into criminals. Oh, and by the way, I don't think you'll have any more trouble with Mr Maugham.'

Harriet stared at him. 'You knew about that? You knew he was stalking me?'

'We've had our eye on him for months. He was arrested yesterday.'

She felt a huge weight roll off her shoulders. 'What for?'

'You don't want to know.'

'Yes I do.'

He sighed. 'He sent obscene photos to his ex-wife, harassed her at her place of work and stole some of her underwear.'

'And can he go to jail for that?'

'I think so. With the right judge. The law's slowly catching up with real life in these cases. Grievous psychological harm is what they'll call it. You don't feel sorry for *him*, I hope?'

She shook her head. 'He frightened me too much for me to feel sorry for him.'

'If it happens again, Mrs Lee, come to us first. Contrary to what you see printed in the press, there are things we can do to warn them off.'

'I will,' she promised, shamefaced.

He moved away. Harriet gazed at the crowd of parents outside St Cecilia's school gate. People were chatting animatedly to one another, smiling, laughing even. They were no longer casting furtive, sullen glances at one other. Life was returning to normal. She heard one mother tell another she had a hole in her tights and did she want to come to the sales with her? She heard a couple of fathers arranging to meet for a drink after work. She caught snatches of discussions about Sports Day and the outing to Flamborough to see the puffins. Mrs Parker came out ringing the bell, with a spring in her step. Mums and dads began waving to their children. Watching them, Harriet suddenly saw them as they were, now that the distorting veil of suspicion had been removed – ordinary, decent human beings, concerned about their children, their homes, their jobs. Just like anyone else, in fact.

She began to walk home. She became conscious of footsteps behind her. Automatically she froze, then she remembered James had been arrested. She turned round. It was Humphrey Osborne, his pipe in his mouth. Her shoulders relaxed in relief.

'Hello. I thought you were still in hospital.'

He took his pipe out of his mouth. 'I discharged myself this morning. Couldn't stick it any longer. They wouldn't let me smoke.'

'How are you feeling?'

'Stiff. I'm still all bandaged up.' He gestured to his shoulder. 'I tell you what, I'd never make a police officer. I never want to go anywhere near a gun again. And as for tracking down criminals, forget it.'

She smiled. 'You know, I thought it was me you suspected.'

His eyes widened. 'I never suspected you. Not for one moment.'

'Why not? I live alone. I have a handicapped son. I might easily be warped.'

'Not you.' He banged his pipe on the heel of his shoe. 'Your face doesn't fit. Besides, you're new to the area. How could you have known all those things about people? It had to be someone who'd lived here all their life.'

'Do you know, I never thought of that. I'm obviously not cut out for police work either.'

'No, I'd stick to painting in future. Listen, Harriet,' he took her by the arm, 'now everything's sorted out, I'd like to invite you to supper one evening. It would be nice to spend an evening not suspecting one another, wouldn't it? And you never did get round to tasting my boeuf stroganoff.' He put his head on one side and regarded her. 'Or does that all sound too cosy and stick-in-the-mud for you? My wife was always saying what a dull chap I was. She never understood that a dull life is just what I need for my work.'

Harriet reflected. She wouldn't mind cosy, feeling as she did at the moment distinctly odd, as if her world had turned suddenly upside down. Yes, cosy might be something she could handle. She lifted her eyes to his.

'Yes. Maybe. In a few days. Give me a bit of time.'

Humphrey released her arm. 'We've got all the time in the world, Harriet. All the time in the world.' With a wave of his pipe, he turned in the direction of his house.

Harriet walked on, thinking over the past few weeks, over all she had learned and all she had lost. She never did do that portrait of Eddie and now she supposed she never would. She'd learned things about people. Painful things. She'd learned how few people could be trusted, really trusted, and how wrong it was possible to be about that. She'd learned about her father whose care and concern for her had saved her life.

She let herself into her house and went up to her studio. Alix was right, she thought, I don't know much about people. Daniel's not the only one in this family who doesn't understand people. She picked up a pencil and sharpened it. But, she added to herself, in a sudden rush of confidence, I know about colour and I know about shape. They are my thing. If Alix had painted pictures instead of writing letters, I'd have been on to her in no time.

She sketched all morning, right up to the moment when she had to leave to collect Nicky. She stood back and looked at the result. An elderly woman, her lovely face haggard and worn, sat in a chair staring blankly out at the spectator. Behind her stood a younger woman, resembling her in features but whose beauty had not yet been ravaged by time. She was clutching the back of the chair so tightly her knuckles were white. Her face expressed a mixture of pity, exasperation and fear. Not bad, thought Harriet. It's a start, anyway.

She left to fetch Nicky. On the way home, he hopped excitedly by her side, telling her about the puffins they were going to see at Flamborough.

'And Mummy, when I get home, can I have a house for my mice?'

'Your mice?'

'Yes. Here they are.' He uncurled his hand. 'There are six of them. Five white and one black. See?' Obediently, she inspected his empty hand. 'I need a house for them to live in when they come back from work.'

'Oh, they work, do they? What do they work at?'

He looked up at her earnestly through smeary glasses. 'They paint pictures.'

She smiled. 'Well, I think I might have an old biscuit tin you can have.'

At home she rummaged through cupboards to find a tin.

'Thank you. And now Mummy, I have some important work to do, so would you mind please sitting quietly? If you want to ask a question, put up your hand.' He cleared his throat and smacked his lips. 'There are many little children without homes so I'm going to decorate this tin for them for houses. Or do I mean mouses?' He glanced up at the ceiling. 'No. Houses. And creatures can live there too. But the thing is, there won't be much room. And if it rains they'll have to put up their umbrellas. Do you think they'll mind?'

And Harriet, leaning against the dresser, thinking how nearly she had lost all this, replied, 'No, darling, I don't suppose they'll mind.' She smiled at him, her eyes full of tears. As she brushed them away, she heard Daniel's voice say clearly, 'Mum, parrots don't cry,' and she thought how odd it was that, out of all the people in her life, it should be her strange, afflicted child who gave her most comfort.

All Fourth Estate books are available at your local bookshop or newsagent, or can be ordered direct from the publisher.

Indicate the number of copies required and quote the author and title.

Send cheque/eurocheque/postal order (Sterling only), made payable to Book Service by Post, to:

> Fourth Estate Books
> Book Service By Post
> PO Box 29, Douglas
> I-O-M, IM99 1BQ.

Or phone: 01624 675137

Or fax: 01624 670923

Alternatively pay by Access, Visa or Mastercard

Card number: ☐☐☐☐☐☐☐☐☐☐☐☐☐☐☐☐

Expiry date ....

Signature ....

Please allow 75 pence per book for post and packing in the UK. Overseas customers please allow £1.00 per book for post and packing.

Name ....

Address ....

....

....

Please allow 28 days for delivery. Please tick the box if you do not wish to receive any additional information. ☐

Prices and availability subject to change without notice.